D1328419

# looking for you

# looking for you

NEW YORK TIMES & USA TODAY BESTSELLING AUTHOR

# KELLY ELLIOTT

# Prologue

## Kyle

"I've never seen anything so beautiful in my life," Everly said softly as she stared out at the view before us.

I chuckled. "I can imagine you've seen a lot of places that are more beautiful than a hiking trail in New Hampshire. I mean, you've been all over the world." Everly was a climatologist for the NOAA, after all.

I'd only known her for a couple of days, but man, had she made an impression on me the moment she flashed that beautiful smile of hers.

Everly was the sister of Hudson Higgins, who was dating my sister, Greer. Greer owned a bookstore in our hometown of Boggy Creek, and Hudson had come to town a few weeks ago seeking solitude to finish a book he was writing. Now Everly and her parents had arrived in Boggy Creek, as well, to spend a few days here to visit Hudson and meet Greer.

I had offered to take Hudson and his family, along with Greer, on a hike today. I loved hiking, and being on the state search and rescue team, I knew these trails like the back of my hand.

She smiled and turned to look at me. She was standing up on a rock, so we were eye to eye. "Every place has its own kind of beauty, I think. You wouldn't see a stunning glacier so blue it takes your breath away here in New Hampshire, but you wouldn't see this particular scenery in Greenland or Iceland either."

I nodded. "Tell me what they look like."

It was her turn to laugh. "What do you mean?"

"Icebergs. Describe one to me."

A look of pure happiness appeared on her face as she closed her eyes and spoke. "They're the most beautiful things to behold. Pure white mountains that erupt from the water." She opened her eyes as she went on. "My most favorite thing about an iceberg is where the waterline is. Sometimes the water is so blue it looks fake. And the ice can take on that color, especially at different times of day. They're majestic, mysterious, beautiful, and powerful. When they reflect on the water, it really makes you pause and think about how fragile life is. How fragile this world is. They're magical."

"Magical, huh? I wouldn't have thought someone would describe an iceberg as magical," I said.

"I don't know why." She shrugged and giggled. "They have this magic about them. I have so many pictures of icebergs, it's unreal. If you ever get the chance to see one in person, you'll know exactly what I mean when I say they have a bit of magic to them."

I stared over at her. "I'd love to see one someday."

"And I would love to show you one someday."

Our eyes locked, and my heart sped up to a crazy-fast beat. The woman standing before me certainly made my body feel things I'd never felt before. She had a bit of magic to her as well.

Her smile faded slightly when her eyes dropped to my mouth, and I had to fight the urge to moan. Her blonde hair was pulled back into a ponytail, and her green eyes had flecks of gold in them. She was stunning.

Maybe it was because all my friends were starting to settle down and live more domesticated lives, or maybe it was simply the woman standing in front of me. All I knew was that I'd wanted to get to know her better from the moment we met. Learn everything I could about her.

She took a step closer to me to where we were only inches apart. "I want to kiss you," she whispered.

I wasn't entirely sure she realized she'd spoken the words out loud. Honestly, I'd barely heard them over the rush of the water behind us.

I looked up the trail and then back to Everly. Greer and Hudson, along with Everly's father, Doug, and mother, Melinda, had already started up the trail and were slightly ahead of us. They were all just out of sight.

I took a step closer to Everly and placed my hand on the side of her face, loving how her head tilted into my touch. Leaning down, I stopped inches from her lips and spoke softly. "I want to kiss you too."

It was Everly who bridged the space between us.

My entire body caught fire as our mouths connected. When I ran my tongue along her bottom lip, she opened to me. The moment our tongues touched, my knees felt like they might buckle. It should have scared the shit out of me. No woman had ever made me feel this way.

She brought her arms up and around my neck, and when her fingers dove into my hair, I wanted to purr like a damn cat.

I knew if I didn't stop the kiss, things would get too heated—at least for me they would. And I was pretty sure for her, as well, especially with the way she gripped my hair and got lost in the kiss.

Drawing back, I leaned my forehead against hers. We both took in a few deep breaths before Everly spoke first.

"Wow."

I couldn't help but laugh as we drew away from one another. Her eyes searched my face before she looked past me to the trail where my sister and her parents and brother had disappeared. It was late fall and almost all the leaves had fallen, yet there was still enough to make the scenery surrounding us beautiful. A gust of wind rained down leaves of deep red, orange, and yellow every now and then, giving the area the most peaceful feeling one could experience. The trail we were hiking was popular, but right then it was like only Everly and I existed in this stunning wonder of nature.

Everly stepped back and gave me a small shake of her head. "We should probably catch up with everyone."

With a quick nod, I replied, "Right, don't want to get too far behind."

Everly took one last glimpse at my lips before she cleared her throat, and I helped her down off the rock.

Four Hours Later

"Are you hiding out here?"

The sound of her sweet voice filled the night air, and I turned to see Everly stepping out of the back door of my parents' house. After our hike, I had suggested we head over to my parents' so everyone could meet. With the way Greer and Hudson were clearly falling for one another, I wouldn't be surprised if we were all family someday in the future.

We had gotten pulled into a few rounds of pick-up sticks, and after losing a few times—and having to pretend that every time Everly laughed or smiled wasn't driving me mad—I found I needed some fresh air. It hadn't helped that Bishop, one my best friends, was also there and flirting with Everly. I had never wanted to punch him like I had a few times tonight.

I turned and leaned against the railing, crossing my arms over my chest. "Not hiding, just taking a few minutes to catch my breath."

Everly smiled and made her way over to me. "Well, I think I need to hide from your friend Bishop."

Laughing, I turned and looked back out over the night sky. There was a forest behind my parents' house, and I stared off into the woods. "Bishop is harmless."

She stood next to me. "How long have you known him?"

I shrugged. "My whole life, pretty much. He's one of my best friends."

She leaned her arms on the railing. "How many best friends do you have?"

There was a bit of humor in her voice, and I found I liked this teasing version of Everly very much. "You don't have more than one best friend?"

4

When she didn't answer right away, I looked at her. She was staring up at the almost-full moon. "I have one. Her name is Kristy. I met her on my first day of work at NOAA. We've been thick as thieves ever since."

"I guess I'm lucky then. I've got four."

She looked at me with a surprised expression. "Four? What are their names?"

"You already know Bishop." Everly nodded. "There's also Hunter Turner, who's a cop for Boggy Creek with me. Then Aiden O'Hara, an ex-Navy SEAL, and Adam Smith, a doctor who spends most of his time in Boston doing doctor things."

She raised one brow. "What exactly are doctor things?"

With a shrug, I replied, "I have no idea. He's recently engaged, so I think that has more to do with him always being in Boston than actual work."

Two little dimples appeared as she grinned.

"Did you enjoy the hike today?" I asked.

She turned her body to face me, leaning her hip against the railing. "I did, very much so. It was nice to be in nature."

Frowning, I replied, "Aren't you always in nature?"

"That's a fair question. When I'm doing research, yes. I spend a lot of time in a lab as well. That part is boring, but I do love my job. But there's something special about being in nature and simply enjoying it for pleasure, rather than it always being something to do with my job. Sometimes my job can be...stressful."

I thought about her words. "That makes sense."

Neither one of us spoke for a few moments and a comfortable quiet settled around us.

When her eyes drifted down to my mouth, I fought the urge to pull her to me. There was something about Everly Higgins that drew me to her. I wanted to explore every inch of her body, then sit and talk to her for hours. Find out everything she liked and didn't like. Her favorite foods, movies, books. She was a puzzle I was dying to solve.

"What are you thinking about, Everly?" I asked quietly.

Her gaze lifted and met mine. "I'm not sure."

I took a step closer, touched a strand of hair that had fallen out of her ponytail, and tucked it behind her ear. Then she closed the distance between us, grabbing my shirt and pulling me toward her as she lifted onto her toes to kiss me.

I wrapped my arms around her, and she placed her own around my neck, allowing me to deepen the kiss. Her fingers went into my hair as I moved my hands slowly over her body. When she inched forward, I took it as a sign she needed to be closer—just like I did.

Dropping my hand to her thigh, I pulled her leg up and she pushed her hips into me, both of us moaning when my hard dick pressed against her core.

I broke the kiss and moved my lips down her neck as I whispered, "Everly."

She dropped her head back, giving me better access. "Kyle."

My name came out on a pant, and I placed my hand on her ass, drawing her closer still. I groaned when she rotated her hips, grinding against my cock. "What are you doing to me, Everly? You're driving me mad."

She whimpered when I moved my hand from her ass to cup her breast. I stroked my thumb over the hardened nipple I could feel through her shirt. It was a chilly night, and she hadn't worn a coat outside.

Then, as if she'd realized what we were doing, she put her leg down and pushed lightly against my chest. Both of us stood there breathing like we'd run a damn marathon.

"I'm sorry. I...I can't do this."

"Do what?" I asked with a confused expression.

She lifted her head, and her eyes met mine. With the moon nearly full, it was like we had our own personal nightlight. "I'm leaving, Kyle. I mean, I only came to visit my brother, and I'm not looking for a one-night stand."

I pulled my head back in surprise, positive my eyes were as round as saucers. "I'm sorry?"

"I'm attracted to you—*very* attracted to you. You're handsome and charming and...I would really like to get to know you better. But I can't sleep with you."

I rubbed at the back of my neck. "I'm sorry, I missed the part where I asked you to sleep with me."

Even in the moonlight, I could see the flush of embarrassment hit her cheeks. "You didn't. I just assumed...well...I guess I figured that was all you wanted."

I let out a humorless laugh. "Wow, well, okay. Never has anyone judged me that quickly before."

She shook her head as she brought her hands up to her temples. "Wait, I didn't mean it like that. It's just...I can't do this. I don't do one-night stands, and that's all this could ever be."

"Why?" I asked.

Her head snapped up and she met my confused gaze. "I'm...I'm leaving. I live in Washington, DC, and my office is usually on an iceberg somewhere. I mean, I was offered a teaching position in Boston but—"

"Teaching what?" I asked.

With a shake of her head, she went on. "No. I'm not giving up field work for anyone."

I held up my hands. "Whoa, hold on a second, Everly. I don't know what you think I'm looking for here, but I would never ask any woman to give up anything for me. It was a kiss—an amazing kiss—but I wasn't asking for your hand in marriage. Nor was I expecting to get a quick fuck out of this. I'm attracted to you and would love to get to know you better. I wasn't aware that was a crime."

She stared at me for a few moments with an expression that seemed to be both embarrassed and a bit angry. It had been a dick thing to say, and I admit it was part of my wounded ego that led me to say it.

"Um, listen," I said, rubbing the back of my neck again. "Let's forget about the last few minutes and agree to be friends."

"Friends?" she asked softly.

With a single nod, I replied, "Yes. I would very much like to be your friend. After all, your brother and my sister seem to be hitting it off, and I'm pretty sure we'll be seeing each other in the future, so let's forget all of this." Between my pounding heart and hard dick, that wasn't going to be very easy. At least for me it wasn't.

She blinked a few times and then looked away. "Right. I guess it was just a couple of kisses that didn't mean anything, anyway."

I swallowed hard because I could see it in her eyes. She wanted me to disagree—and fuck if I didn't want to correct her. I had never felt the way I had when I kissed Everly. Never. But she'd made it clear she wasn't looking for anything.

I wasn't sure how long I stood there before I finally took a few steps back. "If you don't mind, I think I'll stay out here for a bit before I go back in. I need to, um...cool down a bit." It was a jerk move to dismiss her, but I needed to put some distance between the two of us, and I needed to get rid of my problem below before I walked back into the house.

"I'm sorry, Kyle. I didn't mean to lead you on."

Laughing, I replied, "You didn't. It's honestly okay."

The back door opened, and I silently said a prayer of thanks that we'd stopped messing around.

Bishop stuck his head out. "Next game is up! You guys in?"

Everly smiled and cheerfully stated, "Count me in!"

I tried to make my voice sound the same, but I was positive Bishop would pick up on my frustration—if that was what this was. Maybe it was more disappointment. "Yeah, I'll be right in."

As Everly walked into the house and Bishop shut the door behind them, I turned and looked back out over the night, willing myself to forget all about how my body had reacted to Everly...and how easily she had dismissed what had happened between us. I brought my hand to my chest and rubbed at it, hoping the feeling of emptiness I suddenly felt would go away soon.

# Chapter One

## Kyle

*Fall, the next year*

Lifting my glass to my mouth, I took a long pull from my drink and tried not to look at my watch to see what time it was.

When I set the glass down, I glanced anyway and nearly sighed. Ten minutes from the last time I'd looked.

"So, you see, by mixing the two containers together, it caused a huge explosion to occur in the classroom."

My brows lifted. "Was anyone hurt?"

Caroline Morgan let out a laugh that nearly felt like an explosion itself. I couldn't help but glance around the restaurant to see if anyone else had noticed. And at least five or six people had. I simply smiled and then focused back on Caroline.

"Oh, everyone was fine! It wasn't anything big, just enough to scare the kids."

I forced a smile.

Caroline was a sixth-grade science teacher and the product of letting my mom talk me into a blind date. It wasn't like I let her set dates up for me all the time. This one was a favor I'd owed her, and she'd called it in. Fighting the urge to sigh and roll my eyes out of sheer boredom, I glanced around the restaurant once more. I was going to kill my mother.

It wasn't that I didn't like Caroline or find her attractive; it was because the only woman I could think about anymore was thousands of miles away, most likely on an iceberg off the coast of Alaska somewhere.

After a quick look at my watch again, I went to say something, but Caroline beat me to it.

"Do you need to be somewhere else, Kyle? You keep checking your watch."

I drew my eyes back to hers. "I'm sorry. I have to keep an eye on the time. I have a meeting I need to attend."

She smiled and took a sip of her water.

The only way I would agree to this...date...was if it was for lunch and not dinner. Caroline was the daughter of one of my mother's dearest friends from high school. She had moved back to Boggy Creek for a simpler life, and when my mother asked me to "be a dear and take Caroline out to make her feel welcome," I knew what she was doing. Attempting to play matchmaker while scoring brownie points with her friend.

Well, no, thank you.

"I don't want to make you late," Caroline said. "Thanks so much for catching up with me, Kyle. It was so nice of you to do this. I have to admit, I was a bit nervous about moving back to Boggy Creek. I left right after high school, and I vowed to never come back. After the divorce, I needed to be closer to home and family."

I nodded. "I'm glad to have helped."

Caroline smiled and stared at me, as if waiting for me to keep talking. When I didn't say anything else, she cleared her throat.

Turning in my seat, I caught the waitress's eye and held up my hand. "Check, please."

She gave me one nod and quickly made her way back over to the table.

I pulled out my wallet and gave her my card before I focused back on Caroline. She was still staring at me.

*What in the hell is wrong with her? What's she's waiting for?*

Smiling, I said, "It was great catching up. I hope you enjoy teaching at the middle school."

Her shoulders slumped a bit, and it was then I realized she'd most likely been waiting for me to ask her out again. *Shit. I'm never doing this again.*

"Listen, Caroline...I hope that I didn't give you the wrong idea that this was a date?"

Her eyes went wide. "No! Of course not. I...I...well, oh gosh, how do I say this?"

I gave her a playful wink. "Just say it."

She visibly steeled herself. "Right. Okay. I heard you have a bit of a...reputation. I talked to Maggie Goodman yesterday."

*Dear God, no.*

Maggie Goodman was a mistake I'd made a few years back. She had also moved back to town, and we'd gone out on a date. The next thing I knew, we were fucking in the kitchen of her mother's café, The Coffee Pot. It was fun—until Tess, the owner and Maggie's mother, walked in and caught us. I was banned from entering my favorite place to eat for years. I had only recently sweet-talked Tess into letting me back in for the last year or so. She still gave me the evil eye every time she saw me.

Not to mention the three times I'd had food poisoning after going there, and I was pretty sure it had something to do with Tess.

Caroline went on. "And we had a very enlightening conversation."

"Is that so." I kept my voice steady while I leaned back in my chair and waited for what she was going to propose.

Fucking hell. I'd always thought Maggie was a sweet girl, so when she agreed to go out with me, I'd figured we'd have a good time. What I hadn't expected was for her to confess she wanted to fuck me in the middle of her mother's restaurant. The cop in me knew it was a stupid idea, but the guy in me was all in. Christ, I was an idiot back then.

"Yes, and well, she told me how you welcomed her back home after her divorce and...and I was thinking maybe we could go back to my place?"

I raised one of my brows. "Back to your place?"

She nodded. "I know it's the afternoon and all, but I'm totally down for a good round of sex. I need to forget about my ex, and the best way to do that is to sleep with another man. Maggie said you were very good with your, um...you know."

I was positive my mouth was in my lap. I simply stared at Caroline, and she quickly realized I was not on the same page.

"Oh, dear Lord—I propositioned a cop for sex. Please don't arrest me. I just now realized how that sounded."

I couldn't help but laugh. "No, you didn't. Well...I mean, I guess you did. Listen, Caroline, you're a beautiful woman...but I'm not interested in that. I asked you to lunch as a favor for my mother and to be a friend to you. That's all."

She blushed. "I'm so embarrassed. I thought you were..."

*This should be interesting.*

She cleared her throat. "Let's be honest, Kyle. Women talk and you have a reputation as a player. I highly doubt you're a Boy Scout."

It was my turn to clear my throat. "Thanks for that honesty, Caroline. I guess it's a good thing I know what the women of Boggy Creek think of me."

Her eyes went wide with horror. "I didn't mean to offend you."

I let out a bitter laugh because the truth hurt. I *had* been a bit of a manwhore until...

I let that thought drift away. Caroline didn't need to know I hadn't had sex in a long while. My right hand had gotten a good workout over the course of the last year.

The waitress brought back my credit card and thanked us.

Caroline looked down at her hands, then back to me. "I'm so sorry, Kyle. I'm so embarrassed."

I smiled. "You spoke the truth, Caroline."

She shook her head. "I still shouldn't have assumed you'd fall into bed with me."

We sat in silence for a few moments before Caroline flashed a wide smile that was clearly for show and reached for her purse. "I think I'm going to head on out and let you get to your meeting. Thank you so much for lunch and the company."

I got out of my chair and stood. "It was nice to catch up, Caroline." She shook my hand and we said our goodbyes. Once I'd left the restaurant and headed to my truck, I called Hunter. He answered after the second ring.

"Hello?"

"I've got a fucking reputation with the women in Boggy Creek!" I stated as I got into the truck.

Hunter chuckled. "I'm good. How are you, Kyle? I take it your lunch date didn't go as planned."

I sighed. "Do you want to know what she wanted from me?"

"Recommendations on the best places to eat in Boggy Creek, since so much has changed since she left?" The sarcasm was clear in his voice.

"Ha ha. No, she wanted me to go back to her place and fuck her so she could forget about her ex."

Hunter choked on something. "Wh-what?!"

"Yes! Apparently, she had a little conversation with Maggie, who enlightened her on our one damn date."

"And that made her think you'd want to go home with her and have sex?"

I closed my eyes and sighed. "Yes. She said I had a reputation. That the women in Boggy Creek talk. What the fuck is that about?"

It only took two seconds before Hunter lost it laughing.

I dropped back in my seat and waited for him to control himself. "Are you finished yet?" I asked, when it appeared he was starting to calm down.

"Dude, why are you surprised? It isn't exactly a secret that you've hooked up with a lot of women. Both local and not local."

"Well, that was before—" I stopped abruptly and internally cursed.

"Before what?"

I had to think quickly. "Before all of my friends started getting married and having kids. By the way, how's Arabella feeling?"

"She's doing amazing. Only one more month to go."

Smiling, I replied, "I'm really excited for you guys. I talked to Bishop yesterday. I can't believe Abby is due in a few days."

"I know. Bella told me Abby has already started having contractions, but not enough to sound the alarm."

A pang of jealousy hit me, and I quickly shook it off. I truly *was* happy for Hunter and Bishop.

"Wow. It's crazy to think you two are going to be fathers."

"I know. And listen, Kyle, there are worse things that could happen to you. I mean, a woman wanting to hook up isn't so bad. If I remember right, Caroline was a pretty girl."

I closed my eyes and took in a deep breath before letting it out. "I know. Believe me, I know there are worse things. And she's still pretty. Hey, can you ask Arabella if the book club is at two or three?"

"Nice deflection. It's at two. She just left for Greer and Hudson's place. Speaking of Greer, how is she doing with not taking a honeymoon right away?"

That was a subject I didn't mind talking about. My sister, who was also my twin, got married last weekend. Hudson had a book due soon, and another one coming out in two weeks. And October was one of Greer's favorite months at the bookstore. They'd both decided to put their honeymoon off until spring.

"She's totally fine with it. I think they made the right decision. I honestly think they both would have been happy to elope. The wedding was beautiful though. I'm glad the weather was as nice as it was."

Hunter laughed. "For sure. Fall in New England can be tricky. Hey, are we still on for fishing Saturday?"

"I am. Not sure about Bishop, depends on Abby, I guess. Aiden said he had to miss this one. He's busy with work."

"All the more fish for us."

I chuckled. "I better get going so I'm not late."

Hunter snickered. "Did you tell Caroline you were a reformed man? Maybe tell her about your little book club?"

"Fuck no. No one knows about book club except the members of book club. And if it ever gets out—say, at the station—don't think I won't come after you, Hunter."

He faked a gasp. "To think you would even suggest I'd tell your secrets."

"Fuck off, Turner."

"Hey, Kyle?"

"Yeah?" I asked before hanging up.

"If you want to get rid of the manwhore rep and go with the sweet-guy-in-touch-with-his-romantic-side, you should let your book-club secret slip."

I growled into the phone.

"Okay. It was merely a suggestion."

I dried off the last dish and handed it to Hudson, while Greer wiped the sink. She hung up her dishcloth before turning and resting her hip against the counter.

"What do you mean, we can't open up book club to new members?" Greer asked as she folded her arms over her chest.

I sighed. "Greer, this is my safe place. I can't be having any other women sitting in there listening to why I was torn apart about Harper and Chase."

She smiled and covered her mouth with her hand. This month we were reading a contemporary romance novel by Molly McAdams. One that was tearing my heart out bit by bit. Arabella had even mentioned writing to the author to tell her she'd ripped our hearts out, but we'd decided against it.

"Why don't you start another book club, sweetheart?" Hudson asked as he took a seat at the kitchen island.

"Yes!" I said, pointing to Hudson. "Start another book club, but let me and Hudson have this one, please."

Hudson turned to me with wide eyes. "I'm not the one who doesn't want new members."

Rolling my own, I replied, "Please, half those women want to join because they know Greer's famous author husband, *the* Hudson Higgins, is in this book club."

"Why did you say my name in a higher pitch?" he asked with an amused look on his face.

I shrugged. "Because I imagine that's how women say it."

Greer laughed. "Kyle does have a point. Once a few of the customers at Turning Pages found out you were in the club, they suddenly wanted to join. And they've never shown any interest before."

Hudson looked pleasantly surprised. I swore his chest stuck out a bit more.

"It doesn't hurt that there are rumors the town playboy is in the book club, either," Greer said with a wink in my direction.

"I am *not* a playboy! I haven't even slept with a woman since last fall."

Greer and Hudson both focused all their attention on me.

"Why not?" Hudson asked, a knowing glint in his eyes.

*Oh, let's see. Because I kissed your sister twice, and since then, I haven't even wanted to look at another woman.* "I simply haven't met anyone I want to be with," I replied in a casual tone.

"Really?" Greer asked with a smirk. "So, there isn't anyone you're pining over?"

I let out a disbelieving laugh. "Pining over?"

Greer nodded. "Yes, pining over. Someone whom you've let get away, perhaps?"

Narrowing my eyes at her, I prepared to lie. "No, Greer. No one got away."

She folded her arms over her chest again and let out a little huff.

"As a matter of fact," I said, "I have a date this weekend."

That made them both perk up. Greer seemed a little too excited, and I regretted telling her the moment I saw the look on her face. She was for sure going to inform my folks.

"With who?" they both asked.

"Her name is Callie; she works at the station."

"Callie Lewis?" Greer asked.

"Yeah, do you know her?"

"Yes! She's a regular customer at Turning Pages. She loves to read."

Hudson nodded. "She's got my vote."

I laughed. "Don't get all excited. We've talked a few times, and she seems nice. I invited her to dinner and we'll see where things go."

*Nowhere. Because I can't stop thinking about a woman I cannot have.*

The moment I'd seen Everly at Hudson and Greer's wedding last week, I knew something had to give. I couldn't keep pining for a woman I knew would never be in my future.

As if Hudson could read my mind, he said, "Everly's planning on coming back to Boggy Creek soon. She hated that she was only here for the wedding and had to leave so quickly after. Said she needs to get out of the cold for awhile."

Greer laughed. "Does she know it's getting colder here?"

Hudson winked. "Not like Alaska. She has a ton of time off and was hoping to stay a bit longer after the wedding, but she needed to get back to Alaska and finish up the commitment she gave there. I believe she said that she's thinking of stepping out of field work, which surprises me. She loves it. Anyway, she has enough vacation time to take off the whole month of December, and she mentioned coming and staying here in Boggy Creek. She's hoping my folks can join her for a few days."

My eyes went wide. "Wow. She has that much vacation time saved?"

"She does," he answered. "Everly doesn't take time away from her work often. When I suggested she rent out your parents' cabin, she was all about it. I think she needs the time away."

I tried to act like I wasn't affected by the fact that Everly was going to be in Boggy Creek...*staying* in Boggy Creek, for a whole month.

Clapping me on the back, Hudson said, "I'm going to head to my office to get a bit of work done. Good seeing you, Kyle."

I shook my brother-in-law's hand. "Are you sure you want to pass on fishing with me and Hunter?"

He nodded. "I wish I could, but this book won't write itself."

"Sounds good," I called out as he headed out of the kitchen. I turned back to my sister. "Well, as fun as this is, I'm gonna go pick up Cat at Mom and Dad's and then head on home."

Greer walked over to me and leaned up on her toes to give me a kiss on the cheek. She smiled and said, "You could write her, you know."

My brows pulled down. "Write who?"

"Everly."

"Everly?" I replied with a laugh. "Why would I write Everly?"

She gave me a look that said I had asked a stupid question. "She asked for your address a few months back. I think she wants to write you as well. It wasn't hard to notice how the two of you looked at each other last year. And at the wedding, it was obvious you were avoiding each other."

I shook my head. "You've got it all wrong, Greer. She has a life and a career and couldn't possibly want to have anything to do with some cop in a small town in New Hampshire."

Greer gave me a displeased scowl. "You are more than some cop in a small town, Kyle Larson. Don't you ever forget it."

I kissed my sister on the cheek. "You have to say that. You're my sister."

She rolled her eyes.

"I love you, Greer. Thanks for hosting tonight. Talk soon."

"Be careful driving, and tell Mom and Dad I said hi. And kiss Cat for me!"

With a wave of my hand, I headed out to my truck. Once I'd stopped by my parents' and had Cat in tow, we headed back to my place. I used to live closer to the center of Boggy Creek, but I'd recently bought a log home on three acres of land. Cat needed the room to run, and I needed more space for my garden. Another thing only a small handful of people knew about.

Cat barked like crazy as we pulled up to my house. I parked outside the garage, since I still had boxes to unpack and they were currently being stored there. I needed to get them all unpacked before winter hit.

Whining, Cat jumped to get out of the backseat of my truck.

"What in the hell is wrong with you, Cat?" I asked.

She barked over and over until I finally opened the door, then she ran as fast as she could to the front porch.

"Okay, what did Gramma and Gramps do to make you want to get home so..."

My voice trailed off when I saw someone bending down and petting Cat, before she jumped on them and knocked them over, causing the person to let out a very feminine screech and a groan of pain. I hadn't left any lights on outside, even though I knew book club would run well past sundown.

The front porch ran the total length of my house, a good forty feet. With the moonlight filtering down, I could still see the outline of Cat and whoever it was she had run to.

"What in the hell, Cat!" I called out as I ran up the steps—and froze when I saw who Cat had knocked over. "Everly?"

She was in the shadows, so I couldn't really see her face.

"Hey, Kyle."

That was all she said, two words, but it was enough to alert me that something was wrong. Cat whined and barked at Everly, but not in the way she barked at a stranger. It was as if *she* sensed something was wrong as well.

"What are you doing here?" I asked.

I saw Everly look down my driveway and then back to me. "Can we go in and talk?"

After following her gaze, I replied, "Yeah, sure."

I quickly unlocked the door, turned on the small lamp right inside the house, and held the door open for her. Everly kept her head down as she walked by me and into the house. Cat was still all over her, whining and jumping.

"Cat, what the hell are you doing? Down!" *Why in the hell is she acting like this?* She knew better. "Cat—down."

I shut the door and tossed my keys into the bowl on the table in the hallway.

"You moved," Everly said as she walked farther into the house.

"Um, yeah, a few months ago." Something was off. Very off. Reaching over, I flipped the switch to turn on the overhead lights in the small front foyer of my house. It was just big enough to hold a closet for coats and shoes and a side table for my keys and mail. "Do you want something to—what in the fuck?"

Everly had turned and faced me, the light from above illuminating her face. The first thing I noticed wasn't that she'd dyed her dark blonde hair brown. No—it was the black eye, bruised cheek, and busted lip that caught my attention.

I gently cupped her face in my hands as I moved her head from side to side, getting a better look. I was going to kill the motherfucker who put their hands on her.

Kill. Them.

"Everly, what happened? Who did this to you?"

A single tear rolled down her bruised cheek, and I had to fight the urge to kiss it away.

"I'm in a lot of trouble, Kyle," she whispered on a shaky breath. "I didn't know where else to go." Then the floodgates opened, and she buried her face in her hands and cried.

"Shhh," I soothed, pulling her to me. Pressing her face into my chest, she held onto me with a death grip, and I felt her entire body shake. Then she said six words that nearly dropped me to my knees.

"They were going to kill me."

# *Chapter Two*
## Everly

**K**yle's strong arms around me should have given me a sense of peace and eased my sobbing, but once I'd finally allowed myself to cry, it seemed I couldn't turn it off. I was exhausted, hungry, tired, and scared out of my mind. Not to mention my entire body hurt.

I could feel my legs starting to give out, and Kyle lifted me into his arms and started to carry me over to the sofa. When I let out a gasp of pain, he paused.

"Are you okay?"

I shook my head as he started to walk again. He was about to put me down when I grabbed him tighter. "Don't let go of me!" I practically cried out.

He held me closer and sat down with me in his arms. "Shhh, I've got you, sweetheart. You're okay now. I won't let anything happen to you."

My body relaxed into his as much as it could. The pain in my side nearly took my breath away with each sob, but I still wasn't able to stop the tears. I knew every word he said was true. I'd only spent one weekend with Kyle Larson, but it was a weekend I hadn't been able to forget. He plagued my thoughts and my dreams with his smiles and his kisses. His blond hair was still cut short, and those green eyes seemed like they could see into my soul. I knew this was the only safe place I could be right now.

Cat, which was a crazy name for a dog, jumped up next to us and placed her paw on me as she whimpered.

Kyle reached for her and gave her a quick scratch under her chin. "It's okay, girl."

I knew he was talking to his dog, but more tension eased out of my tight muscles at the calmness in his voice. I buried my face into his chest and tried to stop crying. The feeling of Kyle's hand moving up and down my back was so comforting.

"Does Hudson know you're here?" he asked.

Pulling back quickly, I rushed to say, "No! And he *can't* know I'm here, Kyle. No one can. Promise me! Promise you won't tell anyone I'm here."

He placed his hand on the side of my face. His eyes were so dark green that I nearly forgot why I was even there in his house, in his lap, freaking the hell out.

"Hey, calm down. I won't tell anyone. You're safe, Everly."

I let out a shaky breath and shivered.

"Are you cold?" he asked.

"A little."

He reached for a blanket and pulled it over me and then went back to rubbing his hand over my back. My crying finally ebbed, until all that was left was a sob here and there. I wasn't sure if it was from Kyle holding me, being wrapped up in the warm blanket, or the soft motion of his hand moving over my body, but my eyes grew heavy.

"That's it, sweetheart. Close your eyes, I've got you, and I won't let anything happen. Sleep for me."

His request was so earnest and sweet that I couldn't deny him— or my need to rest. I closed my eyes, and for the first time in the last week, I drifted into a deep sleep.

*His fist connecting with my face almost made me pass out. My legs buckled, and I felt like I might be sick.*

"What the fuck, dude? She's a woman, stop punching her," a male voice said from my left.

A deeper voice replied, "The bitch kicked me in the balls."

An evil laugh floated across the dark room as my jaw ached. "She got you good. But I think you roughed her up enough. She looks like she might pass out, and I don't think the boss wants that."

Their words drifted around in a haze in my head. The boss? Who was the boss?

My body was dropped onto a hard chair, and I let out a scream when both of my arms were pulled behind my back.

"Tie the bitch up tight," the guy who'd hit me three times said. He grabbed my jaw and jerked my head up to meet his gaze. "Don't try anything, or I'll make your left eye match the right."

Tears streamed down my face. My cheek stung, and I knew my lip was busted open. I could taste the blood.

"Come on, we need to let him know we got her."

I wanted to scream the moment they opened the door, but I was pretty sure we were in the middle of nowhere by how long it took to get from my apartment to wherever this was.

I thought back to this morning, when I'd walked out of my apartment toward my car. Right before I reached it, something had gone over my head and I couldn't see a thing.

"Get her in the trunk now before someone sees."

It seemed like forever before they'd finally stopped the car and gotten me out of that trunk. It took everything I had not to have a full-on panic attack in there. And now I was in the middle of an empty room, in a warehouse that looked to be abandoned.

Once their footsteps grew distant, I let out a sigh and closed my eyes, praying like I had never prayed before. I had no idea what they wanted from me, and the only thing I could focus on now was how in the hell I was going to escape.

I woke with a start and sat straight up, gasping as the pain in my side hit me full force. Looking around, I tried to push down the instant panic, until I heard a little bark come from beside me. Glancing down, I saw a dog at the side of the bed.

"Cat?" I whispered as I reached out to pet her gently. She moved closer and rested her head on my leg. I ran my hand over her head. "Hey, girl."

My eyes moved from the dog to study the bedroom I was in. A small lamp on a side table lit the space enough for me to make out some of the items in the room. A large dresser sat on the opposite wall, and I could see Kyle's bulletproof vest laying on the top. A picture of a younger Kyle and his sister, Greer, along with their parents, sat at one end.

Sweeping my eyes around the room, I took in the exposed logs and rustic feel of the bedroom. Oh dear...I was in Kyle Larson's bedroom. A strange mix of emotions hit me, but I was too exhausted to try and figure out what it all meant. I was safe, at least for the time being. That was what I needed to focus on.

When I first pulled up to Kyle's house in the hired car, I'd gasped at the beauty of it. There was something so romantic about log homes. My heart had raced when I'd knocked and realized that Kyle wasn't home. I'd sat down in one of the two rocking chairs and focused on attempting to calm my speeding heart. The sun had already set, and I'd waited for about an hour on Kyle's front porch before he finally got home.

After I'd fallen asleep in his arms on the sofa, Kyle must have moved me to his bedroom.

The bed was a massive king-size with a beautiful wooden headboard. The soft down comforter nearly made me want to slip down and fall back to sleep. I knew I needed to get up, though. I pulled the covers back to see I was still dressed in the long-sleeve T-shirt and jeans I had been wearing since I'd escaped Alaska and arrived in Seattle. A friend of mine had gone and bought a few things for me until I could make it to Boggy Creek.

I glanced around again. The walls in the room were bare with a few boxes off to one side. A large, oversized leather chair sat next to the dresser, and there was a dressing bag thrown over the back of it. I couldn't help but wonder if it was Kyle's uniform, or if maybe he was heading to a formal dinner or something. Maybe it was his tux from Greer and Hudson's wedding, although that had been nearly two weeks ago.

On the other side of the dresser was a door that was slightly cracked open. A light was shining through, and I could hear water running, along with a few drawers opening and closing.

"Kyle," I whispered as Cat moved next to me. She sat up and stared at the door, as well, both of us waiting for the man in question to step out.

As if he could read our minds, the door opened and Kyle stepped into the bedroom. I tried not to stare at the sight before me, but it was hard not to. I blinked a few times and ignored the pain in my right eye at the movement. My gaze slowly traveled over Kyle's nearly naked body. I placed my hand over my stomach in an attempt to calm the fluttering going on inside.

Cat jumped down and went to Kyle's side, beaming up at him. It was clear she simply adored the man.

"Did I wake you up?" he asked.

My mouth opened to answer his question, but all I could do was stare at him. Goodness...he was in shape. His abs looked fake, they were so perfect. He stood there in nothing but a towel wrapped around his waist, with his blonde hair now dark and wet from the shower. A lock of it was hanging over his forehead. I looked into his dark emerald eyes after I forced myself to stop gawking at his body.

An instant pull in my lower stomach had me forgetting about the serious trouble I was in. All I could think about was when he'd kissed me months ago. Lord, the way he kissed... I had often dreamt about his soft, beautiful lips on my skin. The feel of his hardness against me.

Cat jumped on the bed and stood in front of me, and for a second, I swore she was attempting to block my view of Kyle.

Finally finding my voice, I cleared it and answered, "No. I woke up and wasn't sure where I was for a few minutes. What time is it?" I tried to look anywhere other than at Kyle. I failed and soon found my eyes back on his handsome face.

Kyle smiled and my stomach did another weird little flip. Those dimples would make any woman forget themselves. "It's six thirty."

My eyes went wide. "In the morning?"

"Yep." He walked over to his dresser and opened a drawer. I watched as he pulled out a shirt and then shut it.

"I slept all night?" I asked.

Kyle headed to the closet and walked inside, only to come right out with a pair of jeans. "You did. You must have been exhausted, Everly."

I nodded. "I...I was."

"Hungry?"

My stomach decided to answer for me with a load roar, and Kyle laughed.

"Let me get dressed really quickly. Then you can take a bath or shower while I make breakfast, if you want to."

I let my eyes wander over his perfectly sculpted upper body before I forced myself to look away. He kept the bathroom door cracked open as he continued to talk.

"I thought maybe we could eat breakfast on the back porch, since it's such a nice morning for October. I was supposed to go fishing with Hunter tomorrow, but I already sent him a text that something came up. Arabella has been feeling a bit sick in the mornings, so he was totally fine with not going."

Wringing my hands together, I nodded, even though he couldn't see me. I wasn't sure why he was telling me all of that.

The door to the bathroom opened and Kyle walked out dressed in a black, long-sleeve Boggy Creek Valley Police shirt and faded jeans. I looked down at his bare feet and had to force myself to swallow.

"That sounds nice," I said quietly before I pushed the covers back and stood up. I tried not to let the pain show.

He let out a soft laugh. "What sounds nice? Me not fishing, or Arabella being sick?"

My eyes went wide. "No, neither. I'm so sorry. I'm a bit out of sorts."

He nodded. "I put a pair of sweats in there for you. They tie at the waist so they should stay up," he said with a wink. "And a long-sleeve T-shirt since it's a bit chilly out. I hope you don't mind, but I looked through the small backpack you had and didn't see very many clothes."

I gave him a weak smile. "Thank you and no, I... I don't have much stuff. I left in a rush."

Kyle gave me a once-over. His gaze lingered on my lip, then my bruised cheek and my eyes.

"I put some medicine on the counter for you to put on that lip and the cut on your cheek. They look like they're healing okay, but I would apply it to both to be sure. The stuff in the round tin is for the bruise on your cheek."

Without thinking, I reached up, touched my cheek, and then winced. When the men who had kidnapped me threw me in the trunk, the side of my face had slammed into something and it felt like my cheekbone might have broken. And it hadn't helped when he'd punched me.

Kyle frowned. "When you were falling asleep last night, I asked if I could take you to the hospital. You said no."

Panic filled my chest. "No! I can't let them find me, Kyle."

He held up his hand. "I know, you were half asleep last night but still freaked out, just like you are now. Will you at least let a friend of mine come and take look at you? He's in town right now, and he's an ER doctor. Please, Everly. He won't tell anyone you're here."

For a moment, I regretted coming to Kyle's house. I knew they, whoever the hell *they* were, could possibly go to Hudson's house or my parents' to search for me. Staying in Alaska wasn't an option, and

Kyle was the only person I could honestly think who might be able to help. The kidnappers would never suspect him—even if he was in Boggy Creek, we had no connection to each other besides his sister and my brother. And I knew deep in my gut I could trust Kyle.

"Where does he normally live?" I asked.

"Boston, but he's originally from Boggy Creek. I've known him nearly my entire life, Everly. His name is Adam Smith. I trust him."

Swallowing hard, I nodded. "You told me about him. His fiancée lives in Boston."

He frowned. "They broke up. He was here for the wedding and stayed a bit longer to visit his family."

"I see," I said as I went to take a step—and sucked in a breath, nearly doubling over from the pain.

Kyle looked at me, then down to where I'd placed my hand on my side. "Your ribs?" he asked.

Nodding, I replied, "They're feeling a bit better."

He sighed and ran his hand through his hair. "Please trust me with this, Everly. *Please.*"

I nodded, knowing that if I even tried to argue with Kyle, it would only result in me having a headache. And I did trust him. With my life. After all, it was why I was here, standing in his bedroom.

Kyle walked up to me and placed his finger on my chin, gently lifting my face until our eyes met. "I'll wait for you to tell me what happened, but you *need* to tell me, Everly. Sooner rather than later. Okay?"

I blinked back tears and nodded. "I'm…I'm sorry I brought you into this."

The corners of his mouth rose slightly before he replied, "I'm not sorry you're here, but I *am* sorry you're hurting. We'll fix this, I promise."

I dropped my eyes to the scruff on his face before I closed them and let out what felt like my first full breath since this nightmare happened. Oh, how I wish he could fix it. But I wasn't even sure what *needed* to be fixed.

Kyle leaned down and kissed me softly on the forehead. "If you want to take a bath, I put some Epsom salt on the counter."

Lifting my gaze back to his, I forced a smile. "As lovely as soaking in a bath sounds, food sounds better. I don't think I could get in and out of the tub right now with how badly my ribs hurt."

He winked. "I could help."

I laughed, then regretted it when a sharp pain hit my side.

He frowned. "I'll let you take care of things." And then he stepped back. I instantly missed the warmth that was Kyle, but knew a hot shower would feel heavenly.

"Stay here with her, Cat," Kyle ordered as he headed out of the bedroom.

Glancing down at the dog, I sighed and then bent down gingerly to give her attention. She was staring after Kyle, and I looked back over my shoulder at the now-closed door. "You love him, don't you, girl?"

She let out a soft bark and I laughed, though it quickly ceased when pain shot through my side again.

After walking into Kyle's bathroom, I carefully stripped out of my clothes and turned the shower to hot. I stepped inside and sighed as the water ran over my aching body. I looked down and saw the bruise on my side from where one of the men had kicked me.

I wasn't even sure how long it had been since I'd last showered. Seattle—when I had gone to Charlie's house. After a few minutes of letting the hot water soothe me, I looked at Kyle's shampoo and conditioner. It was something I had never heard of before and smelled like shampoo a man would use. Beggars couldn't be choosers, so I washed my hair, used his razor to shave, then stood there with my head under the hot water for another few minutes before I turned off the shower and stepped out.

I paused when I saw Cat sitting there on guard duty.

"Wow, you really listen well, don't you, girl?"

No response except for a slight tilt of her head. It almost felt as if she was studying me. Then she turned, looked out the door, and started to sniff the air.

I did the same, and moaned. "Bacon."

Cat barked, and I smiled.

"Right. Let me dry off and get dressed. Then we'll go have breakfast."

I got dressed as quickly as my bruised body would allow and followed Cat down the steps and through the house to the kitchen. I glanced around the large, open floor plan and noticed that all the walls were exposed logs. A large rock fireplace sat on the opposite wall, flanked by two massive windows that looked out over Kyle's property. The view of the forest that surrounded the house was beautiful. I imagined what it looked like with snow covering the ground.

As we got closer to the kitchen, I could hear Kyle moving around. He was standing at the oven making scrambled eggs. He had on a baseball cap that was turned backwards and was humming a song while he cooked.

Cat looked up at me, then at Kyle. No wonder she was in love with him. What woman, human or K9, could resist such a man? He was beautiful in all ways. Not only on the outside, but on the inside as well. It hadn't taken me long to see that.

"Kyle?"

He turned and glanced at me, a wide smile on his face. "You feel any better?"

I nodded. "Some. Thanks for the clothes."

Kyle let his gaze wander over me slowly before he cleared his throat. "Of course."

I jumped when another man suddenly appeared in the kitchen. He had light brown hair and hazel eyes. He smiled at me softly, but before either of us could say a word, Kyle spoke. "This is Adam. Adam Smith, this is Everly Higgins."

Adam reached his hand out to me, and we shook. "Do you mind if I take a look at your injuries?" he asked as he scanned my face. It seemed he was going to get right down to business.

I glanced at Kyle, and he gave me a single nod.

"We don't have to leave the kitchen if you don't want to," Adam added in a soft, kind voice, instantly putting me at ease.

"Okay," I replied, making my way over to the chair he had pulled out for me.

He looked at my eye and then touched around the eye socket. I nearly jumped when he pressed on my cheekbone.

"I'm guessing he punched you?" Adam asked.

My eyes darted over to Kyle. The anger was clear on his face.

"Yes. Twice. I mean, he didn't punch me twice. When they put the bag over my head, they picked me up and threw me in the trunk of a car. The side of my face hit something. Then at the place where they'd taken me, he punched me."

"Fucker," Kyle whispered as Adam's eyes met mine.

"Nothing is broken as far as I can tell, but the bastard had a pretty mean right hook."

I nodded. "Left, since it's all on my right side."

He gave me another soft smile. "Kyle said your side was hurt?"

"Yes. I don't think they're broken, though," I answered.

Adam pointed to the shirt I'd put on after the shower. "May I?"

"Um, I don't have a bra on."

"You won't need to lift it that high," he replied.

Relief flooded my body when I realized he was going to let me be the one to raise my shirt. I lifted it enough, so he could see the bruise on my side and be able to feel my ribs.

"Jesus," Adam whispered, and I jerked my gaze up to see that Kyle was also staring at the large bruise. "He kicked you?"

"Yes," I answered. "A few times."

Adam pushed gently on my ribs for a bit before he looked back at Kyle. "Not broken, but for sure bruised, maybe even cracked. Can't tell without an X-ray." Then he focused on me again. "I'm going to need you to rest. I'm sure breathing deeply doesn't feel good."

I let out a soft chuckle. "No, not really."

"I need you to try though, okay? It's important you breathe deeply, about a dozen times per day."

Nodding, I replied, "Okay, I will."

Adam lifted his phone. "I think we need to document your injuries, Everly."

I glanced over at Kyle, and he winked at me. "We need to, sweetheart. If anything, do it for the police report."

I swallowed hard. There was no way I was going to the police. Not when the two guys who'd kidnapped me were cops. I wasn't a hundred percent sure that both were, but one of them definitely was. I'd caught a glimpse of his badge, and I'd seen him a few times in the local breakfast spot I frequented. Each time he'd had on a police uniform.

After taking pictures, Adam faced Kyle. "I can't write her a prescription for any pain meds."

Kyle looked at me and then back to Adam. "But she's in pain."

"I'm fine," I said. "I've managed the last week or so without anything."

They both looked at me with sympathy on their handsome faces before they focused back on one another.

"If you've got some Motrin, give her three of them, twice a day. You can alternate it with Tylenol if you need to." Adam faced me. "The ribs should start to feel better in a few weeks, as long as you take it easy. Don't go running any marathons or anything."

"I won't be going anywhere for awhile," I stated with a forced smile.

"Put some ice on her cheek and eye, keep using that salve, and it wouldn't hurt to ice the ribs as well," Adam said.

Kyle nodded as he looked from me to his friend. "Thanks, Adam, for taking a look at her."

"Yes, thank you," I added. I started to stand, but Adam lifted his hand to stop me.

"Please, no need to get up."

Kyle turned and opened a cabinet, then walked back over to the table and opened a pill bottle. He pointed to a glass of orange juice. "Take these with the juice."

My entire body ached now, especially since Adam had been poking and pushing on different parts of me. I put the pills in my mouth and then drank nearly all of the OJ.

"I'll show myself out," Adam said after he shook Kyle's hand. "And don't worry, Everly. I won't tell anyone I saw you."

Smiling, I replied, "Thank you so much."

"Later, Adam," Kyle said, and we both watched his friend walk through the open living space and around the corner as he headed to the front door. Without looking at me, Kyle turned back to the stove. He used a spatula and took the eggs out of the pan and placed them onto our plates.

"If you can grab the drinks, I'll get the biscuits and bacon," he said while he put bacon on each plate before giving a piece to Cat.

I took the two glasses and followed Kyle out onto the back porch.

Once we stepped outside, I gasped at the view. A large open meadow led to a tree-filled forest with the mountains as the backdrop. The sky was a wash of blue, while a hint of the morning sunrise still lingered. Or maybe it was the colors of the leaves on the trees that seemed to be casting the orange and yellow light.

"Oh my goodness," I whispered.

"Nothing like a fall morning in New Hampshire. The White Mountains always seem to impress me the most in fall."

All I could do was nod. "Stunning."

Kyle pulled out a chair and helped me to sit in the chair. After easing into the chair, I took the napkin he had placed on the table and laid it across my legs.

"Hope this is all okay. I need to head to the store after breakfast to get some food. I wasn't expecting a guest."

Feeling my cheeks heat some, I replied, "It's perfect. Thank you."

We ate in silence, though I knew Kyle was dying to ask me a million questions. The fact that he was being so patient made my chest warm and reaffirmed that I had come to the right place.

After eating everything on my plate, I set my fork down. Kyle was sitting back in his chair watching me. Waiting for me to explain how in the hell I'd ended up on his doorstep last night with a beat-up and bruised-up face and ribs. Especially since he'd seen me less than two weeks ago at my brother's wedding and everything had been fine.

He finally broke the silence. "Do your parents know where you are?"

I shook my head.

"And Hudson?"

"No," I softly replied. "I sent him a letter before I left Alaska. Dropped it in the mail on my way out of town; he should be getting it any day if he hasn't already."

Kyle lifted his brows. "When was this?"

I thought for a moment. "Today is Friday?"

He nodded.

"A week ago on Tuesday. This all happened that Tuesday morning."

"The beating?" he asked.

I moved in my seat and drew in a deep breath. "The kidnapping and beating, yes. I thought about waiting and mailing it somewhere else, but I needed to let Hudson and my parents know I was okay since I wasn't planning on contacting them anytime soon."

"Why mail it somewhere other than Alaska?"

"I needed to throw off the people who are looking for me. I mean, I assume they're looking for me since I ran away from them."

Kyle frowned. "Who *is* looking for you?"

Shaking my head, I replied, "Um, there were three men. I know one is a cop for sure."

That made Kyle sit forward. "A cop?"

I nodded. "I'm pretty sure he's a cop; I saw him at a local breakfast spot a few times in uniform."

Kyle narrowed his eyes at me but didn't say anything.

"In the letter I wrote to my brother and parents, I said I needed some down time. That since before the wedding, I hadn't felt like myself. I said I was going to a yoga retreat in Arizona."

He leaned forward in his chair. "And is this something your parents and brother would find normal for you?"

"No. Not really. I mean, I've gone to a yoga retreat before. In the letter, I included a phrase that's like a keyword. Actually, we have two phrases. Hudson thought it was something we needed to do, especially since I travel so much and he worries about me."

"Phrases?" Kyle asked.

Nodding, I went on. "Family phrases. Hudson wrote a book a number of years back. The girl in the book gets into trouble and has to go into hiding. In order to let her family know she's okay, she has a phrase she says. So we came up with a family phrase."

The corner of his mouth twitched. "What is it?"

"I need to find myself."

"Not very original, but it wouldn't raise any questions."

"Exactly," I said. "The other phrase, the one that says I need help, is when I said the glaciers are melting and things are out of control."

He frowned. "Which phrase did you use?"

"The first one. I said I was going to a yoga retreat in Arizona. I gave them the name of it. It's a very private resort and not anyone can walk in, and they don't disclose who's there. I thought it would buy me some time."

"Buy you time?" Kyle asked, clearly confused by all the craziness.

"Yes, to figure this out. I couldn't go to Hudson's or my parents' because I thought they would look for me there first. No one knows about you and our...well...our brief past. If you can call two kisses a past."

He winked. "They were pretty awesome kisses."

"Yes, they were." I smiled. "But anyway... You were the only person I could think of to go to. I'm so sorry if you're angry with me. I wasn't even thinking when I brought all of this to your door. I don't think I can go to the police. Not if the one guy was a cop."

"Why not the police somewhere else, Everly? Just because there's one bad cop—if he is even a cop—doesn't mean we're all bad."

I sighed as I closed my eyes. "They wanted to kill me, Kyle. They would have killed me, and I...I'm scared. What if they file a report and it somehow gets back to the police in Valdez?"

When I opened my eyes, Kyle was staring at me. His gaze met mine and I could see the truth in the words he spoke next. "I'll keep you safe."

I shook my head. "I can't. I can't go to the police, at least, not until I figure out why they wanted me killed." Tears slipped free. "I'm so sorry, and I'm sure you're probably furious with me."

He reached for my hand. "Hey, it's okay. I'm glad you came to me. Speaking of which, how did you get here?"

I drew in a slow, deep breath. "I took a charter plane out of Alaska to Seattle. The pilot was the same one who flew me in, so thankfully he didn't ask any questions about why I needed a quick escape. I'm sure my beat-up face was all he needed. I called an old friend of mine who owed me a favor, and I knew I could trust him. He picked me up at a coffee shop and helped me dye my hair and rest up for a few days. He tried his best to talk me into going to the hospital or the police, but I refused. I told him I needed to get back to the East Coast. He bought a Greyhound ticket for me and pretended like he was my boyfriend at the station. I wanted to make it appear as if we were a couple, in case anyone was watching or had somehow followed me."

"Why did he owe you?" Kyle asked.

"I saved his life once when he fell through the ice."

His brows shot up, but he kept quiet.

"He obviously knew I was in some serious trouble. Like I said, at first he tried to get me to go to the police, but I wanted to get as far away from Alaska as I could."

"He lives in Seattle?"

I nodded. "Yes."

"What makes you think they won't look for you there?"

Shrugging, I replied, "They might, if they find out I left on a charter plane. I told Charlie to book me a ticket for Chicago, but at one of the smaller towns we stopped in, I changed it to Salt Lake. Once I got there, I chartered a private plane to fly me to Boston."

"You can charter a private plane? That had to be expensive."

I gave a one-shoulder shrug. "Believe it or not, it wasn't as expensive as you would think."

"Did you use your own name?"

"You'd be surprised what people don't ask when you pay them in cash. Once I got to Boston, I hired a car to drive me to Boggy Creek, to your house. I paid in cash and used a fake name."

He stared at me for a few minutes. "How did you pay for all of this?"

"In Seattle, I withdrew money out of a savings account I have."

"Okay, well, if these men are as powerful as you think they are, they might be able to find out you were in Seattle. Can they connect you to this Charlie guy?"

Chewing on my lip, I shook my head. "No, I don't think so."

"And you don't have any idea why these guys would take you in the first place? Or even who they are?"

"I don't know. The only thing I know for sure is that my ex is involved."

"Your ex?" he asked in a stunned voice.

"Yes, Derrick Mays."

"Wait—Jesus, Everly. Don't you think you should have started with the fact that your ex was involved in kidnapping you?"

I wiped away a tear. "I'm sorry, I'm still a bit shocked by all of this."

Kyle nodded and took my hand. "But you don't know why they took you, or specifically why Derrick would be involved?"

I shook my head. "No, but I know Derrick wanted me gone. Like, as in, not breathing anymore gone. I overheard him talking, and it was clear he wanted me dead."

Kyle frowned and rubbed at the back of his neck. A gust of wind blew through, and I watched as leaves fell to the ground softly. It was all so peaceful, too bad my life was anything but that.

"And you don't want me to let Hudson know you're here?"

"Not yet... please, Kyle. If he sees me like this, he'll fly to Alaska himself."

"No kidding. I want to do just that." He sighed and ran his hand over his jaw. "Everly, your brother is going to be worried sick, not to mention your folks. It's been what, over a week since this happened? I can't imagine you typically go that long without talking to your parents."

"It depends. Sometimes I talk to them daily, other times, like if I'm in a remote area, I could go a few weeks without any communication. I do try and email them, though. Besides the coded phrase, I put in a few more things to Hudson in the letter."

"What did you say?"

A slight chill ran through my body as a cool breeze picked up. "I gave hints about where I was really going."

Kyle frowned. "Hudson has to be going out of his mind worried about you, Everly. If Greer sent me something like that, I would freak the fuck out."

The sound of a car driving toward the house caused me to jump up.

Kyle stood and took my hand in his. "Go up to my room and do *not* come down, no matter who it is. Do you understand me?"

I nodded.

Kyle grabbed the plates and glasses and motioned for me to move. "Go, Everly. Now."

I quickly headed into the house and up the stairs as fast as I could with my sore ribs. The moment I got into Kyle's room, I softly shut the door and went directly to his bed to sit down.

Then I waited for what seemed like forever. I could barely hear voices speaking, but I swore one of them was Hudson's. I buried my face in my hands and silently cried. What in the hell had I gotten myself into?

"Everly?"

At the sound of Kyle's soft voice, I opened my eyes. I straightened and looked at him, sitting on the edge of the bed. "Who was it?"

"Greer and Hudson. He got your letter yesterday and didn't read it until this morning."

My heart started to pound in my chest. "You didn't..."

Kyle shook his head. "No, I didn't say anything. But a part of me thinks he knows you're here. He kept looking around the house."

"Oh, Hudson. I'm so sorry."

"Hudson is beside himself and asked me if I thought he should go to the police."

I sat up straighter. "He can't go to the police. He needs to pretend that I'm at that retreat, especially for my parents' sake. They need to know I'm okay. If they even get a hint that something's wrong, or that I'm in hiding, I'm afraid they'll go to Alaska and look for me. What if those men find them and...and take them? Derrick knows my family!"

Kyle lifted his hand and brushed a piece of hair away from my face. "Hey, calm down. I told Hudson to keep pretending that he believes you're at a yoga retreat, and that you seemed a bit stressed at the wedding."

"If Derrick thinks my family believes I'm at a yoga retreat, maybe he'll leave them alone."

Kyle sighed. "The field supervisor from NOAA called Hudson. He said you sent Kristy—who Hudson said is a co-worker and your best friend—a letter."

I frowned. "Yes, she's both, but wait, I never sent her a letter."

"Okay, well, he said you left a note on her desk Wednesday of last week. It said you were going to be out of town for a few days, that you needed some time to yourself. Kristy thought it was weird, since it wasn't like you to leave without calling her. She called your phone and left a few voicemails. You texted her back that you were okay late Wednesday and would call her soon."

Sickness rolled through my entire body. "I...I didn't leave a note, and I don't even have my phone! They have it. They have my purse and everything."

"Then we can deduce that it was one of those other men, or maybe Derrick, who did it. Most likely to keep Kristy from reporting you missing. Kristy called Hudson right after he finished reading your letter. She said something was wrong and wanted to see if he'd heard from you because she hadn't."

I shook my head. "Oh my God. It had to be Derrick. Only he could get into the NOAA office there and leave a note on Kristy's desk."

Kyle sighed. "My guess is Derrick, or whoever took you, thought they'd find you quickly. And when they couldn't, they came up with this note to try and buy themselves more time to find you. If you up and disappeared, you'd be reported as missing. They probably don't want to draw attention to you or have anyone file a missing person's report."

I stood and paced before facing Kyle. "Do you think they believe I'm not at my brother's?"

"I don't know. I have no idea who we're looking for, how big this is, or if NOAA is involved."

I shook my head. "No, I highly doubt this has anything to do with NOAA."

Kyle narrowed his eyes at me. "How can you be sure? You said Derrick was involved. And if I remember correctly from your first visit, he works for NOAA."

"I don't know what to think anymore, and because I have no earthly idea why they took me in the first place, I can't assume anything. My gut tells me that Derrick is working on his own, though."

"Hudson did say your supervisor mentioned something about some strange things happening at your office the last week or so, and he was really worried about you."

It made me sick that my friends and co-workers were worried. "Poor Dan. I hate that he was worried. Kristy is probably going out of her mind. She won't stop until she talks to me."

"I think the less people who know right now the better, don't you?" Kyle asked.

"Yes. The less she knows, the better. I really don't want to drag her into it. She's been working in Alaska for a few years now and was the reason I headed there. To help her with a research project. I was actually wrapping up my part of it and was planning on leaving Alaska in the next few weeks. Which makes all of this even more strange."

Kyle gave a nod. "And you have no idea why Derrick is involved?"

I shook my head. "I really don't, Kyle."

He looked away for a moment before he focused back on me. "Sweetheart, you have to tell me *everything*. You're leaving a lot out, like how you found out Derrick was involved. Who's the third guy? Did they say anything that might indicate why they took you?"

Swallowing hard, I nodded.

"You said this happened a week ago on Tuesday morning?"

"Yes."

Kyle looked down at my lip. "Christ, how badly was your lip busted open if it's still this bad ten days later?"

I reached up and touched it softly. "It was cut pretty badly. Charlie tried to talk me into letting him stitch it, but I wouldn't let him. It keeps splitting again when I open my mouth too much."

"And you're definitely sure they won't connect you to Charlie?"

With a shrug, I said, "I'm not *sure* they won't make the connection to him. But I don't think so. Derrick doesn't know him, or at least I don't think he does. After Charlie slipped through the ice, he left NOAA. He and Derrick never worked together."

"I asked Hudson when he last spoke to you. He said Monday evening after you got back home."

"Yes," I said with a nod. "I spoke to him the night before the kidnapping." I closed my eyes and let out the breath I hadn't even realized I was holding.

Kyle frowned. "I lied to my sister and her husband—your brother, Everly. Hudson is freaking the fuck out and needs to know where you are. And *I* need to know what I can tell them and what I can't."

Blinking rapidly, I forced the tears back. "I'm sorry I put you in this situation. If you can help me get somewhere safe, I'll leave right away."

His eyes went wide. "You're not going anywhere. Let's be honest, if these guys went so far as to kidnap and threaten to kill you, then it's pretty logical to assume they have someone watching Hudson and your parents'. Thankfully, Hudson coming here shouldn't draw any real attention since he's married to my sister and we're friends."

A wave of nausea hit me so hard I had to focus on not throwing up. "I should have stayed in Seattle, but I wanted to be here near my family. And I knew you would...that I could trust you."

He nodded. "Someone roughed you up for a reason, Everly. They wanted you dead. I think it's safe to say we're dealing with something big here. I suspect they *do* believe Hudson and your parents think you're safe and at a retreat, or at least laying low. But I also think you need to call them."

"But what if these guys can listen in on their calls or trace them coming in or going out?"

"I can take care of that. Even make it look like you're calling from a number in Arizona, if you're that worried about it. I still think we need to be cautious, though. They're going to think you're here in Boggy Creek, and they'll be right about that. You are here."

Kyle gave me a soft smile when he finished speaking. I hated that I'd dragged him into this, but I honestly didn't know where else I could have gone. Had I gone right to Hudson's or my parents' place, I might have been caught immediately. I had spent those few days in Seattle with Charlie on purpose.

My chest was heavy. "I'm so sorry I'm putting you through all of this."

Kyle stood, stepped closer, and brushed a stray hair away from my face, tucking it behind my ear. "Nonsense." He took my hand in his. "Hudson is worried sick, even with your coded message that you're okay. We're going to have to let him know you're *really* okay."

My chin trembled. "I don't want to put them in danger."

He shook his head. "If you ask me, keeping Hudson in the dark is just as dangerous. He's going to want answers and he'll go looking for them, Everly. I think we need to let him know you're here. And you're sure about no police involvement?"

"No police, Kyle. Please. Like I said, I know for sure that one of them was a cop, and what if the other two are as well? The one guy—James was his name—definitely acted like a cop. I don't trust anyone right now—other than you, that is—and I'm scared. I don't even want to talk about this right now. I'm having a hard time trying to tell you everything."

Even I could hear the panic in my voice. Kyle pulled me closer and held me as I fought the onslaught of tears. "I'm so scared, Kyle. What if they hurt Hudson or Greer? Or you? Oh God...I shouldn't have come to Boggy Creek. *Shit.* I should have simply called you and asked what to do. I'm such an idiot."

He ran his hand down my back and spoke softly. "Shhh, it's okay. You did the right thing coming here. We'll protect you, Everly. I swear to you. I need you to trust what I'm telling you, though. Will you trust me?"

Drawing back, I looked up into those dark emerald green eyes. "Why do you think I came here?"

He flashed a wicked grin. "I thought it was because you missed my kisses."

I couldn't help but smile slightly. In any other moment, I would have flirted back. But I simply couldn't bring myself to do so right now.

"It's going to be okay, Everly. I swear to you, I won't let anything happen to you or your family."

"Or *your* family," I added.

He kissed the top of my head. "Yes. Now, how about we get you more comfortable in some clothes that fit you? I seriously doubt you want to wear the few pieces you brought with you over and over. Then when you're ready to tell me what happened, we can talk."

I drew back. "You can't go shopping for women's clothes, Kyle. What if there's someone watching?"

"I doubt anyone's watching me. We have no connection other than my sister marrying your brother. But I'm not stupid. I'm going to ask one of my friends to buy some stuff for you."

I was positive he could see the fear in my eyes. Placing his hand on my cheek that wasn't bruised and sore, he let his gaze travel over my injuries. I could see a flash of anger appear in his eyes and then slowly disappear. When his thumb ran gently over my cheek, I closed my eyes and held completely still until his velvety voice had me opening them again.

"I want to hurt the person who did this to you, Everly. Seriously hurt them."

Our eyes locked, and for the briefest moment, I thought he was going to kiss me. Instead, he placed a soft kiss over my bruised eye. Then another on my cheek.

My heart raced in my chest as I wondered if he would kiss my lips next. I let the memory of our last kiss replay in my mind and nearly groaned. I quickly pushed the thoughts away before I did something foolish, like lean in and kiss *him*.

Kyle looked down at my busted lip, closed his eyes, and drew in a deep breath before slowly letting it out. "I'll ask Brighton to grab some items for you. I trust her with my life. She won't ask questions, and she won't say anything to anyone. I promise you."

I swallowed hard and ignored the sudden disappointment that he hadn't kissed me, telling myself I had bigger issues at hand. "I trust you."

He nodded, then kissed my forehead and moved me back to the bed. "I'll make up the guest room. It's right next door to this one. And I'm going to set the alarm system when I leave."

"You're leaving? Now?" I asked in a panicked voice.

"I have to, Everly. I can't ask Brighton to come here. She'll see you, and you guys met at the wedding."

I brought my thumb up to my mouth and started to chew on my nail. It was a nervous habit that I wasn't even aware of until Kyle pulled my hand away.

"Talk to me, sweetheart."

"How long will you be gone for?"

He gave me a soft smile. "Not long, I promise. I'll leave Cat here with you, and I have a pretty badass alarm system."

Cat was laying at Kyle's feet, and she lifted her head at the mention of her name. "O-okay," I said.

Kyle stood and walked over to his closet. I heard a few beeps, then it sounded like he opened something. A few moments later, Kyle walked out holding a 9mm pistol.

"Do you know how to shoot?"

I stared at the gun for a moment before I nodded. "Hudson took me to a shooting range and taught me how to shoot and taught me a lot about different guns. I have a pistol at my parents' house."

Kyle nodded and then walked over and sat back down. "Do I need to go over anything with you? How to turn the safety off? How to hold it?"

I shook my head.

"It's loaded and the safety is on," he said. "All you have to do is take off the safety and pull the trigger. If someone does break in, don't ask any questions—shoot until there are no bullets left."

My eyes snapped to his. "Kyle..."

"You'll be fine. They won't find you here."

I forced down the bile at the base of my throat and drew in a slow, deep breath. "You'll hurry back?"

He gave me another soft smile, and my stomach did a weird little jump. His blonde hair looked like he had run his hand through it one too many times this morning.

"I promise you. Let me show you the spare room. I'll grab some clean sheets for the bed."

"Thank you," I stated as I stood and followed him out of his room and into the other bedroom. Kyle opened the bedside table drawer and put the pistol in there, and then shut it.

"The bathroom is right across the hall. Don't go outside for any reason. Just open the back door to let Cat use the dog door that's in the storm door. Don't use the phone to call anyone. Do you understand?"

"I do."

He nodded. "Good."

"If I open the back door, though, won't that set off the alarm?"

Kyle smiled. "I'll show you how to set and turn off the alarm. You shouldn't need to go out if I take her out before I leave. I won't be gone long."

"Okay," I said. "Let's do that. If she does need to go out, I can turn it off and then back on."

"Perfect."

Kyle's bedroom was on the west side of the house and had an amazing row of windows that overlooked the mountain range. When I stepped into the spare room, I saw three large windows on the other end of the room. The view was just as beautiful but looked out over a meadow. I thought I saw a small creek running through it.

"It's a queen-size bed; not as big as mine, but it should be comfortable. I'll grab you an extra blanket as well."

"Thank you," I said as I walked over to the large queen bed. The four-poster frame looked antique. "This bed is stunning."

"It belonged to my dad's parents. It wasn't their bed, but was in their guest bedroom. Greer always loved it, too, but I got lucky and was able to snag it. We had to draw straws for it."

Turning back to him, I smiled. "I can see why you both wanted it. It's beautiful."

Kyle cleared his throat in a nervous-sounding manner. "Um, I hate to ask you this...but what size should I tell Brighton for your clothes and...um...other things?"

"Other things?" I asked, knowing darn well what he meant but wanting to hear him say it.

His cheeks turned a bright red, and I had to bite the inside of my cheek to keep from smiling. "Panties, bras...stuff like that."

"Oh. I'll write it all down for you. You sure she won't ask who it's for?"

"Oh, she'll ask, and then tease the hell out of me. But if I tell her how important it is, she won't say a word. Let me get some paper. That way I can write down the alarm info as well."

After Kyle showed me where the three alarm panels were and how to turn the system off and on, I wrote down my sizes for Brighton. I was slightly embarrassed, since I wasn't exactly model thin. I wasn't overweight either, but I had some healthy curves. I worked out, ate fairly well, but I did like a good piece of chocolate cake and Reese's Peanut Butter Cups.

"I'll try to be as fast as I can," he said, standing by the door. "If you need anything, you can call my cell."

"Okay, but you told me not to use the phone."

He looked at me and winked. "You can use it to call me and only me." He squatted down and gave Cat some love. "You watch out for Everly, okay?"

She let out a soft bark, and Kyle smiled and kissed her on the head. "That's my girl." Cat nearly crawled onto his lap as she gave him goodbye kisses.

He stood and looked at me once more. "I'll be back soon."

Trying to sound calm and not terrified, I replied, "Sounds good."

"Try and get some more sleep, Everly. I'll lock the door and set the alarm from my phone when I leave."

With a forced smile and a voice that sounded brighter than I felt, I said, "Okey-doke. I'll be fine."

Kyle stepped out onto the porch and then shut the door. I pressed both hands against the wood and tried to listen to him walk down the porch steps. I locked the door, then turned around and leaned against it. Cat barked and I glanced down at her.

"Well, it's just you and me, Cat."

She pranced over to the sofa and jumped up on it. I followed and sat down next to her. We both stared at the blank TV screen for a few moments while I attempted to calm my racing heart. "I'll be fine. It's going to be fine."

Cat barked in agreement.

"What should we watch?" I asked. We both turned and looked at one another. Cat tilted her head, and I couldn't help but smile. "No wonder he loves you so much. You're beautiful *and* smart."

She let out a little bark before she laid down and put her head on my lap.

"I have no doubt in my mind that you'll protect me, girl."

She sighed as I reached for the remote and turned on the TV. It wasn't long before I was lying on the oversized sofa with a large Belgian Malinois snuggled up next to me. Her soft breathing calmed me instantly, and before I knew it, we were both fighting to hold off sleep.

The fight didn't last long, but I was pretty sure I held out longer than the dog.

# Chapter Three

## Kyle

**B**righton opened the door to her house and smiled when she saw me. "What's wrong, Larson? Run out of beauty products and can't find Candace?"

I flashed her a smirk. "Very funny."

"I'm not giving you any more of my face lotion. You already owe me a bottle."

I looked past her to see if Luke, her fiancé, was there.

"Luke's with Aiden, learning all about apples."

Smiling, I let out a breath. Aiden O'Hara was one of my best friends from high school, along with Hunter Turner, Bishop Harris, and Adam. Aiden was married to Hunter's sister, Willa, who ran Boggy Creek Valley Apple Orchard. Brighton's Husband Luke recently retired from his acting career—his very successful acting career—and was now working as legal counsel for a clinic Aiden opened up with a former Navy SEAL to help people who suffered from PTSD, among other things.

I kissed her on the cheek. "Next he'll be at Bishop's learning all about Christmas tree farms."

Brighton laughed. "Probably. He already asked Arabella if he can visit the apiary, which she was thrilled about." She looked at me with a knowing expression. "What's going on, Larson? You seem off."

Couldn't get anything past Brighton. She was, after all, a lawyer herself. Though she had recently quit her job as a divorce lawyer in Boston and moved back to Boggy Creek to help her parents with Willow Tree Inn, the bed and breakfast they owned.

"I need your help with something, and I really need you to not ask me who it's for, Brighton."

She clearly heard the seriousness in my voice because she replied, "Okay, I can do that."

"And you can't tell anyone, not even Luke, what I'm about to ask you to do."

That made her raise a brow. "If you're about to ask me to help you bury a body, I'm going to have to inform you that we're not *that* good of friends. Share my beauty tips and face cream, I will, but aid in a criminal act, I will not. If you forgot, I'm an expectant mother."

I couldn't help but laugh. "I have not forgotten, and I'm not going to ask you to help me bury a body. Christ, Brighton, you do realize I'm a cop and that my father is the police chief, right?"

She shrugged. "Stranger things have happened."

I pulled out the paper that Everly had given me and waited for Brighton to take it.

After reading over the page, she quickly looked up at me. "No wonder you don't want anyone to find out. Never knew you had a fetish for women's clothing."

"Ha ha. It's not for me."

Her brows pulled down in confusion. "Why do you need women's clothing, Kyle?"

"I just do. I'll need fall and possibly winter clothes, as well, depending on if we get a strong front that moves down. If you could buy it in bits and pieces, it won't draw a lot of attention. And don't come out to the house with anything. I'll swing by the bed and breakfast to pick it all up when you're done. You know how much I love to stop in and try whatever cookies your mother has out in the lobby for guests."

She grinned, nodded, then looked down at the paper. "This is a pretty long list, so I'm going to assume she has nothing. No deodorant, shampoo, soap?"

"She only has a couple of things she picked up before she came to my place. I've got deodorant, soap, shampoo."

Brighton's eyes went wide with horror. "Jesus, you'd really ask a woman to wash with Irish Spring and use Axe deodorant?"

"How did you know I use that?" I asked in a surprised voice.

She let out a mock laugh. "Please. You insult my beauty intelligence...and my nose. She's about my size in almost everything, so let me grab a few things for you to take to her now. With my growing bump I'm not wearing a lot of my clothes anyway. Follow me."

"I think the most important thing she'll need are panties and bras. She only has a couple of days' worth."

Brighton looked back at me from over her shoulder. "I've got brand-new panties I haven't touched. She can have them. Her bra size is bigger than mine, but I do have a new sports bra she can have."

"I've got to say, Bree, I'm surprised you're not asking any questions," I stated as we stepped into her bedroom. I stayed in the doorframe. It didn't feel right to step all the way into the room.

"I did, then you politely reminded me no questions. I trust that you have a good reason for all of this."

"I do," I said, rubbing at the back of my neck.

"She's running from someone?" Brighton asked quietly as she stepped into her closet.

A part of me wanted to ignore her question, but I trusted Brighton. I knew whatever I told her she would keep to herself. "Yes. She hasn't told me the whole story yet, but when I got home last night from book club, she was waiting on my porch. She was beaten up pretty badly."

She poked her head out and looked at me. "*What?* The poor girl. Is she okay?"

I nodded. "She let me have Adam come take a look at her."

Brighton appeared again. "Wait—Adam can go to the house, but I can't?"

With a shake of my head, I replied, "I don't want to get you involved, especially when I don't know who did this to her. She was so upset last night."

Brighton stepped out with a handful of clothes and dropped everything onto her bed before heading for the bathroom. "Did you take pictures of her injuries?"

I nodded.

"Was it her ex?"

Sighing, I replied, "Yes. Well, she said there were a few people involved. I don't know how many yet, just that her ex is somehow a part of it all."

I frowned as I thought about our earlier conversation. *Fucking hell, Everly, what have you gotten yourself into?*

Brighton stepped back out with a few things in her hands. "Kyle, I'm all about you trying to help this woman out...but are you sure you should be?"

"I can't tell her to leave, Brighton."

"Take her to the police."

I laughed. "I *am* the police."

With a sigh, she said, "You know what I mean. Maybe Boston PD, if she doesn't trust a smaller department like Boggy Creek."

"You don't think I'm a real cop?"

She stopped digging through a drawer and faced me. "Of course I do. But if this woman was beaten as badly as you say she was, why do you want to bring that to your door? Or rather, let *her* bring it to your door? She needs to go to the police."

I met Brighton's eyes. "Because I was the only person she believed she could trust. One of the guys—possibly more of them—is a cop. She's afraid that if we go to the police they'll track her here. I've tried to get her to go, but she refuses. She's scared right now. Maybe in a few days she'll change her mind. Plus, I—I, um..." My face heated as I almost admitted I how much I cared about Everly. "I won't let her down. She came to me because she trusts me."

Brighton's mouth fell open. "Oh my God. Is this the woman who's had you tied up in knots for months?"

I let out a bark of laughter. "Excuse me, I haven't been tied up in knots."

She crossed her arms over her chest as she narrowed her gaze at me. The action caused her baby bump to show. Brighton and Luke were expecting their first child in February. "Please. Kyle, you haven't been acting normal at all."

"What in the hell does that mean?"

"When was the last time you had sex?"

I scoffed. "I've had plenty of sex."

She scoffed. "I'm not talking about with your hand. When was the last time you had sex with a woman?"

"Should you really be asking me that?"

"I'm like a sister to you, so yes. I'm allowed to ask shit like that. When was the last time your pee-pee was in a vajayjay?"

I rolled my eyes. "Fine. It's been a while, but I'm tired of mindless hookups. Everyone around me is falling in love, getting married, and having babies. The last thing I want to do is pick up some random chick in a bar and take her back to my house."

Brighton's features relaxed a bit. "Kyle, that's what happens when we grow up. We fall in love, get married, start families. You'll never find anyone if you keep yourself locked up with your dog."

I pointed at her. "Hey, Cat means everything to me. Besides, I don't have time to date anyone, and I'm not interested in a serious relationship right now."

Right at that moment, I remembered my date tonight with Callie.

"Fuck! I need to cancel my date with Callie."

"Who?"

"No one, it's not important—and neither is the question of when I last had sex."

"You don't have time to date, but you're canceling a date?"

"Yes. Because I, um...don't have time to date."

She sighed. "No, you can't go on your date tonight because you're harboring a woman whom someone wants to hurt, and you opened your door to her without a second thought."

"Brighton, I need you to trust me. Please. You're the only person I can talk to about this who won't go blabbing their mouth all over town."

She huffed but finally gave up. "Fine. But are you at least going to let Hunter and your dad know?"

When I didn't answer her, she shook her head and sighed again. "I think you're making a mistake, but you're a grown-ass man. Let me get these things packed, and then I'll slowly start picking up some items I think she'll need. I'm sure she doesn't want to wear all my hand-me-downs. How long do you think she'll be with you?"

I shrugged. "I'm not sure. I guess for however long it'll take me to figure out who's after her—and who we can trust and who we can't."

Brighton put some clothes in a bag and zipped it up. "She doesn't have the same shoe size as me, but she and Candace are the same. She left a pair of sneakers here a while ago, so I put them in the bag as well. I also made up a little bag of goodies with skin care and personal items, in case that time of the month comes while she's with you."

She handed me the duffle bag, along with another, smaller bag.

"I owe you one, Bree."

Smiling, she reached up and kissed me on the cheek. "Yes, you do, because you have no idea how crazy it's making me that you won't tell me anything about this woman. Do I know her?"

I shook my head and avoided making eye contact. "No. You've never met her. She's not from Boggy Creek."

Tossing her head back, Brighton let out a roar of laughter. "Oh my God, you're a terrible liar. I *do* know her! Oh, the twist this just took."

I kissed her forehead. "Tell Luke I said hi. Take care of that baby, and I'll see you soon."

"Did she grow up here?" Brighton shouted as I walked out the door to my truck, still ignoring her. One more stop for food, and then I'd be back at the house with Everly and Cat.

I stood there and stared at Everly, who was fast asleep on the sofa. Cat had already managed to get off the sofa without waking the sleeping beauty when I walked in carrying the food and the duffle bag of stuff Brighton had made up.

Cat whined as she looked up at me. I softly asked, "What is it, girl?"

She let out a bark and then looked back at Everly, who didn't even flinch. She must still be exhausted.

"If I didn't know better, I'd think you were trying to wake her up."

Cat barked again and pawed at me, then looked back at Everly.

Everly stirred. "What time is it?" she asked in a sleepy voice.

"Almost three."

Everly sat up quickly and then reached for her side.

I winced. "Take it easy, you don't want to get hurt any more than you already are."

She nodded and then slowly stood.

"Are you hungry?"

Smiling sweetly, she nodded. "I am."

"Brighton is going to pick up some items of clothing for you over the next few weeks, but she put together a few things she thought you could use now. She said she's the same size as you in most everything. I put it all in your room. The, um...undergarments are all new, she said."

Everly's cheeks turned red. "That was sweet of her." She looked away before focusing back on me. "Did you tell her anything?"

"I told her a little bit about the situation, but that was it. Nothing about you."

She nodded as she wrung her hands together.

"I thought maybe I could pack us a late lunch or early dinner," I said, "and we could take a short walk to one of my favorite spots."

A wide smile grew across her face. "I'd love that. Some fresh air would be nice."

"I'll get everything packed while you get ready."

With a nod, Everly headed toward the steps and started upstairs. Cat seemed to want to follow her but turned back and made her way to my side.

I ran my hand down her neck and gave her a pat. "You're allowed to like her, you know."

She barked and then threw her body against my legs, letting out a soft whine.

"I'm going to need you to take care of her for me, Cat. No being jealous, okay?" I knelt down. "You'll always be my number one girl."

Another bark. It was clear she wanted to discuss this further.

I smiled. "Come on, let's get a basket together. I'll be sure to pack you up something as well."

I had purchased some chicken salad at the grocery store and made us sandwiches, and then added a container of fruit and some chips. I put in a few bottles of water and napkins and then stared into the basket. "What am I missing?"

"Can I help with anything?"

Everly's voice caused me to turn and face her. My breath caught in my throat as I took her in. She had changed into a pair of yoga pants but still had on my long-sleeve T-shirt. It damn near went down to her knees. Her hair was pulled back into a ponytail, and it looked like the bruise on her face had faded a little in the few hours I'd been gone.

"How's your cheekbone? The bruise looks better."

She gently touched the side of her face. "I put some cream on it that Brighton put in the bag, so it covered it a bit. I think it's turning yellow."

I walked up to her and placed my finger and thumb on her chin, tilting her head so I could see it better. "Have I mentioned that I really want to hurt the bastards who did this to you?"

Her eyes met mine, and I would have given anything to be able to read what she was thinking.

"Are you sure you're up for a small walk?" I asked.

"Yes!" she quickly replied. "I need some fresh air, and I think moving a little will help. Sitting around is making me feel stiff." Everly looked at the basket and peeked inside.

Sighing, I said, "I feel like I'm missing something."

She smiled. "It looks like a lot of food in there."

With a shrug, I shut the basket and reached for the other bag I'd packed. "Ready?"

She motioned for me to go first. "Lead the way."

It was a short walk to the spot on my property that I loved most. I wasn't sure why the people who'd built the house hadn't built closer to this area. It was beautiful, and one of the most peaceful places on the property.

Everly gasped as we stepped into the meadow. I could see her wince from the pain of it, but she still grinned. I was glad to see that smile on her face, even though I knew she was also feeling her sore ribs.

"My goodness, Kyle, this is beautiful."

I looked out over the meadow and drew in a long breath before slowly exhaling. The grass was still green and some of the summer flowers were still blooming along the riverbank, but you could tell fall was setting in as you looked toward the White Mountains, which actually looked dark blue against the light blue sky. Splashes of red, orange and yellow dotted the lower levels of the mountains and valleys.

"Why isn't the house here instead?"

Laughing, I set down the basket and bag. I opened the latter and took out a blue-and-white-checkered blanket that had once belonged to my grandmother and grandfather. It had been their picnic quilt.

Some of my favorite memories with them were the picnics they'd take me and Greer on.

"I'm not sure why the previous owners didn't build here. It's a peaceful spot. The little waterfall over there is my favorite. And Cat loves to play in the creek."

"What's the creek called?"

"Our town is named after this creek."

She turned and looked at me. "*This* is Boggy Creek?"

"Yep," I said with a wink. "It's the same creek you can see from your bedroom window."

"How wonderful. Does it flow much all year?"

"It does. I've seen parts of Boggy Creek at its highest level before. It's something to see. Looks like a damn river." I placed the basket on the blanket and then pulled out the paper plates I'd bought at the store. "Do you need help sitting down?"

Everly looked down at the blanket and shook her head. "No, I'll be okay. It just might take me a minute or so."

"Let me help you." I put my hands under her arms and helped guide her down onto the blanket. "Shit, I should have brought a pillow for you. I wasn't even thinking."

She chuckled. "No, no, honestly, this is fine. If it gets to be too much, I'll let you know."

Sitting down opposite her, I started to take out the food. "I hope you like chicken salad. I didn't make it—bought it at the store and made us each a sandwich. On wheat. Damn, didn't even think you might not like wheat either."

With a sweet smile, she watched as I put the sandwiches on plates, followed by grapes, strawberries, and chips. Cat dropped her ball, so I picked it up and tossed it. She wasn't even fazed by the food in her pursuit to go after her ball.

"I actually love wheat bread. I can't stand white."

"Me, either." As I handed her the plate, I added, "Wasn't sure what your favorite chips were, so I got plain old Lay's."

"They're my favorite."

I jerked my head up, and our eyes met. "No kidding? They're mine too. I do believe based on the wheat and chips alone, we must be soulmates."

Her cheeks turned a soft shade of pink. Cat dropped the ball damn near on my plate. Laughing, I picked it up and gave it another toss.

I watched as Everly stared out over the landscape and took a bite of her sandwich. I wasn't going to force her to talk to me, but the sooner I figured out what I was dealing with, the better. I mean, if someone was trying to kill her, they obviously had a reason. I highly doubted it was random with the ex being involved. Not with all the trouble she went through to hide where she was going.

"What else is in the bag?" she asked, drawing me out of my thoughts.

"I, um, brought a book...in case you felt like reading."

Her gaze moved from the bag to my face. She studied me for a moment. "Will you read to me?"

I blinked a few times, stunned that the color of her eyes matched the grass surrounding us. "I can, if you'd like that."

Her eyes widened. "I'd love that."

"Okay, then I'll read to you."

"Right now?" she asked with hopefulness in her voice.

Cat was passed out next to us, already exhausted from me throwing the ball for her over and over once I'd sat down. I pulled the book out while Everly wiped her mouth with a napkin and then set her plate off to the side.

"May I?" She pointed to my legs. I had them stretched out in front of me, and I looked down and then back to her.

"May you what?"

She looked at the blanket with a shy expression before focusing back on me. "Rest my head on your legs?"

"Uh, yeah, of course, if that would be more comfortable."

"It would be," she confirmed.

With a smile and a wink, I stated, "Then my legs are your pillow."

I waited as Everly moved closer, mindful of her ribs, then slowly laid her head down on my legs and stared up at the sky. She closed her eyes and let out a contented sigh. A strange warmth filled my chest, and I fought the urge to rub it away. She looked positively beautiful.

"The sunbeams peeking through feel good on my face," Everly said softly.

I glanced up to see the sun shining through the trees just enough to land on part of Everly's face—the bruised side.

I pushed the building anger away and focused on the moment. "I brought *Jane Eyre,* or I also have *Anne of Green Gables.* We're starting that one for book club."

She giggled and looked up at me. "Your book club is reading *Anne of Green Gables*?"

My cheeks heated slightly. "It is. Do you want something more suspenseful for next time? I can buy one of your brother's books, or you can recommend something."

She frowned. "I think I have enough suspense in my own life right now. Let's read *Anne of Green Gables.* I've never read it before."

"*Anne,* it is."

Everly relaxed as I opened up the book and started to read. "Mrs. Rachel Lynde lived..."

After reading a few chapters, I closed the book and looked down at Everly. She was watching the trees above us. She looked up and smiled. "A girl could really get used to having you read to her. Your voice is so soothing."

"Yeah? Do I win any points for that?"

Her brows rose. "Points? I think you won all the points when you let me into your home last night."

"All the points, huh?" I asked in a teasing voice.

She shrugged. "Well, maybe we should save some for things like this."

"Like this?"

Slowly sitting up, she turned to face me. "Picnics and reading to me. I don't think I've ever met a man like you, Kyle. You know how to make me feel relaxed and cherished all at once. Not to mention, it's utterly romantic to take a girl on a picnic next to a creek *and* read to her."

My stomach flipped like I'd driven over a dip in the road at high speed. "Are you enjoying yourself, then?"

Staring into my eyes, she nodded. "I haven't even thought about what's happening. It's been a nice escape."

I looked out over the meadow and drew in a deep breath. "Then maybe now isn't a good time to ask you to tell me what happened."

Everly crossed her legs and placed her hand on her side while she drew in a slow, deep breath. "I'm dreading reliving it again."

"I get that, but it'll also help to get it all out and let me try and figure out why it happened."

She shrugged. "I can't believe this is really happening." Something passed over her face, and she closed her eyes and exhaled. "Or why my ex is involved and wants me dead."

"I take it that means you haven't come up with any ideas on why they took you?"

She shook her head.

"But you think they were going to kill you?"

"I don't think, Kyle. I *know*. The main guy...was named James. Or that was what Derrick had called him when Derrick arrived. This James guy was upset that they beat me up. He said it needed to look like an accident, and it couldn't if it appeared I'd been roughed up. But then I overheard Derrick and James talking. James said he could possibly make the accident larger, whatever that meant. Something that would explain the injuries."

I slowly shook my head. *What in the hell?* "And you don't think this has to do with work?"

She laughed, then stopped as she put her hand on her side. "My work? I'm a glaciologist. I study glacial deposits and glacial erosion. There's nothing threatening about that."

I frowned. "I thought you were a climatologist."

"I am. I mean, that's what my degree is in. But I specialize in glacial geology and the effects of global warming."

I blew out a breath. "Global warming. Big oil companies and certain people might have a problem with someone like you. I'm sure they don't like climatologists *or* glaciologists."

Her brows drew in some as she thought about it. "When you put it that way, I guess some don't. But I'm not dealing with big oil companies."

She suddenly looked exhausted. I hated to push her, but we needed to get this shit figured out. "Let's go on back to the house, so we can get warmed up and keep talking there," I said.

Everly gave me a weak smile and then nodded.

We walked to the house in silence while Cat ran ahead of us. Then she'd turn and watch to make sure we were both still coming before taking off again.

"Does she ever let you out of her sight?"

"Not really," I chuckled.

Once we were back at the house, Everly helped me clean up and we talked about her job, Alaska, and everything but what had happened to her. It was clear she was putting it off, but I knew I needed to get her to talk. It had already been nearly twenty-four hours since she'd shown up at my door, and over a week since she'd survived the attack. I glanced at the clock and saw that it was already after six.

Clearing my throat, I asked, "Everly, why are you avoiding telling me what happened?"

She sighed. "I don't know." Shaking her head, she said, "I do know. It's just I don't want to relive it and I know the moment I do..."

I took her hands in mine. "The faster you tell me what happened, the faster we can figure it all out."

All she gave me was a weak smile.

"Should we make up the spare bed?" I asked. "I can help with that."

"Yes, if you don't mind."

I motioned for her to lead the way upstairs. Cat rushed to get ahead of Everly, and I laughed. "I don't mind at all, and clearly neither does Cat."

After making up the bed and grabbing some fresh towels for Everly, I leaned against the doorjamb. "I was supposed to go fishing with Hunter tomorrow."

She turned her head and looked at me. "You really don't have to cancel your fishing trip tomorrow."

I could hear the fear in her voice, and I hated it. "I already told him I can't make it, Everly. He was fine about it."

She looked down at Cat. "Won't he ask why?"

I nodded. "Yeah. He will, but I'll come up with something."

Everly glanced around the bedroom, avoiding eye contact. "I'll be fine, Kyle. I don't want you to cancel."

Laughing, I replied, "I am not leaving you alone, so I can go fishing. Christ, what kind of guy do you think I am?"

She smiled. "I just feel bad."

"Well, don't. Besides, we need to finish talking about what happened."

"Okay. I know that we need to talk."

I smiled. "If you want to take a shower and get relaxed, I can make popcorn. We could watch a movie."

A soft smile spread across her face. "Okay. That sounds good."

I would have given anything to hear her thoughts in that moment. I needed to find out what happened to her, but I could also understand her fear of reliving it. I knew I would have to slowly get it out of her piece by piece.

I started to walk backward toward the door of Everly's room. "Come on down when you're ready."

"I will."

I turned and started to pull the bedroom door shut, but stopped when she called out.

"Kyle?"

"Yeah?" I asked, poking my head back in.

"Thank you, for everything."

A strange sensation hit me right in the middle of the chest. "You're welcome."

After I shut the door, I stood there for a moment before I turned and headed back downstairs, willing away the frustration of not knowing what in the hell had happened to Everly. I couldn't fix a problem I didn't know anything about. And that pissed me off.

# Chapter Four

## Everly

After unpacking the clothes Brighton had sent and putting all the products in the bathroom, I turned on the shower and waited for the water to heat up. The moment I stepped into the stream, I let out a long sigh.

I closed my eyes, tensing slightly when I lifted my arms to wash my hair. The bruised ribs reminded me of what I had gone through only days ago.

Focusing on the tile wall ahead of me, I let the water fall over my body, easing away the tension and pain. Kyle was being so patient, but I knew I needed to tell him everything. I was so scared, and that annoyed me. I had escaped. I was safe. I needed to get it all out, for Pete's sake.

Who were the guys who took me? Why did they want me dead? And why in the hell was Derrick involved?

Closing my eyes, the memory rushed back.

*I was outside. Thank God, I was out of that room.*

*After a quick look around me, I ducked low and stayed against the building as I took in my surroundings. "Where am I?" I whispered. The side of the building had barrels lined up and I could smell oil. And gasoline.*

*"Shit. Shit. Shit."*

*I heard noises coming from the building, but wasn't sure what I was hearing. Had James already gone back into the room? What about the other two guys who had taken me? I was pretty sure they were gone.*

*I closed my eyes as it sank in that I had recognized one of the men. He was a cop. I was positive of it. Had he been following me?*

*I quickly ran as fast as I could with my sore ribs and crouched down behind two large barrels. It was then I saw the oil drips running down one of them. The sound of a car pulling up caused me to hold my breath. There was a small gap between the barrels that allowed me to see toward the front of the building. The car that the two kidnappers had driven was gone and a white truck was in its place. That must be the third guy's vehicle. Suddenly a black car came into view, and I watched as the door opened and the driver stepped out. I gasped, closing my eyes in a silent prayer of thanks.*

*Derrick Mays, the man I was once engaged to, started to walk toward the building. I was about to jump up and run to him when I heard the door of the building squeak open and a familiar voice call out. I instantly froze.*

*"About fucking time you got here, Mays."*

*I pressed my hand to my mouth to hold back a scream. It was James, the same man who had yelled at the guy who'd beaten me. I had memorized his features earlier, even with my eye swollen shut and the room dimly lit. He was handsome and tall. He looked to be in his early- to mid-thirties and had a scar across his right cheek. He also looked like a cop, clean cut with short hair. That, or military.*

*"You fucked this up. How could you fuck it up?" Derrick seethed as I watched the two men walk toward each other. They met halfway, and I could easily see their profiles from where I sat.*

*"How are we supposed to make it look like an accident if she looks like she's been in a boxing match? We need to wait a few days,*

or I need to make the accident larger. Her injuries need to match the car accident."

Derrick cursed. "Fuck! I told you to make it quick and painless, James, not beat the living shit out of her!"

My heart pounded in my chest as I realized Derrick was behind all of this. Oh my God. Oh my God. Why in the hell was Derrick trying to have me killed?

I closed my eyes and attempted to calm my heart and slow my breathing.

"It's a minor complication," James said as the men began walking toward the building entrance. "My colleagues got rough with her when she fought back. We need to wait until she's healed up, then we can cause an accident. Or I can make it so they don't even find enough of her to question anything. It's your choice."

I was instantly sick to my stomach. It took everything I had not to throw up or run right then and there.

"Fuck," Derrick repeated. "They're going to report her missing now. Then her family's going to get involved, and people will start looking for her."

James pointed at him angrily. "Then make it look like she's simply gone away for a few days."

Darrick shook his head. "She just got back to Alaska from her brother's fucking wedding! Why would she turn around and take more time off?"

With both hands now over my mouth, I quickly looked around. There was an opening in the fence surrounding the property, probably where an animal had been coming in and out. I was small enough to get through it. Beyond the fence was a hill that dipped out of sight. If I could make it through the fence and down the hill, I could hopefully find the main road and get help. I just needed to ignore the pain in my side in order to accomplish those tasks.

"I told you to make it quick and as painless as possible."

James laughed. "You also told me to kill her. And those two idiots I hired suck at their jobs. They wouldn't last a day on the DC force."

*Oh my God. Were they all cops? How can I go to the police now? The urge to vomit hit me yet again, but I clenched my jaw until it passed.*

*James opened the door to the building. It wouldn't be long before they discovered I was gone.*

*"We're going to have to make up some damn excuse why she's missing," Derrick said.*

*"I'll leave that bit up to you..."*

*The door slammed shut, and I took another look around before running low and fast to the fence. I practically dove under it, ignoring the shooting pain in my side. I crawled over the hill, and once I was down it a bit, I ran as fast as I possibly could, forcing myself not to think about how my entire body felt like someone was still kicking and hitting me.*

*Pushing myself as hard as I could, I cried internally, "Run, Everly! Run!"*

*I wasn't even sure how far I'd gone before I came to a road. I looked around for a clue to where I was and nearly cried when I realized I was close to my apartment. It was so close I paused for a moment. It had seemed like the men drove for hours before they'd finally pulled into the building where they'd kept me.*

*There was no way I could go back to my apartment; James and Derrick had probably already discovered I was gone. The sound of a plane overhead caused me to look down the road.*

*"The airport," I whispered and took off running as fast as I could.*

The sound of Cat's bark had me jumping as I turned to see her standing there, staring at me in the shower.

"A little privacy here, girl?" I stated with a giggle.

She tilted her head and studied me before sitting down.

"Or not."

I quickly got to work washing my hair and soaping up. As I stepped out of the shower, Cat watched my every move—from me grabbing a towel and drying off to getting dressed so I could meet Kyle downstairs.

Picking a pair of cotton sleeping pants and a matching, long-sleeve shirt, I pulled them on. Then I grabbed Kyle's sweatshirt, pulled it over my head, and headed to the door. Cat raced out first and made her way down the steps, letting out another bark once she saw Kyle.

"Hey, sweet baby girl," Kyle said as he dropped down and gave her attention. The dog ate it up, and a part of me was instantly jealous. It was obvious the two shared a special bond.

*Christ, Everly, really? Jealous of a dog?*

I stopped a few feet away and smiled, watching their interaction. Cat licked Kyle and nearly threw herself against him. Then she looked at me, and I swore she gave me a smirk.

"She certainly loves you."

Those dark green eyes met mine, and my breath caught in my throat when Kyle smiled at me.

*How is this man still single?*

He stood, and I took a slow gander over his body. He had on sweatpants and a long-sleeve T-shirt that said Book Nerd on it. My heart beat like someone had kickstarted it after it stalled for a moment or two. Why was it so hot that he liked to read? And Lord, those sweatpants didn't leave much to the imagination. God bless whoever invented men's sweatpants.

"I wasn't sure what you wanted to watch," he said.

I shrugged. "I'm up for whatever you want."

He sent a wickedly charming smile my way. "If you leave it up to me, we'll be watching *Pride and Prejudice*."

"I'm good with that; I don't think I've ever seen it."

A look of pure shock appeared on his face. "What?"

With a shake of my head, I replied, "I've never watched it. I've read the book. We had to read it in high school."

Now his eyes grew wider. "You mean you didn't read it for pleasure?"

I chewed nervously on my lip. "I'm pretty sure I bought the CliffsNotes and didn't even read the entire book."

Kyle took a few steps back. He clutched at his heart, and Cat barked. "I know, Cat. We'll fix this. Starting tonight."

Laughing, I replied, "Will we?"

"Yes. But now I'm thinking we need to start with *Emma*. Have you read that book?"

I wasn't sure if I should tell him the truth or not. Deciding to be honest, I answered, "I haven't read any of Jane Austen's books."

Kyle put his hand to his forehead and slowly drew in a deep breath. "I'm not sure I can allow you to stay in my house even one moment longer, Everly."

Cat barked and made a beeline for the sofa, and I pointed in her direction. "Cat appears to be giving me a second chance."

He glanced over his shoulder. "She wants to get movie time going, if only for the popcorn that will surely end up on the sofa and floor."

"Ahh," I replied, making my way to the sofa and sitting at one end.

"It's a recliner, you can pull it out."

I reached down the side of the sofa and smiled when I found the handle. "Fancy!"

Kyle winked, and my stomach dropped to my toes. "I like to be comfortable. So does Cat." He made his way toward the kitchen. "I'll pop some popcorn. Did you want anything else to eat? You didn't really eat much today."

"I'm good, thank you though."

He paused before he walked out of the room. "A yogurt, maybe? You might want to take something for the pain. We ate a while ago, and Tylenol can make you sick on an empty stomach."

My heart felt as if it might beat right out of my chest. This man was so thoughtful it nearly made me swoon right there. "The popcorn should be good enough. Thank you."

He flashed a boyish smile, bringing his dimples out in full view, and my lower stomach pulled with desire. I looked away before he could see me blush.

"Popcorn, it is," Kyle said as he headed to the kitchen.

I stretched and rolled over to see a beam of sunlight shining through the window. Turning, I saw a note on the pillow next to me. I sat up, mindful of my ribs, and quickly opened it.

*Dear Everly,*
*I went for a quick run. Cat is there with you and I'm not leaving my property. I cut up some fruit for you if you want to have it for breakfast, or I can make something once I get back.*
*Kyle*

I closed my eyes and brought the note up to my chest. "If I thought I liked him before."

With a sigh, I crawled out of bed and walked over to the little dresser where I'd placed most of the clothes Brighton had given to me. Thank God she put in a pair of yoga pants. I slipped them on and then pulled on a long-sleeve pink shirt before I made my way downstairs.

The smell of coffee made me smile as I stepped into the kitchen. It was immaculate. Either Kyle had a cleaning lady, or he was a neat freak. I was hoping it was the latter, because I wasn't sure how in the hell I could hide from a house cleaner.

There was another note on the kitchen island, and I picked it up.

*P.S: You fell asleep during Emma. I'll forgive you this one time. Feel free to watch it until I get back—that's if you even wake up before I get back!*
*K*

I smiled and set the note back down on the counter. I blew out a long breath and walked over to the refrigerator and opened it. I pulled out eggs, cheese, bell peppers, and an onion, and quickly got to work making breakfast. Cat sat by my side watching my every move. As I cooked the meal, I wondered what in the world I was going to do when Kyle had to go to work the next day.

Glancing at the clock, I sighed. Kyle wasn't back yet, so he must have left for his run right before I woke up. I took half of the eggs and started to eat while I tried to think of some meals to make. I wasn't the best cook, but I could throw together a few decent meals, and I wasn't about to let Kyle keep babying me. Although, it was nice to go on that picnic yesterday.

I searched the cabinets—a beautiful light maple with a distressed finish to them—and added to my grocery list for Kyle. His whole house had a very rustic cabin feel, which I loved. I wondered if Greer had helped him decorate. I thought about Kyle's love of romance novels and grinned as I got back to work peeking through each cabinet. I found an Instant Pot, a Crockpot, and a bread machine. "Oh, I've always wanted to make bread!" I said out loud.

I heard someone knocking on the door and froze, then quickly headed into the living room. Cat stood next to me, not seeming the least bit worried.

"Maybe it's Kyle," I whispered, looking down at Cat and back at the door. Then I heard a key sliding into the lock and relaxed.

"It's Kyle," I sighed with relief.

The door opened and a beautiful woman walked in. Her light brown hair was pulled back in a high ponytail and her soft brown eyes met my stunned gaze.

"Oh shit," she said. "Kyle's going to kill me."

"Brighton?" I asked as she closed the door behind her.

"I tried calling Kyle's cell to tell him I was here with some food, but he didn't answer." She gave me a once-over and grinned. "I see my clothes fit you perfectly!"

For a moment I wasn't sure what to do, but then I found my voice. "Um, yes. Thank you. How are you?" I glanced down to her pregnant belly and a strange sensation hit me in the chest. Longing?

Sadness? I shook it away and focused back on Brighton. We'd met at Hudson and Greer's rehearsal dinner, and I had spoken to her and her husband Luke for a bit at the wedding reception.

A soft smile spread across her face. "I'm doing well. I have to say, I wasn't expecting to find you here, Everly." She tilted her head. "The question is, how are you?"

My face heated as she studied me. "I...I...I'm not sure, to be a hundred percent honest." I tried to force calm into my voice. This woman was a close friend of Kyle's, and I was pretty sure he had no idea she'd be coming over. If he had, he wouldn't have left to go for a run, or at the very least, he would have said something in his note. "Um, does Kyle know you're here?"

Brighton's eyes went a bit wide. "He does not. Well, unless he checks his phone. I sent him a text saying I was here and brought some yummies." She looked around and then back at me. "I have to ask, Everly, why did you show up at Kyle's and not Hudson's?"

I drew my brows in. "Why Kyle?"

She nodded.

"Well, he's a friend. I know I can trust him, and honestly, he was the first person I thought of."

The corner of her mouth twitched, and I could tell she was attempting not to smile. What in the hell was there to smile about?

"I can see that," she said. "It was pretty clear with how the two of you were *not* looking at each other during the wedding that there's something between you."

I stood frozen in shock as she moved past me and into the kitchen. I followed and watched as Brighton put a brown bag on the kitchen island. I had been so focused on *not* staring at Kyle that weekend, I hadn't even considered that he might be doing the very same thing to me. Before I could think about all of that, I shook my head and asked, "Wait, you have a key to Kyle's house?"

She nodded. "I do. He gave me a key, and I have his alarm app on my phone. I drop off a lot of...products for him."

A surge of jealousy raced through me. Brighton was married, for goodness' sake. To an actor. A very good-looking actor. Granted, he wasn't nearly as handsome as Kyle, but still. "Are you...do you and Kyle...I mean...are you guys...um...."

One of her brows rose into an arch. "If you're about to ask if there's something between us, let me stop you right there." She shuddered and then fake gagged. "He's a friend...really like a brother. And I trust him with my life. That being said, when he told me about you, the very *little* he told me, I knew I had to come and introduce myself. Despite knowing Kyle was going to be really pissed off about it."

"But you still came knowing this?" I asked.

"I wanted to let you know you're not alone, and I'm here to help in any way I can. Kyle said you won't go to the police, so I thought maybe I could help."

"Help?"

"Yes. Maybe even talk you into at least talking to Lance, Kyle's dad." She held up her hands. "Please don't worry, I won't tell anyone you're here. But does your brother at least know?"

She looked at my cheek, taking in the evidence of my beating, though the bruise was slowly fading with the help of the cream from Kyle and the cover-up she had given me. Still, I could see the anger in her gaze before she deliberately softened it.

"Hudson knows I'm safe, but I haven't told him where I am," I said. "He doesn't know the whole story yet. I'm afraid once he finds out, he'll want to go to Alaska and find the men who did this."

Brighton nodded. "I'd be worried about Kyle wanting to do the same thing."

I opened my mouth to say something, but then snapped it shut.

She smiled gently at me. "Just so you know, Everly, I'm a lawyer, and so is Luke. If you need anything..."

She let her words fade away softly, and I drew in my first full breath since Brighton had showed up only moments ago. I relaxed my body and leaned against the counter. "Thank you, but I don't want to drag you into this mess."

She gave me a knowing look. "I can understand your concern, but I also know you're stuck in this house hiding out with only Kyle and Cat. Plus, I can only imagine Kyle is forcing you to watch Jane Austen movies. I wanted to make sure you were okay, and for you to have a female friend if you need one."

Smiling, I replied, "I am okay, thank you for checking up on me."

"I figured Kyle wouldn't have much in the way of food, since he's a single guy and all."

I nodded, still feeling a bit strange to have her in the house. Nervously, I glanced around the kitchen while I wrung my hands together. Brighton saw the nervous gesture and began to pull out the items in the bag.

"I wasn't sure what you'd want, so I started with the basics. Fruit. Ice cream. Peanut butter and jelly, and Oreos. And lots of fruits and veggies."

"Would you believe I adore all of that? Especially the Oreos."

She looked at me and winked. "You and Kyle will make excellent roomies then, because he's an Oreo whore. A word of advice though, don't let him know I gave you that face cream. He loves it."

My brows shot up. All I could manage to say was, "Ahhh..."

Brighton laughed as she put the ice cream in the freezer. Even though I knew she was married to another man, the fact that she knew her way around Kyle's house so well made me slightly envious of their relationship.

She leaned against the counter. "I know. Kyle is... actually, I'm probably not the best person to say what Kyle is."

It was my turn to laugh. "Why not?"

She met my gaze. "He's one of my dearest friends, but there have been so many times I've wanted to punch him in the face."

"Oh," I said, my eyes widening. "Okay, I have to admit I wasn't expecting that."

"I know," Brighton said with a shake of her head. "I would do anything for him. He really is like a brother to me, and I trust him. He obviously trusts me, since he told me about you, though not by name. I'm glad you came to him, Everly. If anyone can keep you safe and get to the bottom of all of this, it's Kyle."

Tears burned at the back of my eyes. "I hope so. I really didn't want to drag you into this mess."

She waved me off. "Nonsense. It's not unusual for me to drop stuff off here. Greer and I helped him decorate this place. Plus, I'm one of his best skin care dealers."

I smiled. "You've truly brightened my day. Thank you."

Brighton winked. "Where is Kyle, by the way? I thought he was going fishing with Hunter, but Bella said he had to back out."

"He went for a run."

She nodded. "I better go before he gets back and has my head on a platter for not listening to him. Here's my number." She pulled out a business card and slid it my way. "Do you have a cell phone?"

I picked it up and saw it was a business card from Willow Tree Inn, the bed and breakfast her family owned.

I shook my head. "No, I left everything in Alaska. I even tossed out my Apple watch on the way to the airport."

She smiled. "Smart move. If you need any legal advice, please don't hesitate to call me."

"I won't, thank you," I replied as I started to follow her to the front door.

Turning, she held up her hand. "In case anyone *is* watching, don't see me out."

I froze in place and gave a nod. Did she suspect that she was followed here? My heart began to beat in overdrive, though I attempted to look calm on the outside.

"Before I leave, do you need me to get you anything?" she asked. "I have the list of items you wrote down for Kyle. I was thinking you might need a heavy coat, as well, in case you're here longer than you think you'll be."

*Oh God. How long would I have to hide out here? How long would I be a prisoner of my own fear?* I needed to figure out why Derrick wanted me dead. All I could do was nod, unable to form words for a moment.

When I finally found my voice, I replied, "Thank you, Brighton. I appreciate it."

Suddenly, the front door opened and Kyle practically ran over Brighton in his rush to get in. He came to a stop when he saw me, a look of relief on his face. As he turned to Brighton, his expression changed to one of fury. I hadn't known Kyle for very long, but I'd *never* seen anyone look as angry as Kyle did in that moment.

"Oh dear," Brighton muttered.

"What in the fuck are you doing here, Brighton?"

I blanched at Kyle's harsh words while Brighton took a step back. "Hello to you to, Kyle. I brought over some food for Everly. I wasn't sure if you'd left her with only ramen noodles to live off of, and I wanted to make sure she was okay."

The crazy thing was, Kyle had two cases of ramen in his pantry, so it was a fair thing for Brighton to have assumed.

He glared at her. "You wanted to make sure she was okay? Did you ever think that by coming over here you could have drawn attention to the house and actually put her in *more* danger? You turned off the alarm, Brighton! You *turned off* the alarm."

Brighton drew in a breath. "Okay, in hindsight it probably wasn't the smartest thing to do."

"Probably?" Kyle stammered back.

"Well, it's not unusual for me to drop things off at your house. And I know you didn't want me involved, but I got to thinking and I thought maybe she..." Brighton turned to me. "That Everly might need a female friend and someone else to talk to. I didn't mean any harm, Kyle." She tried for a smile. "By the way, that cuticle cream is on back order and won't be in for another month."

I had to try hard not to laugh when I peeked over and saw Kyle nearly ready to blow steam out of his ears.

"I asked you to stay out of this, Brighton. I still have no idea why Everly's ex-fiancé is after her, and you head on over here for a play date?"

I started to speak, but Brighton beat me to it.

She brought her hands to her hips and stood taller, her shoulders squared. "A play date? Did you really just say that? I said I was sorry and that it wasn't the smartest thing to do, but you don't have to be mean, Kyle."

"Yes, goddammit, I do!" Kyle ran his fingers through his hair. "You had to rush over and see, didn't you? So fucking curious that you lost sight of the fact that she's hiding out. Her own brother doesn't even know she's here, for fuck's sake! What a goddamn selfish thing to do, Bree!"

"Kyle—" Brighton started.

"What if someone's watching the house?"

A sudden surge of fear hit me. Not only a fear for myself, but for Brighton as well. She was five months pregnant. "You think someone's watching your house?" I asked.

Kyle quickly turned to me. His expression softened when he saw my own. "No. No, I don't. I would never have gone for a run if I thought that, sweetheart."

The endearment sent a rush through my body.

"I didn't mean to frighten you," he said, "but it was stupid of Brighton to come simply because she was curious."

"Curious?" Brighton called out. "I was *concerned*, Kyle Larson. You don't have to do this alone, you know." She turned to face me. "It's clear you're not going to tell Hudson, which I think is a mistake. You really should tell your brother that you're here, regardless of whether or not he thinks you're safe. He's got to be going out of his mind with worry."

I wanted to tell her that we *were planning* to tell Hudson, but before I could, Kyle spoke again.

"Bree, get out. Now."

She turned back to Kyle and forced a smile. "I'm sorry if I upset you and Everly. I really was acting with my heart and nothing else."

Kyle closed his eyes and drew in a deep breath.

"She didn't put me in any danger, Kyle," I protested quietly. "And honestly, it was good to see another person and have someone to talk to."

He turned to look at me, his face instantly softening. "I know, I'm sorry for blowing up. She did call and text first, I guess."

"I shouldn't have come over, I see that," Brighton said. "At any rate, I left Everly my number in case she needs it for anything."

Kyle nodded. "Thanks, Brighton."

"It was kind of you to stop by, Brighton," I said. I had a feeling that if given the chance, Brighton and I could become good friends. She clearly cared about Kyle, and it was becoming apparent they had more of a brother-sister type relationship. The way he was looking at her—like he was about to lose his patience—was something I was all too familiar with as Hudson's sister.

"Goodbye, Bree." Kyle stepped in front of me, blocking me from the view of outside.

Brighton looked at me once more and waved. "I hope we get to talk soon, Everly!"

"I hope so too," I stated.

After she left, Kyle stared at the door for a few moments before he turned toward me. My breath caught in my throat at the intense look in his eyes. It wasn't anger or fear for my safety, it was something altogether different. It almost looked like...

No. Impossible. But whatever it was, it warmed my body and made my heart rate double and my stomach tumble.

"I'm sorry," he said. "Brighton has a way of pushing my buttons, and when I saw her here...I just..."

I stepped forward, took his hand in mine, and squeezed it. The spot where our skin touched sent a rush of electricity through my entire body. I sucked in a breath, and I couldn't help but notice Kyle reacting similarly.

"I'm okay," I said. "Truth be told, it was nice being able to talk to her. For a few minutes, I felt..."

His brows pulled together. "You felt what?"

Sighing, I replied, "Not scared."

Kyle closed his eyes and pulled me to him, wrapping his arms around me. I hated all the clothing between us because it kept me from feeling his warmth.

"You don't have to be scared, sweetheart. I swear to you, I won't let anyone hurt you."

His words did all kinds of crazy things to my heart, and I tried to push away the idea of staying in Kyle's arms and feeling this beautiful peacefulness...forever. I squeezed my eyes shut. It was a dream, and that was all.

Or...was it possible we could have a future together? I was ready for a change. I needed a change, but at the moment I couldn't even think about the future until this all got figured out.

Stepping back, I willed myself to smile and not think about the instant loss of warmth from his embrace.

"You believe me, right?" he asked.

I snapped my head up to meet his gaze. "Of course I do. I wouldn't be here if I didn't think you'd keep me safe, Kyle. I just...I would never forgive myself if anything happened to you or your family and friends."

He placed his hand on the side of my face, and I leaned slightly into it, stopping myself from letting out a contented purr.

"Nothing is going to happen to anyone," he said.

Cat pushed her way between our bodies, causing the two of us to take a step away from one another. She turned, looked at Kyle, and let out a soft bark.

"What is it, girl?" He ran his hand over her back, and she pressed her body against his.

I loved the bond Cat shared with Kyle, and it was becoming clear we were forming our own bond together as well. She was a precious dog, and I knew she would do anything to protect either one of us.

Kyle looked back up at me. "I should go shower."

I nodded.

"You're okay, though?"

"Yes," I said with a soft smile. "I'm fine."

Kyle nodded, then drew in a breath and looked up the steps.

"Go shower; I made you breakfast, but it's cold now."

He winked. "I'll heat it up."

After making it halfway up the steps, he stopped and turned around.

"I'll buy you a cell phone, one that can't be traced back to you. If you need anything, though, page me. And don't answer the door or the phone."

I put my hand up to my forehead and saluted him. "Got it."

He smiled. "Also, I put a laptop on the coffee table if you want to use it for anything. But whatever you do, don't look up anything about you or where you were working or anything like that."

Nodding, I replied in a whispered voice, "I won't."

I watched Kyle disappear upstairs. Cat had chosen to stay with me.

"Come on, girl, let's go see what Brighton brought for us."

Cat let out a bark and wagged her tail as she led the way into the kitchen.

# Chapter Five
## James - Valdez, Alaska

"**W**e're not getting anywhere here, are we?" Derrick stated as he stood in the middle of Everly's apartment.

"We need to find something that might lead us to where she went," I said. "She clearly didn't go to her brother's place in New Hampshire, but she *has* been in touch with him."

Derrick rubbed at the back of his neck. "Do you really think he believes she's at a resort?"

I turned to face him. "Do you? You know the guy better than I do."

Derrick frowned. "I don't know him that well. Met him once, and I got the impression he didn't care for me."

Laughing, I said, "I like him already."

Derrick sighed. "I think she's still in Alaska. I know Everly, and she wouldn't bring this to her brother's doorstep."

Sighing as well, I closed the drawer of the desk I was searching in the living room. "Why do you say that?"

"Like I said, she wouldn't want to bring him or his new wife any trouble. Do I think she's smart enough to leave Alaska? Maybe. She literally ran out of that warehouse with nothing. No money, no driver's license. How in the hell could she go anywhere?"

I nodded. "We need to find out if that's who she went to or if she did leave Alaska. Someone had to help her leave, if she is gone. Maybe Kristy's the one we need to be focusing on. If she didn't go to family, who else would she trust?"

"Kristy. She'd go to Kristy for help. She's the only reason Everly was in Alaska in the first place."

"I thought she came to Alaska to get as far away from you as she could?"

Derrick shot me a dirty look. "She came to Alaska because one of her best friends is here. They met their first day at NOAA. Kristy asked Everly to come and at first she said no, but then she changed her mind."

"Why did she change her mind?"

With a shrug, Derrick replied, "I have no clue. I've barely spoken to Everly in almost three years. And the little we did speak, it was business only. Once she broke off the engagement, that was it. She wanted nothing to do with me."

"She's not the type of woman to forgive then?"

Derrick smirked. "No, not at all."

I knew Everly had found out Derrick was cheating and that was why she called off the engagement. Or at least, that was *his* side of the story.

Pointing at Derrick, I said, "You need to talk to this Kristy girl."

A bark of laughter filled the room. "Kristy hates me even more than Everly does."

I raised a brow. "Why?"

With a smug smile, Derrick replied, "She was in Greenland for a few weeks when we were there. I met her in a bar, took her back to my place, and we fucked. I had no idea she was Everly's best friend."

Laughing, I said, "Don't tell me that was who she caught you with?"

He nodded. "Yep. Was worth it though. Kristy has the most amazing tits, and man, is she good in bed. Best fucking blowjob I've ever had."

Glancing around the apartment, I felt a surge of anger that there were no leads on where this bitch went. She hadn't gone to the airport. No leads at the bus station and, as far as I could tell, she hadn't chartered a plane. For all I knew, she was dead on the side of the road somewhere.

Nah. If she was dead, her brother and parents wouldn't seem so at ease. Everly clearly contacted them and convinced them she was heading off somewhere for some R&R.

"I need everything on this Kristy," I said. "She's clearly the key to finding your ex. Let's hope Everly keeps her mouth shut until we find her."

Derrick frowned. "I don't even think Everly realizes what she's stumbled into, James."

I met his eyes. "Yet, you were still willing to let me shut her up... permanently."

The corner of his mouth lifted ever so slightly. "I have a lot of money riding on this. She may not have known what she did, but she'll figure it out soon enough. Especially since Jacob ended up dying in a car accident days after Everly filed that report. Luckily, we had someone inside who caught it and got rid of it before alerting us. But I know Everly; she would have followed up with Jacob. She's that dedicated to all this shit. Once she finally figured out that there was no report and that Jacob was dead, she'd either ask questions or file the damn report again. Our guy on the inside can't keep killing people to keep it quiet."

"If only she hadn't stumbled on it. We wouldn't even have to deal with Everly," I muttered.

Derrick shook his head. "From what you told me, she doesn't even know why you took her. Hopefully she didn't say anything to anyone else, but I seriously doubt it."

"Hence the reason we need to talk to Kristy. See if she knows anything."

Derrick pointed at me angrily. "Your henchman fucked it up by beating Everly. Why in the hell did they even lay a finger on her?

Their job was to grab her, drug her, and make it all look like an accident. And these guys are cops?"

I smiled. "I told you. She fought harder than they expected."

A look moved over Derrick's face—and I was almost positive it
was one of regret.

He turned and walked over to the window. "She might already
be dead. She ran from that warehouse with no coat on."

"Is that sadness in your voice I hear?"

Derrick slowly turned to face me. "No."

"You and I both know she's not dead. The family hasn't filed
a missing person's report, so that tells me they've heard from her.
When I talked to the brother on the phone and acted like her supervisor, he didn't seem the least bit concerned. Which tells me she's
contacted him. As far as I can tell, he knows nothing about the kidnapping or her escape."

Rubbing the back of his neck again, Derrick said, "Kristy hangs
out at a bar in town called The Wheelhouse. It's located in the Best
Western."

I pulled out my phone and hit a number. "I need a room booked
at the Best Western here in town. Make it for two weeks. Put it under
Martin Williams." After I hung up, I glanced over at Derrick. "I need
a picture of Kristy and everything you know about her, and I want it
by nine tonight."

Derrick nodded and pulled out his own phone as we walked out
of Everly's apartment.

"Oh, I hope Everly isn't upset with me that I let you gentlemen
in," said Everly's landlord, an older woman. She looked from me to
Derrick, then back to me. We'd told her we were with NOAA, and
that Everly had decided to take an extended vacation, but there was
a report we needed ASAP.

With a smile, I replied, "We didn't find it, but I'm sure she'll be
fine with you letting us in. After all, Derrick and Everly were once
engaged." I turned to Derrick. "Didn't she send you a text saying it
was okay?"

The older woman looked at Derrick and frowned slightly. "Really? You were engaged?"

Derrick tried for a charming smile but it fell short. The old woman clearly didn't think Derrick was Everly's type.

"Do you know when Everly will be back?" she asked.

"I hope soon," I answered as I handed her my business card. "You'll let me know when she returns?"

She glanced down to my card. "Martin Williams, Director of Geoscience?" I smiled again when she looked up at me. "Won't you see her anyway when she returns?" she asked.

Smart old woman. Time to throw her off. "I'll be in the field. We'll get it all figured out."

She smiled.

Derrick and I said our goodbyes and headed toward my rented SUV. Once we were inside, my phone went off, and I pulled up the text Derrick had sent me. It was from the NOAA website and listed Kristy's name and her position.

### Kristy Livingston
### Environmental Research Scientist/Glaciologist

The next text was a picture. I grinned. This was going to be easy. The brunette in the image had stunning blue eyes and a smile that would make any guy want to get to know her better.

"Boyfriend?" I asked.

"Not that I know of. She's married to her work, same as Everly."

I nodded and put my phone down. "It's time for you to go back to Washington, Derrick. The longer you stay here, the more questions it could raise."

"What if you find her?"

Turning to him, I laughed. "What if I do?"

"If she knows I'm here, maybe she'll come to me for help."

I raised a brow. "Or, she saw you that night, and she knows you're in on it. Leave, as soon as possible. I'll take care of things from here on out."

Derrick looked like he wanted to argue, but he knew better. Instead, he added, "You know, if anything happens to Kristy, people will start asking questions. One woman going missing is one thing, but two?"

Narrowing my eyes at him, I asked, "Do you think I'm new at this? I know what the fuck I'm doing. Kristy will be fine. As long as she does what I want her to do and doesn't ask questions, I won't touch a hair on her body."

He nodded and then looked out the window as I put the SUV in gear and drove away from the apartment building.

# Chapter Six
## Kyle

I stepped out of the shower to the sound of my phone ringing.

"What?" I said after picking it up.

"What has you in a mood?" Hunter asked. "Is this why we didn't go fishing? You're having your period?"

"I'm not in a mood," I replied on a long sigh.

"You're for sure in a mood, dude. What's going on, Kyle? You never cancel on fishing."

"I wasn't feeling that great and, to be honest, I wanted some downtime."

"Downtime?" Hunter asked.

Clearly, I sucked at lying.

"Why do you sound so confused?" I asked, hoping to sound more believable. "I honestly wasn't in the mood for fishing."

There was a long silence before Hunter said, "Okay. Are we at least still on for poker tonight?"

I closed my eyes and internally cursed. If I canceled on poker, I'd have Hunter, Bishop, Aiden, and Hudson on my doorstep asking questions.

"Yeah, man, of course. Be prepared to lose."

Hunter laughed. "You keep talking shit, dude."

"Later," I said, smiling.

"Talk soon."

After I hung up, I walked over and opened up my laptop to the page I had been looking at last night when I couldn't sleep. It was Everly's blog. She posted on it a few times a month, and I'd been following it ever since Hudson had mentioned it a few months back.

*"What's It Like Working in Alaska?"*

It was the title of the last entry she'd made, right before she'd left to come back to New Hampshire for the wedding.

*One of the questions I get asked the most is how do I like working in freezing-cold places. The answer: I love it. The last few years, I was in Greenland, and when I was given the chance to head to Alaska to help a colleague study a glacier that's melting at an alarming rate, I didn't hesitate. This is what I love. This is my life's work. This is important work and work I'm proud of.*

*Do I get tired of it?*

*Sometimes. I'm like everyone else who dreams of sitting on a warm beach drinking a cocktail with an umbrella in it. But who can say they get to go to work every day on a glacier? I discover new things all the time, though people laugh when I tell them that. Just the other day, I stumbled upon something that I can't wait to share with you guys. I'm going to make you wait until the next blog post though. Right now, I need to pack for my brother's upcoming wedding in New Hampshire.*

*Until next time!*

*E*

I closed the browser and stared at the computer. Nothing seemed out of the ordinary with her post. Everly was always sharing things about the area where she worked, and some of her finds that she was allowed to share, considering she worked for a government agency. Some of the stuff on her blog was kind of cool.

I pushed my fingers through my damp hair and let out a frustrated sigh. Cat followed my lead, and we both looked at the closed bedroom door. Clearly, she wanted to get back to Everly, and so did I.

Once I was dressed, I opened the bedroom door and Cat made a beeline straight for Everly's bedroom. She reached up with her paw and pulled the handle down, then rushed in.

"Fuck," I said, following behind her.

"Cat! Hey, girl!"

The sound of Everly's voice was the sweetest thing I'd ever heard, and relief rushed over me. I nearly fell as I rushed into the room— and came to an abrupt halt at what I saw before me.

Everly let out a squeak, then attempted to cover her completely naked body with her arms and hands.

"Holy shit!" I said as I spun around, only to realize I could still see Everly in the mirror of the dresser. "Fuck!" I closed my eyes and dropped my head. "I'm so sorry, Everly. Cat came dashing in here and I thought...I thought something was, um, was wrong."

I could hear her moving about before she said, "It's okay, I just came out of the bathroom. I took a shower after I walked on your treadmill for a few minutes. You can turn around, I'm covered up."

Oh, hell no. There was no way I could turn around because my dick was hard as a fucking rock.

"I'll let you get dressed. I need to go change."

"Change? But didn't you just take a shower?"

"Right," I said with a nervous laugh. "I forgot to, um...wash my hair."

And before she could say a word, I quickly made my way out of her room and across the hall to my own bedroom. I kicked the door shut and then leaned over and put my hands on my knees as I drew in a few deep breaths.

"My God," I whispered, closing my eyes and willing my memory to imprint the moment so I would never forget what I had seen. Everly, naked. Gloriously naked and with a body that—Christ Almighty—made me want her even more. With the quick look I got, I couldn't see everything, but what I *had* seen was the body of a goddess. Breasts so stunning that my mouth instantly watered at the thought of sucking on her nipples. An hourglass figure that would bring any man to his knees.

"I need another shower. A cold shower," I huffed and walked farther into the bedroom. I'd never gotten out of my clothes so fast in my entire life. Once undressed, I stepped into the cold shower.

The moment the frigid water hit me, I sucked in a breath and grabbed my still-hard dick in my hand and moaned.

Everly had been naked.

*Naked.*

I placed both hands on the shower wall and closed my eyes as I waited for the cold water to calm my raging hard-on.

After five minutes of standing in the freezing downpour, I realized it wasn't going down. Instead, I took hold of myself again and began pumping my cock. Slowly at first, then faster. Closing my eyes, the image of Everly from moments ago popped into my head. The memory of her smooth skin caused me to move even faster. I squeezed harder, and before I knew it, I was swallowing back moans as I came so hard, my damn legs nearly buckled out from under me.

Once I had wrung out every last bit of cum, I leaned my forehead against the cool tile of the shower and watched the water wash it away. I gritted my teeth and said, "Fuck, fuck, fuck," fighting to breath normally.

A short knock on the bathroom door had me going completely still.

"Kyle?"

Thank God I hadn't said her name when I came. "Yeah...be right out." I prayed my tone sounded casual. I grabbed the soap and started to wash up as she went on.

"It's...your cell phone keeps ringing, and I wasn't trying to be nosy, but it's Hunter. He sent a text that said he was on his way over a little early."

My eyes went wide. Poker night. I had forgotten to tell Everly about poker night.

"Shit!" I said as I turned off the water and pushed open the glass door. "Everly, you've got to—"

Before I could say anything else, my foot hit the slick tile floor instead of the plush carpet and slipped out from under me so fast, I barely had time to do anything. I reached for a towel, but my fingers merely brushed it before I landed flat on my ass with a thud.

"Oh my God, what happened? What was that noise? Are you okay!?"

"Fuuuuuuck," I groaned, positive my tailbone was broken.

That's when I realized I hadn't locked the bathroom door, because I lived alone and there was no *need* to lock my bathroom door. When it opened, and Everly looked down at me on the floor, she gasped. Her eyes quickly took in my naked body, with her gaze landing on my dick, and she slapped her hand over her mouth and closed her eyes.

I looked down. I was still hard. Fucking hell.

"Can you hand me that towel, Everly?"

"Ahh...um...yes." She opened her eyes, looking everywhere but at me. She rushed over to grab the towel, but gasped and grabbed at her side when she stretched her arm to reach it.

I spotted water on the floor and knew if she stepped in it, she could very well slip too.

"Everly!" I called out, which made her jump. And because I had somehow pissed off God, she twisted and started to fall. She attempted to reach for the shower door to steady herself, but missed.

The next thing I knew, Everly was lying on top of my naked, wet body. Her eyes were closed and she was as still as could be, except for her intense breathing.

"Shit, are you okay? Your side—" I said as I placed my hands on her hips. That was a mistake.

Her beautiful green eyes snapped open and met mine, and I saw the tears building.

"Your ribs?" I said softly, trying to ignore the way my body was reacting to hers.

All she could do was nod.

"Shit, let me get you—"

"No!" she cried out. "Don't move for a few moments, okay?"

I froze in place and didn't move. When she dropped her forehead to my bare chest, I cursed silently. I brought my hand up and lightly pushed her hair back, so I could see her face.

"Are you okay, sweetheart?"

It took her about two minutes before she let out a long, deep breath and then said, "I guess we're even now."

I raised a brow. "Excuse me?"

She lifted her head off my chest. "You saw me naked, now I saw you." She let out a nervous giggle and then hissed in pain.

I smiled. "I think you saw more of *me* than I did of you."

She looked down my chest, and I half wondered if she was going to push off me and look down at my dick again. Suddenly, she jerked her gaze back up. "I'm so sorry. I heard you fall and I...I...wait, are *you* okay? Did you hurt yourself?"

"I'm fine. Are you?" I asked in a voice so strained, it was clear I was anything *but* fine. "I'll be fine, I mean. Once I get up."

She nodded but still made no effort to move. Dammit. Her ribs must be killing her.

I lifted my hands, but I wasn't sure if I should touch her or help her up, so I left them up like I was in church singing a hymn. "Did you hurt yourself?" I asked again.

With a shake of her head, she whispered, "No, I landed on something hard—er, *soft*." She closed her eyes and shook her head. "Wait. I mean, you broke my fall."

My mouth twitched, and I somehow managed to find my voice. "As amazing as this feels, I really need to get up, and we need to make sure your ribs are okay. Hunter and the guys are coming over for poker night."

Her eyes went wide. "Poker night?"

She placed her hands on my chest, and I ignored the zip of energy from her touch. As she attempted to get up, she somehow put a knee to my balls, and I sucked in a breath.

"Oh my God! Oh my God! I'm so sorry!" she cried out and jumped up so fast she nearly fell again. She grabbed at her side, and it was *my* turn to jump up when I saw the pain on her face. I wasn't even thinking about covering up in that moment.

"Shit, Everly, you're going to end up breaking your ribs."

Everly let her eyes move slowly over my body. Her brows went up before she turned her head and stared at the shower for a moment, then looked back at me and reached for the towel.

"Here's the towel. For your body. Your...wet body." Her eyes went back down, staring intently at my lower half. When her tongue darted over her swollen bottom lip, I nearly groaned.

"If you keep looking at me, I'm going to have to get another look at *you*," I said.

That seemed to snap her out of her daze, and she pushed the towel she had in her hands against my chest before taking a few steps back and watching as I wrapped it around me.

"Where's Cat?" I asked.

Everly's eyes were fixed on my bare chest, her cheeks turning from soft pink to bright red.

"W-who?" she whispered.

"My dog?"

At that moment, Cat came barreling into the bathroom, knocking Everly forward and right into my arms. I grabbed hold of her and we stood there for what seemed like forever, staring into each other's eyes.

With a smile so sweet it nearly brought me to my knees, Everly said, "We have to stop meeting like this, Mr. Larson."

I laughed. "Maybe we should start locking our bedroom doors."

Was that disappointment I saw flash across her face?

"Maybe," she said quietly before stepping out of my hold. "Poker night?"

I nodded. "Yeah, we play every other Saturday night. I was going to cancel, but I thought not going fishing and then saying no to poker night would look suspicious." I made my way past her and into my bedroom, drawing in a deep breath and willing my heart to stop beating so violently.

"You don't have to cancel, Kyle. I can stay up in my room."

I let out a long breath. "I hate the idea of you locking yourself away, but like I said, if I said no to poker, I'd have four guys showing up at my door asking what's wrong. It can run late into the night though."

She smiled again, and it took my breath away. "I'll pack up some snacks and bring them to my room. If you have some headphones, I can watch a movie on your laptop."

How was it that Everly was able to return to normal, like she hadn't just been spread all over my naked body? I was doing everything I could to settle myself down. Not to mention my still-hard cock that the towel was barely hiding. I was going to have to jerk off again before the guys got here.

"If you're sure," I said.

"I'm positive. I came into your life and turned it upside down, and the last thing I want to do is cause you to miss poker night."

I brought my hand to the back of my neck and rubbed at the ache there. "We needed to really talk tonight. You have to tell me everything, so we could start to figure this out."

The corner of her mouth lifted in a fake smile. "I'm sure it can all wait until tomorrow."

I nodded. "I do have to go to my parents' for dinner tomorrow. It's something we do every Sunday. Me, Greer, and Hudson. I think tonight we need to let Hudson know you're here, Everly."

A look of sadness swept over her face so quickly, I wouldn't have noticed it if I hadn't been watching her.

"Do you think that's wise?" she asked "Won't the other guys ask questions?"

I shook my head. "No. It'll have to be a quick reunion between the two of you."

Everly exhaled, letting out a long breath. "I know you're right, and as far as you and me talking, we can do it tomorrow morning."

She glanced around my bedroom. "I better let you get ready. I brought your phone up; it's on your bed."

I turned to look at my bed. "Great. Thanks."

Everly started toward the door as she said, "I'll go make up some goodies for myself so I can be out of the way when everyone gets here."

All I could do was nod while I watched her walk out of my bedroom and softly close the door behind her. I stumbled back a few steps and sat down on the end of my bed. Cat jumped up and laid down next to me, letting out a heavy sigh.

I moved my hand to her head and gave her a good scratch. "Tell me about it, girl. Shit. I need her to tell me what happened, but at the same time I want to hold her in my arms."

Cat let out a soft bark and then laid her head on my lap.

# Chapter Seven

## Everly

My hands shook as I took some fruit out of the refrigerator and set it on the counter. He'd been naked.

And not only naked—he'd also been hard.

I grabbed the counter, closed my eyes, and counted to ten. When I opened them, my heart was still hammering away.

Why, of all things, did I have to slip? I hadn't even felt the pain in my ribs until after I realized I was on top of Kyle's insanely built body. The feel of his dick pressed into my stomach nearly had me moaning in delight. I probably *could* have moaned and blamed it on my ribs, and he would have been none the wiser.

I drew in a deep breath. "Stop this, Everly."

It was nothing. He'd seen me naked, and then I'd seen him nude. It wasn't a big deal. But...why was he hard? Was it because he'd seen me naked first? I couldn't help but smile at the possibility.

I absentmindedly opened the strawberries I'd washed and cut up earlier today and put them in the plastic container I'd grabbed. Then I made a turkey and swiss cheese wrap, grabbed a bag of potato chips, and placed it all on a tray that I'd found in the pantry. It was the type of tray you'd use for bringing someone breakfast in bed.

I paused as I pictured Kyle bringing another woman breakfast in bed. An instant rush of jealousy came over me. Had Kyle brought anyone back to his new house? Spent the night watching movies before bringing them up to his bedroom?

It wasn't clear to me if he was dating anyone or not. He hadn't brought a date to Hudson and Greer's wedding, and the only people he'd danced with were his sister and mother. I'd prayed that he'd ask me to dance, but he never did. I couldn't blame him. The last time I'd seen him, I told him nothing could happen between us.

If I could turn back the hands of time, I'd take that statement back. Especially if it meant that he would have asked me to dance. Or maybe even kissed me again.

I stared down at the tray and was about to put it back when Kyle walked into the kitchen.

"My mom said that tray would come in handy, and I guess she was right."

Glancing at the tray and then back to Kyle, I asked, "I'm sorry?"

He let out a soft laugh. "She brought it over to my previous house last winter when I had the flu, and she was playing nurse. Then she put it in my pantry for future use. I told her I wasn't planning on serving myself breakfast in bed, but I'm glad she left it. Let me carry that. Your ribs have to be killing you after that fall."

"They're okay," I said as I placed my hand on my side—and promptly winced.

He frowned. "Dammit. Did you take anything for the pain?"

"I took some Tylenol. It'll be fine, and I'll rest for the evening."

Kyle sighed. "I'm really sorry again about poker night."

I waved it off, laughing. "Honestly, it's okay."

"It's not. You've been through so much, and I feel like every time we're ready to talk about what happened, something gets in the way."

I shrugged. "To be honest, I'm not super excited to relive it all."

"But you know we have to talk about it, Everly."

Nodding, I replied, "I know."

He sighed. "I could still call it off, say I'm sick. I don't like having to leave you all alone upstairs."

I smiled softly. "I won't be alone. Besides, you'll find a way to make it up to me." I winked. Then I realized how that sounded. "I mean by watching, like, some chick flick or something like that."

He smiled back at me, and my stomach did a little twist before tumbling to the floor. Goodness, his smile. And those dimples.

I gave him another once-over. His hair was wet and those green eyes of his looked like emeralds when they sparkled with humor.

"I think I can find a way to make it up to you...and it'll be better than a movie," he said.

"Another picnic?" I asked with a hopeful smile.

When I didn't think his smile could get any better, it did. "You liked the picnic?"

A strange ache hit me right in the middle of my chest, and I had to fight the urge to put my hand there to ease it. "I did. Very much."

He winked, and my heart skipped a beat. "Then another picnic it will be." Kyle reached for the tray. "Might want to grab a few bottles of water as well."

I did as he said and then followed him and Cat up the steps to the guest bedroom I was calling mine for the time being.

"Found some earphones for you too," he said. "I also put my cell phone on the side table. If you need anything, you can page me."

"I'm sure I'll be fine, and you'll be downstairs."

Kyle set the tray down on the bed and then looked around the room before his focus came back to me. "You're sure your ribs are okay?"

I nodded. "Yep." When his eyes drifted down to my lips, I tried not to lick them.

The doorbell rang, and the trance was broken. He looked into my eyes. "Wish me luck."

Laughing, I replied, "Good luck. Though I don't know anything about poker."

He paused as he reached the door. "*What?*"

I gave him a one-shoulder shrug. "Never played it."

Kyle gifted me with another brilliant smile. "Well, we're going to have to fix that. Might even have to play strip poker, since we're so good at seeing each other naked."

My eyes went wide, and he quickly stepped out of the room and shut the door before I could respond. After I heard him go down the steps and muffled voices start speaking, I said, "I'd like that very much."

I spent the rest of the night either listening to a group of men laugh, yell, and curse each other out, or to the movie I was watching on Kyle's laptop. I was watching the second new *Jumanji* film, and it was hard to keep from laughing, though I know I needed to. One, it hurt my side when I did. And two, I didn't want Kyle's friends to hear me.

Worse yet, my brother—whose voice I'd recognized when I'd snuck out and slipped into the guest bathroom to pee—was here, and all I wanted to do was run to him. Kyle was right; we needed to let Hudson know I was here and safe. This wasn't fair to him or to my parents.

I took off the earphones to go to the bathroom again and heard a light knock on the bedroom door.

I walked across the room and placed my hand on it as I held my breath. Was it Kyle?

"Everly?"

My heart dropped, and I flung open the door to find my brother standing there. He took one look at me and then cursed. He gently pulled me into his arms.

"What in the hell is going on Everly?" Hudson whispered.

I drew back and shook my head. "Not here, not now, Hudson."

He closed his eyes and cursed again. "Kyle pulled me to the side in the kitchen and told me you were upstairs. I have so many fucking questions."

Wiping at my nose, I replied, "I know. But please know I'm okay and that I'll explain everything to you when I can. I swear. Now you have to go back downstairs. No one knows I'm here, and I'm safe with Kyle. Please."

He narrowed his eyes. "I don't want to leave you here, Evie."

My voice stuck in my throat, but I somehow managed to smile. "I know, but you have to trust me a little bit longer. Please?"

He leaned down and kissed my forehead. "I'm going to kill whoever did this to you."

"You'll have to get in line after Kyle."

Hudson cursed again.

"Please go back to your game. Okay?"

He looked away, and I could see the turmoil on his face.

"Hudson."

"Okay, but I want answers, Everly. Can I tell Mom and Dad I saw you?"

"No!"

His eyes went wide.

"Tell them you spoke to me on the phone," I said.

"They're just as worried."

"Hudson, I never ask you for anything, so please do this for me."

He ran his fingers through his hair and finally nodded. "Fine. Will you be at the Larson's for dinner?"

"No, no one can know I'm here."

"You can't be here alone."

I placed my hand on his chest and pushed him toward the door. "I'll be fine. Now go!"

He took a few steps back and then smiled. "I love you, Evie."

I quickly wiped a tear away. "I love you, too, Hudson."

Then I slowly shut the door and let out a breath when it quietly clicked.

I gave up trying to stay awake around one thirty in the morning. I put on an Apple music playlist Kyle had on his phone and quickly drifted off. It felt as if I'd just fallen asleep when something soft moved down my cheek. I ignored the fear of it being a spider and slowly opened my eyes, only to see Kyle's handsome face looking down at me while he sat on the side of the bed.

"Kyle?" I whispered, starting to sit up.

"No, don't get up. I wanted to make sure you were okay."

I could smell the alcohol coming from him, and I raised a brow. "Are you drunk?"

He chuckled. "I think so. I drank a lot this evening. It was hard for me to look at your brother after he came up here. He's pissed, and he wants you with him."

My heart squeezed. "I'm sorry I put you in that situation."

He stared down at me with a look that screamed he wanted to tell me something.

"Do you normally drink a lot?" I asked, ignoring the way his thumb brushed over my cheek and set my skin on fire.

"No, I don't normally drink much at all," he replied.

His intense stare had my entire body shivering with anticipation for something...I just wasn't sure what it was.

*Liar.* I wanted him to kiss me.

Desperately.

"I want to hurt the person who hit you, Everly. I want to break every bone in their bodies and then tear them limb from limb."

I opened my mouth to say something, but when his eyes moved from the fading bruise to my lips, I lost my voice.

"Your lip is healing," he whispered, leaning closer to me. Our mouths were inches apart, so close I could feel his breath.

His voice was so soft and low, I barely heard him say, "Does it hurt?"

"Does what hurt?" I asked on a swallow.

"Your lip?" he replied in a raspy voice that made my insides tremble with desire.

All I could do was shake my head. Then his thumb was there, sliding ever so gently over my bottom lip. I drew in a sharp breath at the touch. Did he want to kiss me as much as I wanted him to?

"I haven't been able to stop thinking about you, Everly," he confessed.

"I've been fine, Kyle. I watched a few movies and fell asleep to some music. Didn't even hear you guys down there."

His eyes bored into mine, causing the entire room to feel as if it had shifted on its axis. "That's not what I meant."

With a barely there voice, I asked, "It's not?"

Slowly shaking his head, he replied, "It's not. Since the first moment you walked into that Greek restaurant, I haven't been able to stop thinking about you."

*Oh. My. Goodness. Please don't be the alcohol talking.*

I started to tell him the same, but before I could respond, Kyle lowered his lips onto mine.

The kiss was so soft and tender, I couldn't help but let out a soft moan. When his tongue moved gently along my lower lip, I was positive I melted into the bed with a long, deep sigh.

He drew back and leaned his forehead against mine while he drew in a shaky breath, and I worked to steady my own. I wasn't sure how long we stayed there in the dark, his body touching mine in the most innocent of ways, until he finally spoke. The word was so quiet, yet somehow it filled the entire bedroom with unspoken longing.

"Everly."

Then he stood, and I instantly missed the loss of his touch.

"Get some sleep, sweetheart."

He turned and headed out of my room, Cat following close behind. The soft click of the door latch alerted me to his absence.

I sat up and stared at the closed door while my heart raced in my chest. It took everything I had not to follow after him. The only thing that kept me at bay was knowing he'd been drinking. Would he have kissed me if he hadn't had so much alcohol? The last two days, he'd been nothing but a gentleman.

Dropping back onto the bed, I let out a frustrated groan, drew the covers up over my head, and willed myself to stop thinking about the last few minutes. Or what he'd confessed.

Or that kiss.

His tongue had touched the cut on my lip so gently, yet it had been filled with so much erotic intention... I nearly slipped my hand into my panties to relieve the ache that was now pulsing there.

I told myself to forget what had happened as I laid there and stared up at the ceiling for what seemed like hours. After tossing and turning until my side ached, sleep finally found me.

Something cold and wet against my face made me open my sleepy eyes. I smiled when two big, brown eyes stared back at me.

"Good morning, sweet girl," I murmured, running my hand down the side of Cat's neck. She had her face perched on the bed as she watched me. "Are you trying to get me up?"

Her soft bark was my answer.

My eyes drifted toward the door to see it was barely ajar before I focused back on her. "So, you know how to open doors, huh?"

She lifted her head off the bed and then slanted it to the side, giving me another soft bark.

"Is your dad still sleeping?"

Cat looked back at the door, then at me.

"Let me guess, you need to go potty?"

She stepped back and gave a low, barely audible bark, as if she was worried about waking Kyle. It warmed my heart how much she loved him. And I had to admit, I liked that she'd come into my room to wake me.

Throwing the blankets off, I swung my legs over the edge of the bed and carefully stretched before I stood and grabbed a sweatshirt. I had fallen asleep in a pair of sweatpants Brighton had given me. After slipping on a pair of shoes, I motioned to the door. "Come on, girl. Let's go potty."

Cat ran ahead of me and down the steps. I paused outside of Kyle's door, tempted to knock, but decided against it. Easing down the steps, I made my way to the back door and smiled at Cat, who was patiently waiting. I turned off the alarm and opened the door.

"Holy crap!" I said. "Why is this cold so different from Alaska or Greenland cold?"

Ignoring me, Cat bolted off and into the backyard, where she proceeded to run around for a good five minutes before she found a spot to do her business. I rubbed my hands over my arms in an attempt to keep myself warm while I watched her come barreling back toward me.

With a bark, she skidded to a stop at the door.

"I guess that's your request for breakfast, huh?"

Another bark.

I opened the door and came to an abrupt halt when I saw Kyle standing in the kitchen. He was bent over looking in the refrigerator. When he heard his dog come racing in, he straightened and turned. My breath stalled in my throat.

Kyle was in a T-shirt and low-slung sweats and...God help me... bare feet.

*Kill. Me. Now.*

Cat barked, and Kyle closed his eyes. "Shit, Cat, keep it down, will you?"

I quickly shut the door and took in Kyle's messy hair; it looked like he'd run his fingers through it at least a dozen times. "How are you feeling?" I asked, making my way into the kitchen.

"Like someone hit me with a massive truck and then backed over my head."

I tried to hide my smile. "Are you hungry?"

He shook his head and shuffled over to where Cat's food was kept. I wondered if Kyle remembered anything from last night. When he came into my bedroom. The things he'd said. The kiss. My heart deflated a bit at the thought that he might have been too drunk to remember any of it.

Clearing my throat, I said, "Let me feed her. Why don't you go on back to bed?"

Kyle shook his head. "That's okay. I'll feed her. Would you want to maybe go for a walk, then come back and talk?"

My eyes widened in shock. "You want to go for a walk with a hangover? I mean, it's not a run but..."

He looked over his shoulder at me and winked. "Fresh air is the best cure for a hangover. That is, if you don't have Hunter's magical hangover drink. I have no idea what's in it, but it works."

Smiling, I stood awkwardly at the kitchen island and watched Kyle feed Cat.

When he noticed me standing there, he asked, "Have you eaten yet?"

"No," I replied, forcing myself to stop wringing my hands. "Cat woke me up to go outside."

"I'm sorry about that. I should have warned you that she knows how to pull down the door handles. Lock your door at night, and she won't bug you."

My stomach dropped at the thought of locking Kyle out of my room. What if he wanted to kiss me again...and maybe do something else?

*Ugh, stop this, Everly.*

I let the thought drift away. "It's fine," I said with a slight chuckle. "She doesn't bother me at all."

Kyle reached for the orange juice he'd taken out and poured himself a glass. "Want one?"

"No, thank you. I, um, I think I'll make some oatmeal, unless you want to go for a walk right now."

He frowned, and for a moment I thought he was going to say something. But then he stopped himself.

"If you'd rather go for a run, Kyle, I'll be fine here."

After glancing around the room, he finally met my gaze. "Do you run?" he asked.

"Yes, I actually love running, but I can't with my ribs, obviously."

His eyes moved down to my side and he frowned. I instinctively wrapped my arms around myself.

He jerked his head back up to meet my gaze. He held it for a moment or two before he looked away. "I'm going to get some Motrin and get changed. I need to shave, so if you want to make breakfast first I can wait."

I shook my head. "Honestly, I think I'll grab a protein bar. Brighton brought some. Then we can go for a walk and...talk."

How I wanted him to say something about that kiss.

He smiled, but it didn't reach his eyes. Shit. He either had an excruciating hangover or he regretted what happened last night. Though there was still the possibility that he didn't remember coming into my room at all.

Kyle turned to leave, and I suddenly had the urge to find out if he did, in fact, remember. "What time did the poker game last until?"

He stilled and then faced me again. "I don't even know. Last thing I remember, I was losing, and then I woke up in bed this morning. Must not have drank as much as I thought, since it appears I was able to make it to my bed and change my clothes."

I forced a smile, trying not to let my disappointment show that he didn't remember the kiss. That amazing, soft, beautiful kiss. "I'm sorry you lost."

He gave me a half shrug. "Win some, lose some."

Nodding, I let out a sigh and then made my way to his pantry to get breakfast.

Kyle cleared his throat. "I'll meet you on the porch in about fifteen minutes?"

I forced myself to keep my voice light and easy. "Sounds good."

A feeling of emptiness crashed over me as Kyle headed up the stairs. I had laid in bed for hours last night, replaying those few minutes. His confession of not being able to stop thinking about me for all those months. The tender, yet most erotic kiss I'd ever experienced.

*And Kyle didn't remember any of it.*

Closing my eyes, I willed the hurt and disappointment away. I ripped open a protein bar and took a bite as I headed upstairs to change for our walk.

After brushing my teeth and putting my hair up, I put on yoga pants and a sweater, since the temperature outside was on the chilly side. I grabbed the sweatshirt Kyle had given me and made my way back downstairs and through the house to the back door. I stopped on the porch, pausing and looking out into the woods. I hated being scared. I not only hated it, it pissed me off. I sat down in a chair and stared into the forest as I waited for Kyle, so I could finally tell him the story of what happened to me nearly two weeks ago.

I didn't expect the wave of loneliness that came over me as I sat and stared off at the mountains in the distance. The mix of emotions running through me were enough to cause my eyes to burn with unshed tears.

And just like that, the tears broke free. I was hit so hard by the memory of almost being murdered that I couldn't breathe, each inhale harder than the last until I was gasping for air. The pain in my side made it even worse.

I closed my eyes and tried to will myself to calm down, but my lungs were being squeezed.

"Can't, breathe," I gasped.

Suddenly warm hands were on my cheeks, and I jerked my eyes open.

"Breathe, Everly. Deep breath in, then out."

Kyle was there. Those emerald eyes stared back into mine with a hint of panic.

"Can you take a deep breath in, Everly?"

I tried, but it still seemed like something was keeping the air from moving. "Can't!" I gasped.

"Yes, you can. If you couldn't breathe, you wouldn't be able to talk. Take a deep breath."

I did as he said—and something snapped inside of me and a rush of air came in.

"That's it. Now let it all out."

Doing as he said, I continued to take in deep breaths while Kyle counted. "One. Two. Three. Four. Five. Exhale. One. Two. Three. Four. Five. That's it, sweetheart."

After what felt like forever, I was breathing normally again.

Kyle used his thumbs to wipe away the tears on my cheeks.

"I hate this," I finally managed to say.

With a gentle smile that still somehow managed to showcase his dimples, he replied, "I do too."

"I started to think about what happened, and then I thought about walking in the woods and how I couldn't do it alone. And I just..."

He closed his eyes and cursed under his breath before he looked at me again. I could tell he was holding back something he wanted to say.

My eyes darted toward the woods where a layer of fog had now settled, giving it an even eerier look. I shook my head. "I don't want to go for a walk."

From the corner of my eye, I saw Kyle nod. "Later then—when it warms up."

With my eyes still on the fog, I whispered, "Maybe."

"Do you want to go inside, sweetheart?"

It was then I noticed Cat was resting her head on my thigh. I brought my hand to her soft fur and stroked it slowly. "Please, don't worry about me, Kyle. Go for a run."

A deep crease appeared between his brows. "No, I'm not leaving you like this, Everly. I want to..."

His words floated off into the air like the fog in the distance.

"You want to what?"

"Nothing," he answered, rubbing at the back of his neck. Then, he sighed. "We need to talk, Everly."

My heart began to race in my chest. How honest could I be about my affection for this man? Would I be able to tell him he was one of the reasons I ran to Alaska, because I was afraid of the strong feelings I'd instantly had for him?

"About?" I softly asked.

"What happened to you. I know it's hard to talk about it, but I need to know. The sooner I hear the whole story, the sooner we can start to figure this all out. Hudson wants to know as well. He said it's taking everything in him not to come back over today. I told him I'd get the story from you and fill him in tonight."

I raised a brow. "Really? And he was okay with waiting?"

Kyle let out a humorless laugh. "Hardly. But I talked him into it. Let's go inside and talk about that day."

I was positive my body slumped over a little bit. Of course that was what he wanted to talk about. Because he didn't remember last night. The things he'd said, the feel of my lips on his.

Before I could stop it, I brought my finger up and absently ran it over my lip.

Kyle watched and the crease between his brows deepened. "Is it hurting?"

Shaking my head, I replied, "No, it's okay."

"Do you want to sit out here and talk, or go inside?"

A part of me wanted to go upstairs and lie down. The panic attack or whatever it was had zapped all the energy out of me.

"Do you mind if I go upstairs and wash my face? I need to regain a bit of...composure, I guess, before we start talking about what happened."

Kyle stood. "Yeah, sure. Take your time. I'll be in my office; come in when you're ready to talk."

It was my turn to stand. With a single nod, I turned and made my way back into the house as fast as I could, not sure if I was running from what happened last night or the idea of facing what happened last Tuesday.

# Chapter Eight
## Kyle

The moment the back door shut, I let out a soft curse. "Fuck." Stabbing my fingers through my hair, I sat down in the rocking chair Everly had just vacated. "You stupid fucking idiot."

Cat whined, and I glanced down to her. "I am one, Cat. First, I go to her room last night, drunk. Confess I've been thinking about her, kiss her—then see her this morning and pretend like it never even happened. Then I say we need to talk and let her down again. I saw that look in her eyes. She thought I meant about the kiss. I'm an idiot."

This time, my dog barked at me. I was positive she thought I was an asshole as well.

"And then what do I do? Instead of trying to make things better, I tell her she needs to relive the moments that led up to her being kidnapped and nearly killed. Good move, Larson."

Cat rested her head on my knee, and I rubbed behind her ears.

I had kissed Everly last night. Shit. What in the world was I thinking? Actually, it wasn't *me* thinking, it was the damn alcohol thinking for me.

For the life of me, I wasn't sure why I'd decided to pretend like last night didn't happen. Maybe because when I'd finally kissed Everly, I had envisioned a whole other scenario. Not me drunk and confessing to her in the middle of the night like a coward.

After a deep breath in, I exhaled and headed into the house and to my office. It wasn't long before Everly knocked lightly on the door and poked her head in.

"Feeling better?" I asked, studying her.

Smiling, she replied, "I think so."

"Want to talk in here or go back downstairs?"

A light pink color hit her cheeks. "I made us some hot apple cider. I thought we could sit in the living room and drink it while we talked."

Standing, I noticed the chill in the air for the first time. "Of course we can. I'll build a fire, as well, if you want."

Her eyes lit up. "That would be amazing."

I motioned for her to lead the way. As I built the fire, Everly brought in the tray with the apple cider and some fruit she'd cut up, setting it on the coffee table. I noticed she even had a few dog treats on the tray, as well, which made Cat perk up. I loved how Everly always thought about Cat.

When I turned again, I saw Everly staring into the fire. I walked over and sat down next to her, taking her hand in mine.

"I'm not going to let anything happen to you," I said. "You know that, right?"

Her head turned and our eyes met. It felt like someone sucker punched me in the stomach when I saw the unshed tears and the fear in her beautiful green eyes.

She managed a weak, "I know." She cleared her throat. "Where do you want me to start?"

I sighed. "Let's start with the morning you were kidnapped."

After taking in a long breath, Everly steeled herself and started to speak.

"I was heading out to my rental car when someone put something over my head. They grabbed me and threw me into the trunk of a car. That's when I hit the side of my face on something hard. I fought and tried to scream, but they'd covered my mouth. It was still dark out; the sun doesn't come up until about eight thirty in Alaska at this time of year."

"Where were you heading? The glacier?"

She shook her head. "No. I was going into the field office to catch up on some notes and reports I needed to get done since I'd been gone for a few days for the wedding. Plus, I was finishing up all the notes on my work, since I was planning on leaving Alaska and coming back to DC. All I remember is one of the guys telling the other one to hurry up, so I knew there were at least two of them."

Anger raged inside of me, but I held it back.

"I could hear the guys talking, but it was muffled. I kept kicking at the backseat of the car and the trunk, praying someone would hear me. The trunk was so small, and I couldn't find my purse—if I even still had it. I was going to look for a latch to get out, but after feeling everywhere in the trunk, I finally gave up. But I kept screaming."

I wanted to pull her into my arms and tell her how brave she was.

"Apparently, me making a fuss made one of them angry. When we finally stopped after what seemed like hours of driving, he pulled me out of the trunk and slapped me so hard across the face, I crumbled to the ground. Whatever they'd put over my head fell off, and I could see a large building, maybe some kind of warehouse, but I wasn't able to get a good look around before they pushed me inside. I turned and kicked the guy who'd slapped me as hard as I could in the balls, and he dropped to the floor. I tried to run back out the door, but the other guy grabbed my hair. When the first guy finally stood, he grabbed my arm and pulled me into a small room. I kept fighting against him, and I tripped and fell. That's when he kicked me in the side." Tears streamed down her face and she wrung her hands together to keep them from shaking as she went on. "I could hardly breathe, but he pulled me up and punched me again. I nearly passed out that time."

I scrubbed my hands down my face. "Fuck. I'm so sorry, Everly."

She wiped at her tears and attempted to smile but failed.

"How long were you in the trunk, do you think?" I asked.

"A while. I had assumed we'd driven a good ways away from Valdez. But when I escaped, I realized I wasn't that far from the main road or my apartment. Maybe it simply felt like I was in that trunk forever, or maybe they drove around a bit to make it seem like it was farther."

"And where did you go when you got away?"

She paused and took in a few breaths before she went on. "All I knew was I needed to get out of Alaska. I knew I wasn't far from the small airport, so I ran there. I saw the guy who'd flown me in the first time I arrived in Alaska from Seattle. I stopped him and told him I was in desperate need of getting back to the mainland. He must've thought it was a domestic violence type thing, because he took one look at me, took me by the arm, and gently walked me toward his plane. He didn't ask anything other than where I wanted to go. I said Seattle. I told him no one could know where I was or that I'd even left."

"You trust him?"

Everly nodded. "Yes. And I don't think anyone would even think to talk to him. I was terrified they'd come after me, so I went directly to Charlie's place. I stayed there for a few days; he helped me dye and cut my hair and pick up a few items, and then gave me some money to make it back to the East Coast. When we were at the bus station, he bought me a ticket for Chicago. Later, I changed it to Salt Lake City. That's where I rented the charter plane. The guy didn't ask any questions. I think, given my bruises, he was happy to get me the hell out of Salt Lake. He flew me into Boston, no questions asked."

I smiled. "Smart girl."

She shrugged. "I'm not sure how long it may have been before they realized I was gone. If I had gone in the opposite direction, I would have been lost in the woods, and who knows what would have happened. But I knew if I stayed, I'd die for sure."

I nodded. "Okay, let's get back to the car ride while you were in the trunk. What happened after they brought you into the building and into the room?"

Everly closed her eyes. "That one guy kept bitching about me seeing them. Then I realized that one of them was a cop. He was mad my head covering had come off, but the other guy kept saying it wouldn't be an issue."

"You could identify them, that's why I'm guessing he was mad."

She nodded. "Yes. He said I could identify them both now that I'd seen them. The other guy laughed and said it wouldn't matter when I was dead. That freaked me out, and I started to struggle. I managed to kick the guy, and that's when he punched me again, cutting my lip."

I balled my fists and clenched my jaw until it ached.

"He would've hit me again, but the other guy pulled him away. They dropped me onto a chair, and I let out a scream when they pulled both of my arms behind my back. The one guy who had hit me said to tie me up. He said if I tried anything again he'd make my left eye match the right. Thinking back now, the guy never tied me up, which was weird. They left to go get the boss—as they called him."

"Would you be able to recognize any of these men again?"

Everly nodded. "I know the third guy's name is James. I'm not sure if it's his first name or last."

I grabbed a small notebook I had on the coffee table and wrote down a few notes. I underlined the name James. "Then what happened, after the third guy came in?"

She swallowed hard. "He was mad. *Really* mad at the other two guys. Yelled at them and said something about me needing to heal up now. That my death needed to look like an accident. That first guy said maybe they'd think it was from the car wreck I was supposed to have...the injuries they'd given me...but the third guy shook his head. That's when I knew I absolutely had to get out of there."

"Did this James guy talk to you?"

"Yes. He walked up to me and lifted my chin, so he could see my face. I remember him shaking his head in disgust and saying what a waste, that he hated to have to kill me, but I'd interfered."

I frowned. "In what?"

Everly shrugged. "I don't know. I asked him what he meant, and he ignored me. He told the other men to go and get some things for my face—I'm guessing he meant medicine? They both left, and I was alone with James. He paced back and forth in the small room, and a part of me thought maybe if I pleaded with him, he might let me go. For the briefest moment, I thought he might have regretted taking me. I got the feeling he might have been a cop as well. I'd never seen him around Valdez before, though."

"What happened to change your mind about him having regrets?"

"The way he looked at me," she replied, her body shivering. I wasn't sure if it was from the memory or if she was cold. "His eyes were void of any emotion. Then I saw anger. He asked me why I had to stick my nose into it, and I started to cry. I said I had no idea what he was talking about. He said he had to kill me, and he really wasn't a fan of killing people. But I'd left them no choice."

"Them?"

She nodded and wiped a tear away. "I have no idea what he was talking about, Kyle. I thought maybe they had the wrong person, and I told him that. I told him I was a glaciologist, and I had no clue what in the world he was talking about. He laughed, like he thought I was lying."

I took her hands in mine. "Take a moment, then tell me how you got out of the room."

After a few deep breaths, she went on. "Um, the third guy, James...he shut the door and locked it. It was one of those old-fashioned locks with the type of key that people use on necklaces now, or for decorating...what are they called?"

"A skeleton key?"

"Yes! That's it. I don't think the three of them even knew that on the wall in the corner there was a rusty key hanging up on a nail. I saw it when I started looking around the room for another way out. There was a small window up high that I couldn't reach, even with the chair, so that wasn't an option. Then I saw the key and grabbed it. I have to admit, I was stunned when I realized It unlocked the door. I slowly opened it. I could hear James somewhere in the opposite direction from where the two men had brought me in. He was on the phone with someone."

"Did you hear what he was saying?"

"No," she said with a quick shake of her head. "I wanted to get the hell out of there. I'd heard the other two guys drive off. At least, I was hoping they'd both left. I quickly made my way to the door and ran toward the back of the building. I worked my way around the building and heard a car pulling up, so I ducked behind some barrels."

"Wood or metal?"

She looked confused. "What?"

"The barrels, were they metal or wood?"

"They were...metal. And I smelled oil. Gasoline, as well, but at least one of the barrels definitely held oil, because it was running down the side of it."

I wrote that down and motioned for her to go on.

"The car pulled up and I saw Derrick get out. I was so relieved I almost ran to him, not even caring why he might be there, but that James guy...he started talking to him as he walked out of the building. It didn't take me long to realize Derrick was in on it. That it was actually *him* who'd wanted me...um...he wanted them to..."

"Kill you and make it look like an accident."

She nodded and started to wring her hands again.

I leaned back and let everything she'd said soak in. "Was Derrick working up in Alaska with you?"

"No," she replied softly. "I hadn't physically seen him in over two—or maybe three—years."

"Did you know he was in Alaska?"

Everly shook her head. "I thought he was back in Washington working on some special project."

Sighing, I rubbed at the back of my neck. "So, your ex was in town without telling you, and he wanted you killed for interfering in something. But what?"

"I don't know," she answered, wiping at a tear. "I was working at the glacier site taking core samples with Kristy, Mitch, Lou, and Craig. We've been studying the rate of glacier melt off and the amount of emissions in the ice, but that's nothing new. There'd be no reason for anyone, let alone Derrick, to kill me because of that. I was one of a dozen NOAA employees there."

I drew in a deep breath and slowly let it out. "Everly, I'm going to ask you something personal...and I'm sorry."

"O-okay."

"Your relationship with Derrick...why did you call off the engagement? Did he beat you or threaten you for any reason?"

"He cheated on me with my best friend Kristy."

That shocked the shit out of me. "Your friend in Alaska?"

A smile moved over her face, but it didn't reach her eyes. "She had come to Greenland to work for a few months when both Derrick and I were working there as well. She met Derrick in a bar, had no idea who he was, and he took her back to our place. I happened to walk in on them together. Derrick clearly hadn't expected me to show up."

"Ouch. And you're still friends with her?"

Everly nodded. "She didn't know who he was. And truth be told, I knew deep in my heart that Derrick wasn't the one for me. There was always something about him that bothered me. The more I got to know him, the less I liked. I had actually planned on calling off the engagement and breaking up with him before that. Kristy simply gave me an easy out."

"So you don't have anything on Derrick then?"

"Anything on him?"

"Yes, like he was involved with something shady, or was counting the icebergs wrong on purpose, something like that."

She laughed, and I loved how the sound made me warm inside. With her hand on her side, she replied, "No. I honestly have no idea why the man would want me dead. I'm pretty sure he was glad we broke up as well. I think maybe we both liked the idea of being married to someone in our own field of work. If that makes sense."

"What an asshole," I mumbled.

"I think so. I *know* so! The jerk tried to have me killed."

I stood and began to pace while Cat curled up next to Everly and started to drift off to sleep. "Something isn't right here. They wanted you gone for a reason, not simply because you broke up with him years prior. You interfered with something, and they needed you gone, but they needed it to look like an accident. Why?"

Turning to Everly, I asked, "And you're sure you have no clue what it could be? Anything from Greenland, perhaps?"

"No. I have no idea why they'd want me dead. Nothing in my life has changed. Nothing with work, nothing personal. I basically worked on site, then went home. Rinse and repeat."

I started to pace again. "You must have stumbled onto something, and you're not piecing it together yet."

Everly frowned.

"Who's Martin Williams?" I asked. "Hudson had mentioned he called him and was from NOAA. Do you know him?"

"I have no idea who that is. I can look him up, but I'd have to log into my work account. If you look it up on the main website, it'll give you an employee's email and phone number."

"And you've never heard of him before?"

She shook her head. "No, I'm sorry. If I have, I don't remember."

I sat and leaned back in the chair. "I think what you need to do is recount the last couple of weeks before you left for the wedding. We'll go through it all day by day if we have to. You clearly stumbled onto something that you just haven't realized yet."

She swallowed, then nodded. "I'll try, but I don't have my laptop with me. It'll all be from memory."

With a frustrated sigh, I replied, "That'll have to be good enough."

# Chapter Nine
## Kyle

Later that evening at my parents' house for dinner, Hudson and I excused ourselves to get some fresh air. It wasn't too cold out, so it was believable that we might want to sit on the back porch to enjoy the evening air. Instead, we started up with some small talk as we walked down the porch steps and then headed off toward the wooded area behind my folks' place.

"How's my sister?" Hudson abruptly asked as soon as we were away from the house.

I stopped, turning to look at him. "Okay. She's okay."

He shook his head. "Kyle, I've got to tell you: I want her with me, not at your place."

I raised a brow at him. "Do you not trust that I'll keep her safe?"

Hudson's jaw ticced. "Yes, I trust you. It's just that I'm going fucking crazy here. What in the hell happened to my sister? And why is she hiding out at your house?"

"I want to tell you everything, but Everly asked me not to. She wants to tell you herself." I sighed. "At any rate, it's probably best you don't see her just yet, or you'd be on the first flight to Alaska tracking these assholes down."

He looked angry. "Why is she being so goddamn stubborn about this? I saw her face the night we played poker, Kyle. Someone beat the living shit out of her, and I want to know who it is so I can go kill them."

I totally got where he was coming from, but I drew in a breath before I spoke. "Hudson, this is why Everly didn't go to you or your parents. It's complicated and dangerous."

He sighed, clearly upset. "Then why in the hell didn't she go to the police?"

"One of the kidnappers was a cop."

Hudson's eyes went wide. "One of the kidnappers? Someone kidnapped her? What in the living fuck?"

He started to pace across the lawn. If I didn't get him under control soon, he'd be racing back to my house to get his sister.

"Hudson, I know Everly is your sister. And I know if the roles were reversed and it was Greer, I'd be going out of my mind. But I really need you to trust me on this. Please. Please just wait to talk to Everly."

He leaned over and put his hands on his knees as he drew in a few deep breaths. When he finally stood, he nodded.

"I need you to do something else too," I said. "Let your parents know you've spoken to her on the phone. Tell them she's fine, that she's at that yoga retreat. The less they know, the better it is. If they think everything's okay, the safer they'll be."

He pushed his fingers through his hair. "Holy shit. What did she get herself tangled up in?"

"Now that I have the entire story, I'm going to try and figure it out."

Hudson raked his hands down his face and let out a bitter laugh. "I'm not surprised she went to you."

I jerked my head back. "What do you mean by that?"

He lifted his eyes to meet my confused gaze. "She got beat up, is in some kind of danger, and won't go to the cops. So it's no wonder she'd run to the guy—who also happens to be a cop—she has a thing for."

"A thing for?" I asked in a surprised voice.

He smiled. "It isn't hard to see the way the two of you look at one another. And it wasn't lost on me or Greer how you both did everything possible to avoid each other at the wedding, yet you couldn't stop staring when you thought no one was looking. Plus, my sister isn't stupid. She'd want to be close to family at a time like this. She knows you're a cop, and she also knows no one would put the two of you together. It just makes sense."

Sighing, I ran my fingers through my hair. "You haven't told Greer?"

Hudson shook his head. "No. I just told her and my parents that Everly needed some time to herself. She's done this once before, so I don't think it's too surprising for my parents—especially if I tell them that I talked to her."

"Done what before?"

"Gone to a yoga retreat thing. The last one was like three weeks long. Greer knows I'm lying, but she's being Greer and patiently waiting for me to fill her in."

"Listen, I want to tell you everything, believe me, I do."

Hudson looked out into the woods and then back at me. "You think it's safe?"

I nodded. "If you and Greer come over to the house, I think that's perfectly normal. If someone is watching you—which could be possible—then it won't seem out of the ordinary for you to stop by a friend's place. I have security cameras all over my place. If anyone else gets close to the house, I'll know."

"And then I'll know if I'm being watched."

"That too."

"Fuck. I write this shit, I'm not supposed to live it."

All I could do was nod.

"I'll try and replay my conversations with Everly from the few weeks or so before the wedding," Hudson said as we started walking back toward the house. "She was pretty busy with work and trying to finish up her assignment there, and she told me a bit about it."

"Sounds good. I'm going to try and pick her brain again as well. Now that she's told me the details of what happened, I think she can start to focus on the days and weeks leading up to the kidnapping."

"For fuck's sake. That just sounds so crazy. *Leading up to the kidnapping*. My sister being beaten."

I gave a slight nod. "I know it seems crazy, but unfortunately, it's really happening. And I'm going to tell you up front, I wouldn't be surprised if someone was watching your house and your folks' house."

Hudson stopped again and faced me. "Do you think my parents are safe?"

"Yes, as long as you can keep them believing the story that Everly came up with."

"Shit."

"There are at least four men out there who want your sister gone for some reason. They know she's still alive because she contacted you. They also know they're on borrowed time, and at some point, she'll have to resurface or contact you again. They're just waiting for her to make a mistake."

Hudson frowned. "Should we play it the other way? Make people think she's missing?"

"No. As long as we keep her hidden and safe, I think that's best. I just need to figure out what in the hell she knows that scared them so much they decided to kill her."

"And you really think they're watching me and our parents?"

I thought for a long moment before I answered, "Yes, I do. Especially if they're willing to go as far as kidnapping her and trying to make her death look like an accident. Something big has to be going down. And whether Everly knows it or not, she's stumbled upon something that's threatening whatever plans these guys have. Also, the man who called you, Martin Williams? I told Everly his name, and she doesn't know who he is."

Hudson nodded. "I'll let you know if he calls again."

"I think I'm going to sneak out of here early; I don't like leaving Everly home alone."

"Yeah, I agree," Hudson said. "Your dad seemed surprised you left Cat at home."

I laughed. "Yeah, I think he assumes I've got a girl there."

Hudson smiled. "You do."

"I guess so," I replied. "I better get going; I've been gone long enough."

Hudson and I headed back toward my folks' house. I stopped before we got to the porch, and Hudson did the same.

We had reached the part of the conversation I didn't want to have. "I'm not exactly sure how to tell you this, but it appears Everly's ex-fiancé is involved."

Hudson's eyes went wide. "What do you mean? Involved how?"

"Derrick was the one who wanted her death to look like an accident."

Hudson looked as if he might throw up. His face went pure white and he swayed just a bit before he regained his composure.

Clearing his throat, he finally growled, "I never did like that asshole. Where is he now? Alaska?"

I already knew where Hudson's mind was going, because mine had gone there too. "You can't go after him, Hudson. Believe me, I'd like to go myself, but he can't know we're on to him. If you go running in to question or accuse him, you're putting yourself, as well as Greer and your parents, in danger."

His anger cleared a bit. "I want to hurt him, Kyle."

"You and me both, Hudson. You and me both."

I brought my hand to the back of my neck. "She has some bruised ribs, but the black eye and bruise on her cheek are healing well. So is the cut on her lip."

Hudson looked ready to jump out of his own skin. I could see his rage, and I let him handle it in his own way. He turned and paced, clenched and unclenched his hands, then bent over and drew in several breaths.

Eventually, I said, "She was on my front porch when I got home from book club Thursday night. I took one look at her and wanted to kill someone."

"Did she go to a doctor? Are her ribs broken?"

"Adam came to the house the morning after she showed up at my place."

Hudson spun and looked at me. "What?"

"Everly refused to go to the hospital. I managed to talk her into letting Adam come take a look at her. Besides the ribs, I think she's okay, physically."

My brother-in-law closed his eyes, and I knew he was holding back tears. When he finally met my gaze, he said, "We need to find these men, Kyle."

I nodded. "I know. I will, I promise you."

I opened the door and heard the TV going. Cat popped her head up from the sofa and barked but didn't bother to come greet me. I couldn't help but smile.

"Hey, how was dinner at your parents' house?" Everly asked as she sat up, swinging her feet off the sofa right before Cat jumped up and nearly landed on top of her.

"It was good. I talked to Hudson alone. He'd like to come back over with Greer and talk to you."

Everly's eyes filled with concern. "Is he very mad?"

I smiled, sitting down on the coffee table. "He is, but not at you. He's worried about you. He's a good brother. And I should know— I'm one, too."

Her lips tilted upward in a slight smile, and the gesture made my chest feel warm and tight. I loved seeing her smile, even if just a little.

She opened her mouth to speak, then closed it.

"Talk to me, Everly."

With a sigh, she said, "I've been thinking...maybe I *should* go to the police."

I raised a brow. "Is that what you want to do?"

She wrung her hands together, then dropped them and shook her head. "No. I mean, a part of me does, so I can stop hiding. But the other part of me thinks that if they find out where I am, they'll come for me regardless of the police knowing or not. I don't think this James guy is someone to mess around with. And if he is a cop, well...I just can't trust anyone."

I nodded. "I agree. I think he hired some bad cops who messed up the job. He knows you've seen him, so he isn't going to stop until he finds you. And if Derrick thinks you know he's involved...well, they're both pretty motivated to find you."

"That's my thought as well. I just feel so bad for putting you in danger and causing my family to worry."

"They're not worried. Hudson knows you're with me, and he's going to let your parents know he talked to you and that you're loving the yoga retreat."

"Do you think it's wise to let Greer know? I mean, if anything ever happened to her, I'd never forgive myself."

Reaching for her hand, I gave it a light squeeze. "It's going to be fine. I won't let anything happen to you or Greer or Hudson. The more normally we behave, the less we'll draw attention. And maybe we can even sneak you out for a hike when you're feeling better or when we figure this shit all out."

Her eyes lit up. "I'd love that."

I smiled and stood. "Have you eaten? I brought some leftover lasagna my mom made."

"I made some soup and had a few crackers."

"I'll just put this in the fridge then."

I made my way to the kitchen to put away the leftovers, and Everly followed.

"May I ask you a question?" she said.

After putting the container away, I leaned against the counter and folded my arms. Everly's eyes did a quick sweep of my entire body before her gaze met mine. "You can ask me anything you want," I said.

A sweet smile played across her face. "Why did you name your dog Cat?"

"It's short for Catherine."

She tilted her head. "Okay, why did you name your dog Catherine?"

I dropped my hands to my sides as I pushed off the counter and cleared my throat. "If I tell you, you have to promise not to judge or laugh."

Everly raised her index finger and crossed her heart. "I promise not to do either."

"I named her after Catherine, a character from the novel *Northanger Abbey*."

After a few short blinks, Everly simply stared at me. "Who?"

I placed my hand over my heart and closed my eyes. "I'm not sure I can let you live under this roof any longer, Everly Higgins."

When she giggled, I opened my eyes and nearly lost my breath. The sight of Everly happy and carefree was enough to steal the air from my lungs.

"I'm going to guess Jane Austen wrote this *Northend Abbey*."

"*Northanger Abbey*, and yes, she did. I forgot you haven't read any of her work."

Everly looked down at Cat, who was laying on the floor and not paying any attention to our conversation. "I think it's cute. She's a dog, but you call her Cat. I like it."

Smiling, I replied, "So do I."

"Does anyone else know who you named her after?"

"Abby, Bishop's wife. She figured it out almost immediately, but she's a huge fan of Jane Austen too. And I'm sure Greer knows but just hasn't said anything. Hunter teases me about it a lot."

"I like it," Everly softly repeated. She looked down at Cat lovingly and then back up to me.

I winked. "So, how about a little game night tonight?"

Her face lit up with excitement. "Game night? Please tell me we're not playing pick-up sticks."

I feigned a disappointed expression. "You wound me, Everly Higgins. Pick-up sticks is the bomb."

She rolled her eyes. "How about you teach me how to play actual poker?"

"Actual poker, huh?" I asked with a teasing tone, remembering I told her I'd teach her how to play strip poker not that long ago.

"Yeah, I've always wanted to learn and keep my clothes on."

A part of me wanted to tell her I only knew the rules for strip poker, but I knew that wasn't the way to play this.

"Then, poker, it is."

Everly clapped her hands, and for the first time since she'd shown up on my front porch, a touch of genuine happiness filled those beautiful eyes of hers. I decided in that moment I would do whatever it took to keep it there.

# Chapter Ten

## Everly

I sat at the kitchen table with a warm cup of coffee in my hands and gazed out the window. I hadn't been able to sleep much last night. Not after the night I'd shared with Kyle. Who knew poker could be so much fun? I'd laughed too much, and I was paying for it with a sore side this morning. But goodness, it had been so nice to just relax. From the very first moment I'd met Kyle, I knew he was carefree and could make me laugh. He was so easygoing. His sense of humor was off the charts, and he made learning poker more fun than I could have ever imagined.

"Morning," Kyle said as he walked in and headed straight to the coffee pot. "I think I like this roommate thing we have going on. Keep making coffee in the morning, and I'll never want you to leave."

I smiled. "You say that now, but you'll get sick of me soon. I've only been here a few days."

Kyle winked, and I tried to ignore the way it made my heart flutter.

"I talked to Hudson a few minutes ago," he said. "He and Greer are coming over for dinner tonight."

My fluttering heart now pounded with dread. "Tonight? Are you sure it's..."

Kyle lifted a finger, and my words faded. "It's fine. I don't have to work today, so I thought I'd head to the grocery store and pick up what we need for dinner."

"What do you want me to make?" I asked, slightly worried since my culinary skills were lacking in a big way.

With a huff, Kyle replied, "I don't expect you to cook. *I'm* making dinner. I make a really good chicken in the Instant Pot. I'll pick up some tortillas, and we can have shredded chicken tacos. If that sounds good to you."

My mouth watered, and my stomach picked that moment to make it known I hadn't eaten breakfast yet.

Kyle grinned. "You hungry?"

I nodded. "I thought I'd wait and see if you wanted to have breakfast together."

Pushing off the counter, Kyle looked outside. "It's a beautiful fall day, warm for this time of year. What do you say we have a breakfast picnic?"

"A breakfast picnic?" My brows rose. Kyle and his picnics. I knew they stemmed from memories of his grandparents, and I loved that he'd come up with the idea for a breakfast picnic. Another point in the romantic column for Kyle.

"Yeah."

Cat got up and stretched before she made her way over to Kyle and pushed against his legs. She had come into my room earlier to wake me up. It appeared she liked me to let her out in the mornings, so Kyle could sleep in. I honestly didn't mind in the least bit. I was so much more at ease with Cat by my side.

Kyle bent down and gave his dog some pets and love. "Hey, girl, you snuck out of bed again this morning."

For a moment, I was insanely jealous of Kyle's canine partner. She clearly held the key to his heart, and he adored her. "I think she's assigned me the duty of letting her out in the mornings."

Kyle looked down at Cat and smiled before looking back at me. "Remember, you know you can just lock your door at night."

With a half shrug, I replied, "I don't mind. I like having her come in. She jumped up in bed with me around four in the morning, and I have to admit, I enjoyed snuggling up with her."

Kyle's eyes went wide. "She slept with you?"

"Um...yes. Is that okay? It wasn't for long; she woke up around six, so maybe two hours."

Kyle bent again and kissed Cat on the top of her head. "You're such a good girl. Are you taking care of our Everly?"

Cat licked his face, and he laughed. "You go change," he said to me, "and I'll get everything ready for our breakfast picnic."

My heart melted, and I couldn't help but stare at Kyle. Had he realized he'd said *our Everly*? The idea of being Kyle's was something I could get used to. Standing, I said, "Why don't you let me help you?"

He shook his head. "Nope, go do what you need to do, and I'll take care of the food. Grab a sweatshirt. It's going to get warm later, but it's still a bit chilly out now."

He was so sweet and thoughtful. I wasn't entirely sure Kyle knew he was being super romantic, and I wasn't about to point it out. I enjoyed the picnic we'd gone on a few days ago, and the last thing I wanted to do was have him stop suggesting sweet things like this.

"You're sure you don't need any help?" I asked again.

"Positive," Kyle said, waving his hand and motioning me to leave.

Thirty minutes later, I was back down in the kitchen, and Kyle was putting the last of what he had packed up in the basket.

"You look cute," he said, giving me a quick once-over. I glanced down at the black yoga pants and Boggy Creek Valley PD sweatshirt I was wearing. Considering I was in someone else's clothes, the compliment made me feel good. Especially since my face was still bruised and my lip wasn't healed all the way yet. But whatever it was that Brighton had given me had made such a huge difference in just a few days. I'd even found some amazing lip balm in her little spa package, and it was doing wonders for my lips. They weren't cracking open any longer when I smiled or yawned.

"Thanks, but I'm just wearing yoga pants and *your* sweatshirt."

Kyle winked. "And you look cute in both. I also like your hair up like that."

I instantly touched the sloppy bun I'd quickly piled on my head, my cheeks heating when my eyes met Kyle's.

He frowned slightly. "I'm not used to the different color yet."

"Me either. It's a bit of a shock to see brown hair when I look in the mirror."

"It makes your eyes pop more."

I blinked a few times before I glanced at the picnic basket, a feeling of awkwardness making me flustered. "All set?"

"All set. Did you want me to bring a book to read while we're there?"

"I finished *Anne of Green Gables* last night, so you might have to pick another one. I'd like a Jane Austen novel, I think. Maybe the one with the character you named Cat after."

One of his brows rose, and I could see the smile he was trying to hide. "*Northanger Abbey?*"

"Yes. Let's start that one next."

"I'll grab it on the way out."

I allowed myself to slowly roll back onto the quilt as I stared up at the blue sky. It was a beautiful warm day. Growing up in Boston, I knew winter was right around the corner, so I wasn't going to complain.

"It's almost borderline hot out." Kyle wiped his brow. "I mean, it's already up to seventy-five, and it's only nine in the morning."

"It's a heat wave," I murmured, closing my eyes and letting the sun shine on my face. "I'm so full. When did you buy those muffins?"

With a slight chuckle, he said, "My mother made a huge batch, so I grabbed some along with the croissants. I already had the homemade jam. It's a recipe from my great-grandmother."

I smiled and turned my head to watch as Kyle finished packing up all the food and grabbed the book to read. "How sweet. Does your mom make it or your dad?"

"Mom makes it; it was her grandmother's recipe. But this batch, I made."

My stomach did a little flip. "You make jam?"

He smiled. "Why does that surprise you?"

I gently pushed myself up into a sitting position with Kyle's help. "It's just that not every guy admits to liking picnics, and cooking, and reading romance novels. You're one of a kind, Kyle Larson."

A blush swept over his handsome face. "Why, thank you, Everly Higgins. I've been telling Brighton that for months now."

I couldn't help but laugh, and I noticed the pain in my side had eased just a bit. "In all seriousness, Kyle, you're pretty amazing."

He waved off my compliment. "Nah. I'm just a guy who likes what I like."

I pulled my knees up to my chest the best I could without straining my ribs. "I think that's what I like most about you."

"What's that?" he asked.

"You're in touch with your sensitive side, even though you appear so rough and tough."

Kyle laughed. "Rough and tough?"

"Yes," I replied. "When you're in your uniform, especially."

He leaned back on one hand and extended his legs, crossing them at the ankles. "Don't tell me you're a fool for a guy in uniform?"

The words were out of my mouth before I even realized I'd thought them. "Not all guys, just you."

His smile faded some, but his eyes... Lord, his eyes turned dark with desire, and I felt it in my core.

"Is that right? I think next time we play poker, I'll wear my uniform, and we'll definitely try out the strip version."

My mouth watered at the thought, and I wanted more than anything to reply with...*yes, please!* "I don't know. You said yourself I was a fast learner. You could be the one sitting there naked at the poker table."

Kyle shook his head and looked away for a brief moment before focusing back on me. "We should probably talk about something different, Everly."

I raised a brow and smiled.

Pointing at me, he shook his head. "You are a naughty girl."

With a one-shoulder shrug, I added, "Well, I *am* on the run."

"From killers!"

"True," I said with a giggle. "Will you read to me?"

Kyle's face turned serious. "I'll do anything you ask of me, Everly."

*Kiss me.* I didn't say it out loud, but I prayed he'd somehow hear it.

When he opened up the book, I let out a slow sigh of disappointment before I laid back down and waited for Kyle to start.

After clearing his throat, Kyle began. "No one who had ever seen..."

I was soon lost in the story and could see why Kyle loved Jane Austen's writing. Closing my eyes, I let the heat of the sun and Kyle's soothing voice relax my entire body.

"Everly."

Sighing, I mumbled, "Yeah?"

A slight shake on my shoulder had me jerking my eyes open to see Kyle's green gaze staring back at me. "Was the book so boring it put you to sleep?"

"Sleep?" I asked in a groggy voice as I attempted to sit up.

"Yeah," Kyle chuckled. "I was reading, and I looked over, only to find you sound asleep."

"I'm so sorry, Kyle. The story wasn't boring at all! I didn't sleep very well last night, and we were up so late...I think that's all it was. The heat of the sun and your voice just lulled me to sleep."

He nodded. "Another charming quality I have. My voice puts women to sleep."

I playfully pushed at his shoulder. "Stop it. You know what I mean. I really did love the story. How much did I miss?"

Kyle shrugged. "I'm not sure. When I looked up, you were out."

With a pout, I replied, "I'm so sorry."

Kyle stood, then reached for my hand to help me up. "No worries. But we do need to head on back. I have to run to the grocery store and pick up stuff for dinner tonight."

"Wish I could come," I replied as I helped him gather everything and then folded the quilt. Cat had taken off to go do her business. Kyle whistled, and she quickly returned.

We started to head back toward the house when Kyle asked, "Have you thought of anything else? Any reason they could be after you?"

I shook my head. "If I'm being honest, I haven't even thought about it. I know I should, but I just...wish it was a dream. Not this part, though."

Kyle turned his head, and I could feel his eyes on me. "What do you mean?"

With a half shrug, I replied, "This. Me being here with you. I mean, I hate being in hiding, but I've loved staying here the last few days. I haven't been this happy—and felt this safe—in a long time."

He smiled, and we both turned to concentrate on the path. "I'm glad you're happy, and that you feel safe."

As we walked in silence, I forced myself to think about the weeks before the kidnapping. Nothing unusual had happened. At least, nothing I could think of.

"Is there anything you'd like me to pick up for you at the store?" Kyle asked. "I've got tomorrow off, as well, so we could make anything you'd like."

I grinned. "I'd love anything on the grill."

"The grill, huh?" Kyle mused, looking lost in thought. "How about I pick us up some salmon. What kind of veggies do you like?"

We stopped at the bottom of the steps that led up to Kyle's back door. "All of them. I don't think there's a single vegetable I don't like."

He screwed up his face. "Not one? Asparagus?"

"One of my favorites!"

"Brussels sprouts," he stated with confidence.

"One of my favorites too."

He slowly shook his head. "Something is wrong with you. No one likes Brussels sprouts."

"That is not true, Kyle Larson. Lots of people like them. I bet you'd like them the way I make them. Maple syrup, bacon, with a touch of soy sauce...sounds good, doesn't it?"

When he scrunched up his nose, my knees went weak. "You give me a list for this Brussels sprouts dish, and you can make them tomorrow. I'll make my famous cauliflower."

"Oh, I'm intrigued. What's in it?"

He shook his head and motioned for me to head up the steps. "Oh no, that's a secret recipe. You'll just have to wait to eat them tomorrow."

I chuckled as I walked into the house, Cat pushing past me to get to her food bowl where she patiently waited for her dad to give her lunch.

# Chapter Eleven

## Kyle

"**D**o you need any help at all?" Everly asked as she walked into the kitchen that evening.

With a quick shake of my head, I replied, "I've got it all covered. Though, you could set the table, if you want."

Everly made her way over to the cabinets and took out four plates before opening the silverware drawer. Cat looked between the two of us, trying to decide if she should stick by me or follow Everly. When she laid back down at my feet, I couldn't help but laugh.

"Figured I was the one with the food, huh?"

Everly stopped and glanced down at Cat. "I think she just loves you that much."

"I would pet you, girl, but then I'd have to wash my hands for the millionth time."

Everly made her way out of the kitchen and to the dining room—and that's when I heard a groan.

"No, no, no! Not pick-up sticks!"

I chuckled. Cat let out a soft bark and placed her snout on my shoe. "I know, girl. I wish you could play too."

"Seriously doubt the dog wants to play that game," Everly called out, "especially if she knew how competitive you and Greer are about it."

"Hey, we take our pick-up sticks very seriously in the Larson family."

Everly walked back in, rolling her eyes, and took four wine glasses out of the cabinet. "I'm going to need something stronger than this if I'm forced to play that game. The only saving grace is Bishop won't be here."

I let out a bark of laughter. "Okay, he does get into it just as much as the rest of the family, but that's only because he's practically a Larson."

She sighed. "You don't want to do something different, like Monopoly?"

"Oh, if we played Monopoly, we'd need a few days."

Pausing on her way back into the dining room, she turned to me. "Why?"

"We take that game seriously as well. My parents had to buy three games, so we could add up all the money. Me, Bishop, Greer, Aiden, and Hunter would play for days. One time, we had a game going for nearly three weeks before I finally bankrupted everyone."

Everly stared at me with her mouth slightly agape. "Adam wasn't in on this?"

Laughing, I said, "He quit after the second day."

"I hope my brother realizes what he married into."

At that moment, the doorbell rang and Cat stood up. I wiped my hand on a towel and motioned for her to stay. After a quick glance at the monitor for the front door, I smiled.

Turning back to Everly, I said, "Wait here, just in case."

She saluted me. "Yes, sir."

I opened the door and did a quick visual sweep of the driveway, making sure no one had followed them. The main road was far enough from the house that you couldn't see it, but it looked empty. "Well, hello there!" I finally said, holding out my arms for a hug from Greer. Then I shook Hudson's hand as my sister headed into the house. "Thanks for coming over."

"Couldn't pass up dinner with my favorite brother-in-law," Hudson said, walking in. I shut and locked the door. The second it was closed, he asked, "Where is she?"

I pointed and said, "Kitchen."

He quickly made his way over as Greer and I followed.

"Remember, she has bruised ribs," I said quietly.

The moment Everly saw her brother, she started to cry and rushed into his outstretched arms.

Hudson wrapped his sister in a gentle hug. "Shhh, it's okay, Evie. It's okay."

I raised a brow at Greer. "Evie?"

"That's what Hudson used to call her when they were kids."

All I could do was nod as I became instantly jealous of my brother-in-law. It was stupid; he was hugging his own sister...but what I wouldn't give to be able to hold Everly in my arms whenever I wanted.

"How is she?" Greer asked in a hushed voice.

Jerking my head to the living room, we walked away to let Hudson and Everly spend some time alone.

"I think she's okay. I mean, someone *did* try to kill her."

Greer looked sick to her stomach. "No idea why yet?"

I brought my hand up and ran it through my hair. "No. Everly can't think of any reason, but something clearly happened. I just need her to remember what it was."

"Do you think she's too afraid to tell you?"

"No, I think she honestly doesn't know. Or it's something so mundane to her, she doesn't realize it's related."

"She studies melting icebergs. Why in the world would anyone want to kill her? Unless she's involved with something she doesn't want anyone to know about."

I shook my head. "No. You didn't see her that first night, Greer. She was terrified. And I believe her when she says she has no idea."

"And the ex is involved? That makes me think it *has* to have something to do with her job. Have you looked to see if there's anything odd going on around the area where she was working?"

Frowning, I asked, "'Odd' meaning...?"

Greer shrugged. "I don't know, a pipeline, the new construction of an oil plant, something big that people wouldn't want NOAA involved in."

"But she isn't the only climatologist there. There are a dozen or more. So why her?"

Greer looked toward the kitchen, then back at me. "Have you looked up any accidents that happened *before* the kidnapping?"

My heart dropped to my toes. "No—but that's a damn good idea, sis. I'm pissed I didn't think of it."

She smiled. "I *am* the daughter of a police officer...and the sister of one."

"I'll do that tomorrow."

Everly and Hudson walked into the living room, Cat following closely behind. She'd clearly picked up that Everly was upset and was staying close to her. Damn, I really loved my dog.

"Greer, I'm so sorry to bring this to your doorstep," Everly said.

My sister made her way over to her and drew her in for another gentle hug. "You didn't. And for the record, I'm so glad you sought out Kyle first. I know he can help you figure this out."

Everly's eyes met mine as her cheeks turned slightly pink. She looked back at Greer. "I'm just so glad to see you both. I want to hear all about married life and how the honeymoon planning is going."

"We're still in the early planning stages, but I think we're narrowing it down to either Hawaii or Fiji. And we're planning it after Brighton's due date," Greer said. "It just made sense to wait with Hudson's book coming out and all the upcoming births."

Everly's eyes lit up. "Oh, to go somewhere warm."

Greer laughed. "When you get married, I can imagine you'll demand somewhere warm too."

Smiling, Everly nodded and peeked over at me before she turned to Hudson. "Have you talked to Mom and Dad?"

"Yes," he said. "They think you're at a yoga retreat, but now Mom suspects you fell into a depression because I'm married and you're not."

Everly's mouth dropped open. "What? Did you correct them?"

Hudson's smirked. "I thought about it, but where's the fun in that?"

"Hudson!" Everly let out a soft laugh.

I clapped my hands together and said, "Who's ready for some pulled chicken tacos? We should eat before the tortillas get cold."

"You touched the other stick!" Greer called out, pointing at me.

"Are you *sure* it moved?" Everly asked oh-so-sweetly.

Greer shot me a dirty look. "Oh, I saw it move. He touched it!"

"You're seeing things," I retorted as I slid my stick out and smiled. "My hand-eye coordination is the best.

Greer pointed her finger at me again. "Bullshit! It moved, Kyle!"

"It counts!" I shouted back.

Hudson let out a long sigh and looked at Everly. "I don't even know why I allow them to play this game."

Greer turned to her husband. "*Allow?*"

Everly covered her mouth to hide a smile while Hudson attempted to recover from his faux pas.

"Did I say allow? I meant to say I don't even know why I join in on this game."

Greer narrowed one eye. "That's what I thought you said."

"Are you going, Everly? It's your turn," I prompted.

Everly surreptitiously glanced at Hudson, who seemed to give her a slight nod of encouragement. With a deep breath, she went for one of the yellow sticks and successfully slid it out without moving the others.

Smiling, I cheered, "That's my girl! Hudson, go."

"Christ Almighty, I hate this game," he mumbled as he pulled a green stick out without even trying, rattling the other sticks.

"Hudson!" Greer complained. "You have to at least try. We're a team, and you're bringing me down!"

He shook his head. "Why can't we play something different? Like—oh, I know! We should play Monopoly!"

"No!" Everly called out. "You don't want to play that game with them either."

Drawing his brows in, he asked, "Why not?"

Everly shot Greer and me a look before she focused back on her brother. "They have to combine sets to get more money because their games last for days."

"Sometimes weeks," Greer added.

A look of horror moved over Hudson's face. "Weeks?"

Greer and I both nodded.

"Okay, so no Monopoly. Clue?"

"Oh, I love Clue!" Greer clapped.

"No," I said with a sharp glare in my sister's direction. "We're playing pick-up sticks, and we are not stopping until a team has won."

She gave me a nod. "Right. I don't know what I was thinking."

I cracked my knuckles and studied the sticks.

"Everly, do you enjoy birds?" Greer asked, in a sad attempt at throwing me off with a stupid conversation.

"I, um...I do enjoy birds. I noticed Kyle has some feeders but no food."

Greer grunted. "That doesn't surprise me."

"I forgot to pick some up," I said. "And hush! I'm trying to concentrate."

"Wait until you see the feeding station we have set up at our house," Greer said.

Everly looked curious. "What's a feeding station?"

I let out a low growl.

"Oh, it's amazing!" Greer smiled. "It's a pole system, and you can have more than one feeder on it. I've seen some beautiful birds I'd never spotted before with it. It allows me to put different types of food out."

I carefully drew out a yellow stick and smiled as I put it in our pile. "Your turn, Everly."

She nodded and looked over the pile of sticks. "I actually stumbled upon some unique seaducks while I was working in Alaska. They're called Steller's eiders."

"Never heard of them," Greer replied.

"They're a threatened species in Alaska. The breeding population has dropped so low that biologists are really trying hard to build their numbers up once again. Last time I saw one, I had to report the sighting to U.S. Fish and Wildlife Service. Actually, you're supposed to report it anytime you come upon a nesting spot."

"Why do you need to report it?" Greer asked.

"Since they're a threatened species, biologists want to know where the nesting spots are so that they don't disturb them. They once had to reroute a pipeline in Canada because of a threatened species."

I instantly stilled when a thought occurred to me. "Wait—you reported the seaducks' nest?"

Everly glanced at me. "Yes."

What if Everly reporting this nest had something to do with her kidnapping. "Did you talk to someone specific about it?"

She nodded. "Yeah, his name was Jacob West. Nice guy. Asked me out when I came in to fill out the paperwork about the sighting."

I instantly didn't like the guy, but on a hunch, I pulled out my phone and typed in his name. "Was that in the same town where you lived?"

Frowning, Everly asked, "Yes. Why?"

"Everly...this might be connected to your kidnapping," Hudson said as I typed in Jacob's name and Valdez, Alaska. He was clearly thinking the same way I was.

My heart dropped and my stomach rolled over when the first news article popped up.

"You think so?" Everly asked her brother.

I skimmed the first paragraph of the article.

*Jacob West, local resident of Valdez, died in a single-car accident in the early morning of September 29. He worked at the U.S. Fish and Wildlife Service for the last five years.*

Slowly putting my phone down on the table, I looked at Everly. "Do you know if Jacob got around to putting the report in their system?"

Looking confused, she replied, "I'm assuming he did. Why wouldn't he? I stopped in the day I left to fly back to New Hampshire for the wedding. He was going to email me a copy of it."

Hudson and I looked at one another, both of us clearly thinking the same thing.

"Is there any way you can access your email? To see if Jacob sent that?" I asked.

Everly's eyes went wide. "What if they're monitoring it? And why would I need to know?"

Before I could answer her, Hudson said, "I know a way to get around that. There's a guy in Boston whom I've used for research on some of my books. He can ensure the IP address is scrambled. If Everly is on and off quickly enough, there's no way they can trace it."

I ran my hand through my hair. "We need to find out if he filed that reported sighting, but I'm not sure it's worth the risk of having Everly log into her email."

Everly dropped back in her seat and gave me a confused look. "Why do we need to find out about the report?"

Picking up my phone, I opened it and handed it to Everly.

"Because Jacob West died in an accident two days after you told him about finding those seaducks."

# Chapter Twelve
## James/Martin - Alaska

"**D**o you mind if I take a seat here?" I asked as I walked up to the bar. I had just observed Kristy come in with a man and another woman, and all three of them had gathered around the bar, waiting for their drinks. I had seen her the first few days after I'd checked into the hotel, but I had managed to keep a close eye on her and wait for the perfect moment to move in and make contact.

With a wide smile, Kristy replied, "I don't mind at all."

She glanced down to my badge briefly. "You work for NOAA, Martin?"

"I do."

Motioning to the others, Kristy said, "So do we. My name's Kristy Clarkson. What brings you to Alaska?"

"I'm working on a small project, just lending a bit of time and ideas to it. It worked out well, since I usually come here at least once a year anyway."

She raised a brow in question.

"My mother grew up here, and I still come back to visit the town every year since she passed away. Makes me feel closer to her."

Kristy blinked a few times in rapid succession before she said, "I'm so sorry for your loss."

I smiled. "Thank you. it's been ten years, but sometimes it feels like it was just yesterday."

On a long exhale, she said, "I know what you mean. I lost both of my parents a few years back, and I still sometimes find myself reaching for my phone to call them."

I nodded. "Know that feeling as well. What do you do for NOAA?"

"A little bit of everything," she replied with a smile. "I specialize in glacial geology."

I nodded and looked at the bartender, who walked up to take my order.

"What can I get for you tonight, sir?"

"Give me any local beer on tap."

I could see Kristy watching me from the corner of her eye. When I glanced back at her, she gave me another friendly smile. Any other time or place, and I would have loved to get to know this woman better. But right now she only had one purpose for me.

"So, what do people do around here for fun these days?" I asked as I took the beer from the bartender and nodded my thanks.

"What's fun?" She chuckled. "I seem to work all the time, so if you're looking for something fun to do, you'll have to seek out someone else's advice."

I laughed. "I thought a friend of mine who works for NOAA was up here, too, but I haven't been able to contact her."

Kristy raised a brow. "What's her name?"

"Everly Higgins. I haven't seen her in a number of years, and last I heard, she was working around here. Thought since I was here I might say hi. Do you know her?"

"Yes!" Kristy said, her eyes full of light. "Unfortunately, she's not here right now. She took some time off. The little bitch didn't even tell me she was leaving for a few weeks. I'm supposed to be her best friend, and all I got was a note on my desk saying she needed some time away. Her brother just got married, and I think maybe that put her in a weird place."

"Weird place?" I asked.

She nodded and took a sip of her wine. "Yeah. Depressed, maybe? I think that Everly thought she'd be married by now. Problem is, she loves this job and puts it before anything else."

I let out a dry laugh. "I know that feeling. You said she wrote you a note? Why wouldn't she just tell you herself?"

Kristy shrugged. "I'm not sure. I called her brother to make sure she was okay, and he said she just needed some time away and went on a yoga retreat. She's been on one before, after she found out her ex was cheating on her."

"Never understood why people get into that," I replied.

"Cheating or yoga?" she asked with a teasing smile.

"Both."

She gave me a look I couldn't read, but I did notice her gaze move to my mouth and then back to my eyes. "Me neither. I can't stand yoga. I do like to run, though."

I smiled. This was something I already knew about Kristy after watching her for the last few days. She had a routine that she followed every day. Run two miles in the morning. Head back to her rental. An hour later, leave for the office. She hadn't gone out to do any field work in the last two days.

It was time to make my move. "Same here. I usually run in the mornings."

"Me too!" she said, excitement in her voice. "I can't find a running partner here; everyone says it's too damn cold."

I winked. "I could be your partner. I'm staying for a few weeks to finally get my mom's estate settled."

Kristy chewed on her bottom lip. "Are you staying here at the hotel or her house?"

"At the hotel. The house just sold," I said with a grin.

Glancing down at her drink and then back up at me, she replied, "I like running on the trail system they have here. It's one of the best I've seen. I'm usually there around seven thirty if the weather permits. We could meet up tomorrow if you'd like."

I finished off my beer, stood, and took out a business card that had my name and cell number on it. "I'll meet you there. If you can't make it, just text me. Maybe we can meet for dinner tomorrow, instead—or if I impress you with my running skills, we can do both."

A blush moved up her neck and into her cheeks. "I'll see you in the morning, Martin."

"See you then, Kristy."

I didn't need to turn and see if she was watching me leave; I could see her in the reflection of the glass windows as I walked away.

# Chapter Thirteen

## Kyle

**"W**hat are you looking up?" Hunter asked as he walked into our shared office at the police station.

"Nothing," I said as I turned in my chair and focused on him. As much as I wanted to tell Hunter everything that was going on, I knew I couldn't. At least not yet.

It had been four days since Everly mentioned the seaducks she'd stumbled upon. It turned out we didn't need to get into her email after all to see if Jacob West had filed the report about the nest of Steller's eiders. Hudson had come up with a better idea. I'd simply called the U.S. Wildlife Department and said I was a nature photographer with *National Geographic* who wanted to capture some nesting sites of Steller's eiders. I asked if any had been reported in the Valdez area.

There wasn't one even close to where Everly had seen them. Which meant that the report obviously hadn't been filed.

I wanted to ask about any preliminary reports Jacob may have filed, but I wasn't sure if he'd ever typed up the report and someone on the inside had made it disappear.

"Something's up, Kyle," Hunter said. "I noticed it days ago. You seem to forget that we're best friends, and I've known you my entire life. You're more like a brother to me than anything. So, what's going on?"

Sighing, I rubbed the back of my neck. "Will you just trust me if I say I can't tell you right now, but I will soon?"

He narrowed his eyes at me before his features relaxed. "Okay. I'll let it go for now."

"Thanks, Hunter. How's Bella feeling?"

A wide smile grew on his face. "Miserable."

I laughed. "And that makes you smile? That's fucked up, dude."

"No," he replied with a chuckle. "I hate that she's feeling miserable, but she's also over-the-moon excited. Have you heard from Bishop? We haven't had a chance to see him or Abby in a while."

"Talked to him earlier. Abby's started having stronger contractions that are closer together."

"I bet she's relieved, since she's well past her due date."

I nodded. "I can't wait to find out if they're having a boy or a girl."

"At least their puppy isn't still a puppy."

"How do you think Jack's going to handle *your* new baby?"

Hunter glanced down at his partner, who was asleep, curled up on a bed with Cat. The two of them were like two peas in a pod. Best friends, just like me and Hunter.

"I think he's going to be a great big brother. He loves Bella and is so protective of her, I'm going to guess he'll be the same with the baby."

Smiling, I looked at Cat. "Yeah, Cat's a bit jealous of..." I let my voice trail off when I realized what I'd been about to say.

Hunter raised a questioning brow. "She's a bit jealous of who? Dude, are you dating someone and didn't tell me?"

"No, I can promise you, I'm not dating anyone."

"Who are you having sex with then?"

An image of a naked Everly popped into my head and I had to quickly push it away. "Unfortunately, I'm not having sex with anyone but my own hand."

Hunter snarled his lip. "Dude, that was way too much information. Christ, I'm not going to be able to get that image out of my head now, you jackass."

Laughing, I turned back to my laptop and finished my daily reports. I couldn't wait to get home and see Everly. I had the next couple of days off after talking to my father and telling him I needed some personal time. He hadn't asked any questions, but I could tell it was killing him not to ask. Everly's ribs had been feeling better, so we were going on a hike tomorrow. She needed to get out of the house before she went stir crazy. Even if my house was being watched, I knew no one could get on my property, so letting Everly in my car wasn't an issue.

"What are you doing tonight?" Hunter asked.

"Nothing," I lied.

"Bella was wondering if you wanted to come over for dinner."

*Shit. How am I going to get out of this?* I never turned down an invite to their place. "I would, but I've got, um, I've got..."

*Christ, think, Kyle!*

Laughing, Hunter asked, "A book to finish for book club?"

*Okay, I'll go with that.* "You guessed it. Tell Bella thank you, though."

Hunter stared at me a little too long. "I will. If you change your mind, just come on over—you don't even have to call to let us know."

Smiling, I replied, "Thanks, bro. I'm pretty sure I'll just be staying in tonight, so I can finish up that book. I'm going to take Cat up to Cloudland Falls tomorrow."

He nodded, but before he could say anything else, my cell phone rang.

Smiling, I answered, "Hey, Bishop."

"Hey, is Hunter there with you?"

I looked over at Hunter. "Yeah, he's right here."

"Great! Good. Perfect!"

"Why?" I asked, already knowing the answer from how manic he sounded.

"Abby's in labor. We just got to the hospital. I haven't called anyone else, so do you think you and Hunter can let everyone know? Her contractions are coming fast, and—what? Now? *Right now?*"

I laughed. "Go be with Abby. We'll let everyone know and get up there as soon as we can."

"Great, thanks," Bishop managed to say before he hung up on me.

"Abby's in labor?" Hunter asked.

"Yeah," I said with a chuckle. "And it sounds like the baby is almost here. I'll call Greer and Hudson, then Candace."

Hunter nodded as he picked up his phone. "I'll call Aiden and Willa."

After making my calls, I stepped outside and called the burner cell I'd bought for Everly.

"Hello?"

A warm feeling spread through my entire body at the sound of her voice. "Hey, I just wanted to let you know that Abby, Bishop's wife, is in labor, so I'm going to head to the hospital. Not sure how long I'll be. I'm sorry to leave you alone like this."

"How exciting!" Everly exclaimed. "Don't worry about me. I was planning on making little pizzas for us, so I'll just keep yours in the fridge."

My stomach did a weird little dip, loving how that sounded. I could get very used to Everly being in my life. The sound of her voice first thing in the morning and the last thing at night made me want things that I didn't even realize I wanted. But I knew whenever we figured everything out and she was finally safe, she'd go back to her life. The life she loved and wasn't ready to give up for anyone.

"Sounds good," I replied. "I'll try to keep you updated."

"What about Cat?"

I turned back toward the door to the station. "I was going to let my dad take her home with him, but I could drop her off at the house first."

"If you wouldn't mind, that'd be great. You might be at the hospital for a while, and it'd be nice to have her with me."

My heartbeat felt like it paused for a moment. "Everly, I know you said you're not afraid to be there alone, but are you telling me the truth? Are you okay when I leave you home alone?"

She let out a soft laugh. "Yes. It's just...lonely sometimes."

I closed my eyes and inwardly cursed. There was no way I could skip the hospital without people asking why. Bishop was one of my best friends, more like a brother to me.

"Stop what you're thinking," Everly said. "I would never expect you to *not* go to the hospital. Honestly, I'm totally fine—I just thought I could puppy-sit for you."

"You realize she's a police dog, not a puppy, right?"

"I thought she was still in training?"

I could hear the humor in her voice. "You would be correct. But she's still my partner and partakes in police-type shit."

Everly let out a bark of laughter. "Police-type shit? Okay, then."

"Kyle! What are you doing?"

The sound of Hunter's voice had me looking back toward the entrance. I held up a finger, silently asking him to give me a minute. "Hey, I've got to run. I'll see you in a bit."

"Okay, see you and Cat soon."

Hitting End, I took the steps up to where Hunter waited and was about to walk back inside when he stepped in front of me.

"Dude, you're totally dating someone."

"What?" I asked.

Hunter slowly shook his head. "I've never seen you smile like that while on the phone. Let's not even bring up the fact that you went *outside* to make your call. You're seeing someone, and you didn't even tell me!" He took a step back and put his hand over his heart. "You lied to me, dude."

I rolled my eyes and pushed him out of the way. "I'm not dating anyone. It was a friend, that's all."

Hunter followed me through the station to the office we both shared. "A friend? Is it someone I know?"

"They're not from around here."

"He or she?"

I looked over at him. "I'm not doing this with you right now. We need to get to the hospital before Abby births that baby."

"I'm only letting this go for now. Is your dad taking Cat?" Hunter asked.

*Fuck. Fuck. Fuck.* "Um, no."

He gave a smirk. "Dude, I know how much you love her and all, but I'm pretty sure she's not allowed in the hospital."

"I'm dropping her off at home. I'll meet you there."

I grabbed my laptop, slipped it into my backpack, and zipped it up. Tossing it over my shoulder, I called for Cat. We started to head out of the office. When Hunter didn't say anything, I glanced back at him.

He smiled. "Like I said, I'm letting it go...for now."

A loud commotion came from the elevators as Candace stepped out and fell right onto the floor when her heel got stuck.

"Candace!" Greer and Brighton shouted, rushing to help her up with me and Hunter hot on their tails.

"Are you okay?" Greer reached for her best friend from college's hand and pulled her up.

"I am," Candace said, drawing in a breath and letting it out. "I had to close up The Queen Bee—I couldn't very well tell people to get the hell out because my friend was in labor."

"I'm glad. That would have been bad for business," Arabella stated.

Arabella had once owned a small café at the apiary on her parents' property. Once they retired, and Arabella and Hunter got married, she'd moved the apiary to their new property and went in on a partnership with Candace. One side of The Queen Bee was now a café, while the other was a retail spot that sold local items such as honey from the apiary, flower seeds from Abby's parents' seed farm, and various items from Hunter and Willa's family apple orchard.

Candace laughed and replied, "Trust me, business is doing well! Everyone loves New Hampshire in the fall." With a quick look over at Arabella, she asked, "How are you feeling? Still having the contractions?"

I turned to gape at Hunter. "You didn't tell me Arabella was having contractions."

Before Hunter could answer, Bella said, "They're not those types of contractions. They're just Braxton Hicks, which are not uncommon in your third trimester."

A wave of relief washed over me. Arabella wasn't due for another few weeks. "I'm glad to hear everything's normal."

"Any updates?" Candace asked Brighton as she headed to the large waiting room to greet everyone else. Bishop's parents were on their way in from Boston, but they were stuck in traffic.

Pete and Crystal, Abby's parents, had already been there for hours. Her dad had been pacing the room since I'd walked in twenty minutes ago.

"Pete's so nervous," Arabella said quietly. She wrapped her arm in mine, and we moved a bit away from the group. "Abby said he's been nervous the whole pregnancy."

"So has Bishop. He tried to act like he wasn't, but I could tell he was worried."

Arabella smiled softly. "The two of them have kept going to therapy, and I think it's really been helping."

"What about you, Arabella. How are *you* feeling?"

Her smile turned into a full-on grin. "The happiest I've ever been. I'm still going to therapy twice a month too. Hunter comes with me to one of the appointments. It's really been helping him as well."

I nodded and took a quick peek at Hunter before focusing on his wife. "Bishop said *everyone* should be in counseling."

She laughed. "What's going on in your world? Hunter seems to think there's a woman in your life."

With a shake of my head, I stepped back and faced her directly. "Did your husband set you on me to pry for information?"

Her cheeks turned slightly pink. It was adorable. "Maybe."

"Unfortunately, I'm not in a relationship with anyone."

She jutted out her lower lip in a pout. "But you're such a great catch, Kyle Larson! What kind of woman do we need to find to capture your heart?"

*Oh, you wouldn't have to look far, considering she's at my house with my dog right now.* "When I find her, I'll be sure to let you know."

She smiled once again, and I guided her back over toward the waiting group.

"What's taking so long?" Pete stopped his pacing and glanced from his watch to the clock on the wall.

Crystal sighed. "Pete, sweetheart, why don't you sit down before you give yourself a heart attack. If you do, and I miss the birth of my first grandbaby, I'll kill you!"

"If the heart attack doesn't do it for you," Candace said with a wink.

"Yes!" Crystal pointed to Candace. "What Candace said."

Willa walked over to me and spread her arms out. "Hey, how are you?"

I pulled her close and hugged her. "I'm fine."

She reached up onto her toes and whispered into my ear, "Liar."

Drawing back, I gave her a look. "What?"

"I know when something's off with you, and something is way off. I just can't seem to put my finger on it."

"Could you be pregnant?" I asked teasingly.

She grinned. "No, but not for lack of trying."

I rolled my eyes and fake gagged. Willa and Aiden had two kids, Ben who was three, and Ciara, who would be turning one in January. "I really don't need that visual."

"Enough about my and Aiden's very active sex life."

I gagged again.

"What's going on?" she asked. "Hunter said you took Cat home and didn't leave her with your dad. You never leave that dog alone."

"I do too."

"Why won't you just..." Her words trailed off as she looked over my shoulder, then she pushed me out of the way and cried out, "Bishop!"

Crystal and Pete rushed to their son-in-law. "How is Abby? The baby?" Crystal asked.

Bishop had a huge smile on his face. "Abby did amazing! I've never been more proud of her in my life. And the baby is...beautiful. Wonderful. Everything I ever dreamed of."

"*Bishop!*" Arabella said, exasperated. "Boy or girl?"

Wiping a tear away, Bishop said, "It's a boy."

The entire waiting room erupted in a bevy of cheers as everyone took turns congratulating him.

Then came the part where we all waited to meet the newest member of our tightknit group.

# Chapter Fourteen

## Everly

The lock started to turn and Cat was off the sofa and to the front door faster than I could even register that someone was walking in.

Kyle shut the door and bent down to give her some love while I stood and waited to hear about Bishop and Abby's baby.

"How did it go?" I asked when I couldn't take it any longer.

Glancing up with a smile on his face, Kyle replied, "They had a little boy."

I brought my hand up to my mouth as a gasp escaped. "What's his name?"

Kyle stood, and I could see it on his face. Happiness. Surprise. Clearing his throat, he said, "Noah Kyle Harris."

Tears filled my eyes. "How sweet of them to name their son after you."

He nodded and tossed his keys into the bowl on the table before heading into the living room. "I thought so."

"Have you eaten?" I asked. "I made those homemade pizzas, and I think they turned out pretty good."

Kyle grinned. "Sounds delicious; I hope you weren't waiting on me to eat."

"Not at all! Cat and I ate already."

I headed into the kitchen to heat up Kyle's pizzas.

"I should have called to let you know I wasn't going to be here to eat dinner," he said. "I'm sorry."

"You don't have anything to be sorry for. I wasn't sure how long Abby would be in labor. I bet the baby is precious."

Something moved over his face, but it was gone as quickly as it appeared. "Yeah, he is. I wish you could have been there."

I let out a somber laugh. "Me too. I'm starting to go a bit stir crazy."

Kyle dropped his head and sighed before looking back at me. "I'm so sorry, Everly. I know you're bored and probably afraid being here alone. I should have just come home once the baby was born."

"Don't be ridiculous. They're your friends, Kyle. You have every right to want to be there and meet your little namesake."

His gaze met mine, and my breath caught in my throat at the way he looked at me. "I really wanted to be here, with you."

I frowned. "You did?"

Kyle nodded and took a step closer. "I did. Don't get me wrong, I'm very happy for Bishop and Abby, and Noah is a precious little angel. But all I could think about was getting home to you."

My heart started to beat faster the closer Kyle got to me. "And Cat."

*Ugh. Why did I just say that?*

With a smile so sexy I nearly let out a groan, Kyle replied, "I do love my dog, and I love her kisses...but not as much as I love yours."

"M-mine?"

He stopped only inches from me, and I held my breath while I waited for his next move. He leaned in, and I reached for the kitchen island, afraid my knees would buckle at any moment.

"I'm going to kiss you, Everly."

Swallowing the frog in my throat, I managed a weak, "Please do."

The moment Kyle's hands cradled my face, a rush of energy moved through my body. I wanted that kiss more than I wanted my next breath.

Closer. Closer.

Lord, he was only a breath away from my lips. I could almost feel the tingle that I knew would come from Kyle's mouth on mine.

I closed my eyes and inched up onto my toes, bridging the gap between us. My body melted completely against his while I snaked my hands around his neck and he deepened the kiss.

Part of the whole reason I left for Alaska was because of Kyle Larson's kisses. Now it only made me want to crawl inside of him and never leave.

He drew back just enough to speak. "Your ribs?"

"Are fine," I panted back.

Kyle lifted me oh so gently onto the kitchen island, and before I could even have another coherent thought, his lips were back on mine. I slid my fingers through his hair, and when I tugged slightly, he groaned with delight.

"I'm not going to make love to you in my kitchen, Everly...but I really want to taste you."

I dropped my head back, and this time it was my turn to moan. "Yes, Kyle. Yes!"

His hands slid up my yoga pants to my hips. I placed my hands on the island, prepared to lift myself off the counter so he could take them off.

*Ding-dong.*

Kyle and I both froze.

I pulled back and stared out into the living room where Cat had bounded off to while Kyle looked over at the security monitors.

"No, no, no," I whispered.

Cat gave one bark, then a whine.

Kyle closed his eyes before he dropped his head into my lap. I smiled and ran my fingers through his soft brown hair. "I'm going to kill him," he said.

"Who?" I glanced toward the monitor for the front door as Kyle took a step back, then helped me down off the island.

"Hunter."

"Hunter is here...with his wife," I said, more to myself than anything.

With a nod, Kyle said, "Stay in here, Everly."

"I'm not going anywhere. I don't think I could walk if I tried."

He turned and looked at me, one brow raised. "Hunter or the kiss?"

"Ha!" I let out a strangled laugh. "It was the promise of you tasting me."

Kyle's eyes turned dark. "*Fuck*," he said before he walked out to go deal with his unexpected visitors.

Turning around, I held onto the island and drew in a few deep breaths. Maybe it was a good thing Hunter and Arabella had shown up.

A minute later, I heard voices coming closer to the kitchen. Before I could even react, Hunter and his very pregnant wife walked in.

"Everly?" Hunter asked, looking at me and then back to Kyle. "What's going on?"

"Are you okay? You look flushed?" Arabella said with concern in her voice.

*Lord, if she only knew.* "Um..." I looked over at Kyle.

"Everly Higgins, this is Arabella Turner. Arabella, Everly Higgins."

A wide smile broke out across the woman's face. "Yes! We met at your brother's wedding a few weeks ago."

As Arabella made her way toward me, Cat rushed by with another dog who looked nearly identical. Kyle opened the backdoor, and they both took off into the backyard.

"I think Jack has a thing for Cat," Hunter said with a smile.

Not knowing what in the hell to say or do, I just stood there like an idiot.

"Of course he does. Have you seen how beautiful she is?" Kyle opened the refrigerator and took out two beers, then looked at me. "Want one?"

"No, thank you," I said with a slight shake of my head.

Hunter cleared his throat. "Okay, so I guess I need to address the elephant in the room. Why is Hudson's sister here? And why are you keeping it a secret?"

"That's the elephant?" Kyle scoffed. "I thought it was you dropping by unannounced and uninvited."

"Ouch," Hunter said with a teasing tone in his voice.

Kyle lifted his beer to his lips, and I couldn't help but be envious of the bottle. Those lips had just been on mine, ready to explore my body.

I quickly looked away and down at my hands, where I was rubbing them together nervously.

Kyle cleared his throat, and I glanced up. When our eyes met, I nodded my head slightly. With a frustrated sigh, meant for Hunter and not me, Kyle said, "Come on, let's head into the living room. It's a long story."

After Kyle finished telling them everything that had happened to me, Arabella looked white as a ghost. Hunter was still pacing the room— he had started about five minutes into Kyle's explanation.

"Wait," Arabella said, holding up her hand. "You think someone tried to kill Everly because she found some endangered seaducks?"

I drew in a breath. It did sound insane.

"Yes, I just haven't figured out why yet. My gut is telling me it has to do with oil or gas," Kyle said.

I snapped my head up to look at Kyle. "What?"

"That's what I was thinking," Hunter added.

"Oil or gas?" I repeated. "Why didn't I think of that the moment I remembered the seaducks? But what about the report?"

Kyle turned to me. "I talked to them today, Everly. There are no reports of that seaduck nest anywhere near Valdez."

"And why does that lead you to believe it has something to do with oil or gas?" Arabella asked.

Kyle stood and rubbed at the back of his neck. "Listen, I've already told you both too much. The last thing I want is to put either of you in danger—"

Hunter lifted a hand. "You're not. Like you said, they don't know she's here. They probably have no idea *where* she is."

"But they know she's alive because Hudson said she was at a yoga retreat. You can't use that excuse for much longer. How long do those things even last?" Arabella asked.

"I once went to one that was three weeks," I answered.

The tension was clear on Kyle's face. "I figure we have maybe a few more days before they realize Everly is in hiding and her family knows where she is. I need to figure this out before they come for the family in an attempt to flush her out."

"Why haven't you just gone to the police?" Hunter asked.

"No!" I said. "I know it probably sounds crazy to you, but I know for sure that one of them was a cop. Maybe even all three of them. I don't trust anyone right now. I mean, I found out *my ex* wants me dead. And if Jacob was killed because he knew about the seaducks, then someone on the inside had to have alerted Derrick or James or whoever."

"I think this is bigger than we first thought. It may go pretty deep," Kyle stated. "We might have to go to the police soon, Everly."

Hunter cleared his throat. "Okay, the first thing we need to do is figure out if there are any oil or gas permits or plans for a future pipeline near where Everly found the endangered ducks."

"I've already done that," Kyle said. "And there is no *we* in this, Hunter. I didn't tell you about Everly and this whole situation because I want to keep you and Arabella safe."

Hunter grinned. "I appreciate that, but I'm not letting you handle this alone."

"We're not," I interjected. "Hudson is helping."

Hunter glared at Kyle. "Hudson knows Everly's here?"

Kyle nodded. "Yes. I had to tell him; he had a right to know."

"But you didn't trust me with this information?" Hunter asked.

"Okay, just stop right there," Arabella said before I could cut into the conversation again. "Hunter, it's not fair to put that on Kyle. I completely understand why he informed Hudson—it's his sister, for heaven's sake. And as far as not telling *you*, I see his point on that as well."

Turning to face Kyle, Arabella went on. "But I'm going to have to agree with Hunter about letting him help you. And what about Everly? The faster we figure this all out, the safer she'll be. I'm sure she's going to lose her mind soon having to look over her shoulder constantly."

"That's already happening," I said with a sigh.

Arabella pointed at me. "See! So, this is what I suggest: You let Hunter help you."

Kyle tilted his head and sighed. "I feel like there's a but in there somewhere."

She smiled. "Not a but, an *and*."

Kyle motioned for her to go on.

"And you let me steal Everly for a night."

That made my eyes go wide. "Steal me?"

"Steal her?" Kyle asked.

Arabella looked at Hunter, then at me, before finally settling her gaze on Kyle. "Yes. Not away from the house; she can stay here. But I think it's time for a girls' night."

Both Hunter and Kyle groaned as a wide grin spread across my face.

# Chapter Fifteen

## Kyle

I stared at Arabella like she'd lost her mind before I finally found my voice. "No way."

"Kyle, she'll still be here and safe. And you could even be here. It's just some one-on-one girl time." Arabella folded her arms over her chest, letting them rest on top of her belly. She looked so darn cute it was hard to even want to argue with her.

"Arabella, I know your heart is in the right place, but this isn't a good idea," I said.

"Kyle's right," Everly said with a nod. "As fun as it sounds, the last thing I want to do is bring attention to the fact that I'm here."

Arabella pouted. "I hate it that you're both right. I just really wanted Everly to have one night where she wasn't worried."

Everly smiled. "Thank you, Arabella. Maybe once this all unfolds and everything goes back to normal, we can plan a girls' night."

Arabella started to pace. "What if we do a book club meeting over here instead? Just me, Greer, and you?" She looked at Kyle. "You, Hudson, and Hunter can play poker or something."

The moment Arabella said poker, Everly lit up like a Christmas tree.

"Or we could play couple's poker!" she said. "Kyle's teaching me how to play."

"Couple's poker? I love that idea!" Arabella bounced with excitement.

My heart did a weird jump at the idea of Everly and me being a couple.

When she looked at me, she must have seen the surprise on my face because she quickly added. "I mean...Kyle and I aren't a couple in that sense, more like partner's poker, I guess."

With a wave of her hand, Arabella said, "Minor details. This is perfect! Shall we plan it for tomorrow night?"

I sighed. "Are you sure, Everly?"

She gave me a sweet smile. "If you think it's okay."

Nodding, I said to Arabella, "I'll text Greer and Hudson."

Arabella let out a little squeal of laughter. "You're truly doing me a favor." Placing her hand on her stomach, she added, "'Cause once this little one gets here, we won't be able to do things like this for a while."

Everly let out a soft laugh. "Then it's my pleasure. Do you know if you're having a boy or girl?"

Arabella shook her head. "We want to be surprised."

They both drifted off into a conversation about baby clothes, and how Arabella was nesting in preparation for the baby.

Hunter and I made our way into the kitchen, farther away from the girls.

"What's your next move?" he asked.

"I don't know," I said on a long exhale. "I need to figure out how to look into this Jacob guy's death without bringing attention to it."

Hunter nodded. "What can I do?"

"I'm not sure. It's not like I can call up there and ask for information on this guy."

We stood in silence for a bit before Hunter spoke. "Let's go over what you *do* know. Everly stumbled upon some endangered seaducks. She reported the sighting before she left for the wedding. This

Jacob West was the one who took the report. The day after he filed it, or we think he filed it, he ends up in a one-car accident and dies. Then Everly comes back from the wedding and the next morning, she's kidnapped."

"Yes. And if the idiots hadn't beaten her, she'd most likely be dead already."

"Okay, think about this: They could have just tampered with her car. Why take her?"

That made me pause. "We don't know that they *didn't* take Jacob. They might have."

Hunter nodded. "That's true. And we can't go asking questions because it will only lead them right back here. If they have the means to wipe away a report, who knows what else they can do."

"Exactly. And since one of them is a cop, Everly won't go to the police."

"What if you have Hudson contact Everly's best friend? Ask her about the ducks."

"I've already thought about that...but I have a feeling this James guy is on the inside."

"Of NOAA?"

"Yeah," I replied, turning to grab a couple more beers. "He knows Derrick, Everly's ex. And if my gut is right, he's the same guy who called Hudson claiming to be Martin something or other. With NOAA."

"You think it's the same guy?"

I took a drink before I answered. "My gut is telling me it is. Either way, I need to find this guy before he finds Everly."

"Maybe he's still in Alaska. Is Derrick?"

"No, I already looked up his flight details. He stayed in Alaska for a bit after Everly's kidnapping, then he left to go back to DC."

"At some point, Kyle, you're going to have to go to the police in Valdez with all of this. Or at the very least, to your dad."

Glancing out into the living room, I watched Everly smile at something Arabella was showing her on her phone.

"I know. Everly doesn't want me to, but I think I need to. Sooner rather than later."

Everly sat across from me at the card table I'd set up after Hunter and Arabella left.

"Okay, so usually the dealer decides what kind of poker the table is playing. We played five-card draw the other night. Tomorrow night, we'll probably play Texas Hold 'Em, so that's what I'll teach you right now."

With a smile, Everly asked, "And what's the difference?"

"The other night, we were both dealt five cards. In Texas Hold 'Em, we're dealt two pocket cards and then there are five community cards, or bard cards, that are revealed. There are four rounds of betting before we show our cards."

She nodded.

"First, do you remember the terms I taught you?"

Everly looked up in thought. "Let's see. There was ante, which was the minimum amount you had to bet. Um, call, which is when a new wager has been placed and you want to match the raised amount. Check is no new wager, and you don't wish to raise. Raise is when you want to increase the table bet. Fold is when you decide not to even go on with the game, and you slide the cards away from you."

Smiling, I replied, "Fast learner."

Everly winked.

"Okay, so in Texas Hold 'Em, you have to make your best hand with the two pocket cards, or sometimes they're called hole cards, and any combination of the five cards."

She shook her head. "Maybe we should just play Go Fish."

I couldn't help but laugh. "You'll catch on quickly enough. Want to try a hand?"

Her eyes met mine. "What does the winner get?"

My dick jumped in my pants. "Whatever the winner wants."

Everly's brow rose. "Anything? Nothing's off limits?"

I swallowed hard, thinking back to earlier in the kitchen, before Hunter and Arabella had interrupted us. "Nothing's off limits."

With a wave of her hand, she said, "Then let's play."

Clearing my throat, I picked up the deck. "Dealer always shuffles the deck. Normally the dealer doesn't play, but in self-dealt games at home, he does. Dealing is shared among the players. Person to the left goes first, and then it moves in a clockwise rotation."

"Okay. Keep going."

"Right, um, the first two people to the left of the dealer put an amount we all agree on into the pot before any cards are dealt. Usually the small blind, who's to the left of the dealer, puts in half of the bet, then the large blind puts in the remainder."

"Got it," Everly said with a smile.

"Each player is dealt two cards. The object is to make a hand with your cards and the board cards. For instance, you can use two of your cards and three on the board. Or one of your hole cards and four on the board."

She nodded.

I went on with my instructions while Everly watched and nodded every now and then.

"This round is the river round..." My voice drifted off. "Everly, are you even listening?"

Her cheeks went red, and she moved about in her seat. "Honestly, you lost me after the first betting round."

Laughing, I said, "We can't play if you don't know how."

She chewed on her lower lip. "Maybe I can learn all this as we play tomorrow? Arabella said she's still trying to learn as well."

"Okay, then do you want to stop altogether now?"

"No!"

I raised my brows and she smiled sheepishly at me. "I mean, we need to play something," I said, "since there's a bet on the table. Go Fish?"

She nodded. "That sounds amazing."

I dealt out seven cards each, and we started playing. After nearly half an hour, I looked at all of Everly's pairs. "You've got to be cheating."

She giggled. "You're literally telling me every card you have in your hand!"

"Well, how else am I supposed to get pairs?"

With a shrug, she asked, "Do you have a seven?"

I glanced down to my cards and then back to her.

"Do not even tell me to go fish, Kyle Larson! You asked for a seven a few turns back."

With a long exhale, I took the seven out and handed it to her. "I'm folding."

She jerked her eyes up to meet mine. "You can't fold."

"I'm making a new rule. You're going to win anyway."

She smiled as she looked down at all her pairs. "It's true, I *am* going to win."

I leaned back in my chair. "Tell me, Everly, what is it you want for winning this hand?"

She swept her tongue over her lips, and her eyes drifted down to my mouth. It didn't take my body long to catch up with what she was clearly thinking.

"I want to finish what we were about to do in the kitchen."

"Is that so?" I asked, hoping my voice sounded normal because my heart was about to beat out of my damn chest. "Do you want to go back to the kitchen?"

She shook her head. "I want to go to your bedroom."

I nearly knocked the chair over, I stood up so fast. Before Everly could even move, I swept her into my arms and headed for the steps. Cat was hot on my trail, letting out a few barks as we walked.

Everly wrapped her arms around my neck and laughed as I took the steps two at a time. "Don't drop me! I'm just now feeling normal."

Walking down the hall to my bedroom, I replied, "Trust me, I wouldn't dream of dropping you."

I stopped at the edge of my bed and gently placed Everly down. The second her feet hit the floor, I pressed my mouth to hers. Her arms came up and around my neck. I pulled her closer to me, and we both let out low, soft groans of pleasure.

"I've been wanting to do this since the first moment I saw you," I said.

She dropped her head back to allow me access to kiss down her neck. "Do what?"

"Kiss you, touch you...make love to you."

Everly let a sigh escape and then allowed me to lift her shirt and gently pull it over her head. Her lip was healed, and you could barely see the bruise on the side of her face anymore. I ran my thumb gently over it and whispered, "I want to kill the person who did this to you."

She reached up and kissed me before pulling my shirt up and over my head. I didn't want to break the kiss, but had to.

Everly worked at unbuttoning my jeans while I sealed my mouth over hers once more. Then I gently guided her onto the bed. I placed soft kisses all over her face, down her neck, and across the swell of her right breast. "Fuck, I want to see you naked...well, again," I whispered. "And I see you have some new panties and bras."

She blushed. "I do."

Arching her back, Everly practically purred when I placed my mouth over her bra to suck on her nipple. "Kyle."

Smiling, I moved my hand around her back and found her bra strap. Everly arched up more and I unclasped it. I admired the pretty lace bra before I pulled the straps down Everly's arms and tossed it to the side of the bed.

"Everly," I panted as I took in her perfect body. I loved that she wasn't stick thin. She was in shape but she had curves—and fuck, if they weren't sexy. Her breasts were perfect. Not too small, not too big. They fit nicely in my hand, and I nearly came when I touched them at last. I started to play with her nipple with my left hand while I took her other breast into my mouth and sucked.

"Oh God!" she gasped, pushing more of herself into my mouth.

"Do you like that?"

"Yes." She gripped the bedspread with her hands, watching me touch her.

Moving to her other breast, I gave it the same amount of attention before trailing kisses down her body. I took hold of her yoga pants and gently pulled them off as she lifted her hips. Then I slipped off her panties, growling when I saw a patch of blonde hair between her thighs.

"I can't wait to taste you."

"Wait, Kyle..."

I stopped and looked at her. "What's wrong?"

"It's just...I haven't exactly been a good girl. But I've only been with five guys, and I've never let them do...that."

Raising a brow, I asked, "You've never had oral sex?"

"No. I've given it before though."

An instant surge of jealousy hit me. "I want to kill them all."

She laughed. "Only one. Derrick."

"Now I have another reason to kill him."

Smiling, she chewed nervously on her lip. "It's just...I don't shave down there, and I—"

I spread her legs wide, cutting her off. "That doesn't bother me at all, sweetheart. I want to taste you, and the longer you make me wait, the more painful it becomes."

Everly frowned. "What do you mean?"

"My dick. It's so hard now I can hardly stand it. Can I taste you?"

Her breathing increased, and she managed to say, "Yes, please."

I settled my body between her legs and slowly spread her open. Blowing softly, I moaned at the sight before me. "So fucking pretty."

Everly grabbed for the comforter again, and when I ran my tongue through her lips, she cried out in pleasure.

Before I could place my mouth over her, I felt a rush of hot breath on my neck. I pulled my head up, only to find Cat with her front paws on the bed, staring at me with a *what in the fuck do you think you're doing* expression on her face.

"Cat, down."

"W-what?" Everly asked, lifting her head. "What is she doing?"

Everly attempted to scramble away from me, but I stopped her. "Don't move."

I got off the bed and walked to the door. "Cat, out."

The damn dog jumped up on the bed and stared at Everly.

"Um, Kyle? Why does your dog look like she wants to attack me?"

I laughed. "She's jealous. Cat. Come."

She finally listened, but when I motioned toward the door, she walked out of the room totally pouting. I closed the door and then made my way back over to Everly.

I pulled down my jeans and kicked them to the side before doing the same with my boxer briefs. When I looked back at Everly, her eyes were on my dick. Clearly all worries about Cat were gone.

"I hope you like what you see, sweetheart."

Color instantly filled her cheeks, and she looked away.

"Don't ever be embarrassed to look at me, Everly." She turned back, and our eyes met. "*I'm* certainly not when I look at your body. I could stare at you for hours and never get tired of it." She smiled at me as I got back into position between her legs and asked, "Now, where was I?"

Before she could answer, my mouth was on her. I sucked and licked while she whimpered and moaned. God, I loved the little sounds she made. She tasted like heaven, and a part of me hoped like hell I wasn't dreaming.

"Kyle!" Everly cried out, arching her back. "Oh my God, yes."

I slipped two fingers inside her and sucked on her clit. Everly fell, calling out my name over and over as she let her orgasm take control. Her hands slipped into my hair, and I couldn't tell if she wanted me closer or needed me to stop.

"Oh God. Oh God. Kyle, I can't. No more. Yes!"

I held onto her while I brought out the last waves of her orgasm, and soon she lay spent on my bed. "Condom?" I asked.

She shook her head. "On the pill."

I smiled and went back to worshiping her body with my lips. Then I positioned myself at her entrance and took her mouth with mine. She moaned when she tasted her pleasure on my tongue, and I had to fight not to slam into her.

I drew back and looked into her eyes as I slowly slid inside of her. My eyes closed for a moment while I enjoyed the most amazing feeling I'd ever experienced in my life.

Everly's hands moved over my back, and she wrapped her legs around me, urging me to go deeper.

"It feels too good," I whispered and stopped, afraid if I moved another inch, I'd lose control.

I opened my eyes when her hand touched my cheek. She was looking at me, and I could see it in her eyes. This wasn't simply two people satisfying an itch.

No, this was so much more.

"Everly," I whispered as I leaned down and kissed her softly on the side of her mouth. "I don't want it to end."

"Neither do I, but I need you to move, Kyle. God, I need to feel you inside me, all the way inside me. Please."

Her words nearly shattered me. I pushed in as deep as I could and dropped my forehead to hers. "Holy hell, you feel like heaven. I never want to leave."

Then I began to thrust—and I knew nothing would ever be the same again. Everly and I fit together and it was perfection. When I moved, she moved; it was like a beautiful, erotic dance that I didn't want to end.

"Oh, Kyle... Yes. It feels so good."

I found her neck with my mouth as I slowly moved in and out of her. Then I licked up to her ear, where I gently bit on her earlobe, causing her to gasp and tighten her legs around me. "Everly, my God, the feel of you."

"I know. I know! More. Kyle, please, I need more."

I moved faster, going deeper and harder until the sound of our bodies slapping together nearly drove me over the edge. I wanted Everly to come again and was about to slip my hand between our bodies when she arched her back and moved faster against me.

"Yes! Yes! I'm going to come. Don't stop, please, don't stop!"

"That's it, sweetheart. Let me hear how good it feels."

And that's when Everly cried out my name, and I felt her squeeze my dick. It was more than I could take.

"I'm coming. Fuuuuck...Everly, I'm coming!"

We both fell together, and it was the most amazing moment of my life. As we lay there after our lovemaking, I couldn't ignore the strange feeling in my chest—I'd never experienced it with anyone else.

Everly nestled next to me, and I soon drifted off to sleep, dreaming of a future I wasn't sure I could have.

# Chapter Sixteen

## Everly

Kyle's breathing steadily slowed, and I sensed the moment he fell asleep. I opened my eyes and looked up to see the most handsome, caring, and utterly romantic man I'd ever known adrift in what I hoped were happy dreams.

I snuck out of the room and opened the door to let Cat back in.

"Cat, come girl," I whispered.

She immediately got up and made her way onto the bed. It looked as if she wanted to slip in between me and Kyle, but she laid down at our feet and rested her head on my legs, looking directly at me. I saw something in those eyes, and it moved me so much I nearly cried.

"I won't hurt him, I promise you."

She let out a soft bark, and Kyle mumbled something and then returned to his slumber. I snuggled closer to him, watching as his chest rose and fell. My entire body was still tingling from our love-making...and from two of the most intense orgasms I'd ever had in my life.

It wasn't like I'd had bad sex with my ex-lovers, but it hadn't been anything close to what I'd experienced with Kyle. I'd never experienced such feelings like when Kyle had slipped inside of me, and when he'd moved. We'd been like one. When he'd kissed me... Lord, when he'd kissed me, it had seemed like I was the very air he needed to breathe.

I closed my eyes and let out a soft sigh. What was it I'd felt, exactly? I'd never experienced it before, not even with Derrick. I'd always somehow known there would never be a future with him. It had been smart to listen to my gut and break things off with the asshat, of course him cheating on me helped make the decision too.

For the longest time, I laid there thinking about what he'd done. It didn't make sense to me that all of this was because I'd stumbled upon the nest. There had to be more to it...and I needed to think harder. Was there something I'd missed? A conversation? Something I'd overheard, perhaps? And who in the hell was James—and what were he and Derrick up to?

The weight of my exhaustion eventually made my body relax completely, and I drifted off to sleep next to the man I was head over heels for.

*Ding-dong.*

Kyle groaned as he pulled me closer. "Please tell me that wasn't the doorbell."

Smiling, I kissed the side of his handsome face. "It wasn't the doorbell." Though I was pretty sure it had been.

The sound of Cat barking downstairs had Kyle bolting upright.

"Who do you think it is?" I asked, watching Kyle get dressed faster than I could even process. Before I knew it, he was in sweatpants and a T-shirt, heading out of the bedroom.

"Don't leave this room," he said. "Remember, there's a loaded pistol in the side drawer."

My heart started to pound. "Kyle, why in the world do you not have monitors in here?"

He stopped and looked back at me. "Because I can look at them on my phone, which is downstairs. But that'll change this week." Taking a breath, he attempted to relax his features. "It's okay, sweetheart. Just stay here until I come back, all right?"

I nodded. "Okay."

The bedroom door clicked, and I stayed still and held my breath so that I could listen. Faint voices drifted up, but I could barely make out if they were male or female. I jumped out of bed and searched for my clothes to put back on. When I couldn't find a shirt, I slipped on one of Kyle's. I drew in a deep breath and sighed. It smelled like him, and that instantly calmed me.

There was a light knock, and then the door opened to Kyle saying my name. "It's Hunter; can you come down as soon as possible?"

My knees nearly buckled. "Is everything okay?" I asked.

"Everything's fine, but he has some new information. I'll start breakfast while you get ready."

Nodding, I rushed out of Kyle's bedroom and into the guest bathroom, where I brushed my teeth and pulled my hair up into a ponytail before heading downstairs.

The smell of coffee should have been reassuring, but all it did was make me anxious. The scent of bacon became stronger as I walked into the kitchen to find Hunter leaning against the counter.

"Hunter, what are you doing here?" I asked, and Kyle looked up at me from where he was pouring cups of coffee. He handed the first cup to me, the second to Hunter. "Thank you," I said.

"I'm sorry it's so early," Hunter replied, "but last night I remembered that when I was at the academy there was a guy there, named Bill, from Alaska. He'd left the state for a few years to go to college, but his father was some political guy there. Well, I looked up the congressman for Alaska—and lo and behold, it's Bill's dad. So I gave Bill a call. Turns out he's back in Alaska and living in the capital. I mentioned we were thinking of doing a fishing trip up there. We got to talking, and I found a spot in the conversation to ask if there were any gas or oil lines going in and, if so, should we avoid those areas."

"Wow, what great thinking." I sat down on one of the stools at the kitchen island. Hunter smiled and Kyle rolled his eyes. "What did he say?" I asked, nearly ready to bounce out of my seat.

"He said, yeah, there's a private company that's put in a bid to do an oil pipeline. They've met with a lot of pushback from environmentalists and such and have been delayed a number of times. He said it looks like they're going to be getting the go-ahead soon, though, if they don't run into any other problems."

Kyle and I looked at each other. "Is the line anywhere close to Valdez?" Kyle asked.

Hunter pulled out a piece of paper. "He told me to keep this on the down low, but this is the projected path of the pipeline."

I took the paper...and nearly felt sick when I saw it. It wasn't going through the direct area of the nest I'd found, but it was only a few miles away—enough that the state would *not* allow a pipeline if they knew about it.

I pressed my hand to my mouth, trying to hold back a rush of queasiness. Collecting myself, I dropped my arm and looked at Kyle. "The nest. If the state found out about that nest, they wouldn't be able to put the pipeline through there. It would be blocked for sure."

"For one nest, though?" Kyle asked.

I shook my head. "If there's one nest spotted, there's likely to be more nearby. I happened to stumble upon that one."

Hunter cleared his throat. "Are you the only one who knew about it?"

I slowly shook my head. "Kristy knows. I told her, and I believe another climatologist was standing there. Um, his name was Richard...I don't know his last name. He'd shown up a few weeks prior to me leaving."

"I'm guessing Kristy doesn't realize that your sighting was never reported," Kyle said.

"No," I confirmed, chewing on my thumbnail. "She would have no reason to follow up if I was the one who found it."

"That's not all," Hunter said, causing me and Kyle to focus back on him. "When I looked up the board of directors for the private company that's building the pipeline, I found an interesting name listed."

"Who?" Kyle and I asked in unison.

"Derrick Mays."

My heart dropped to my stomach.

"I looked for a James but didn't see one. No Martin either," Hunter added.

I started to pace the kitchen. "So, I stumbled upon that nest and reported it. And they assumed that if I found out about the pipeline, I'd still be a threat since I could report about the Steller's Eider's nest."

"And Derrick is on this board, clearly in their pockets, and he somehow found out about the nest from someone inside Fish and Wildlife Services," Kyle stated.

"If the construction company had already been delayed once," I said, "it would stand to reason they might do something drastic, or pay to have something drastic done while playing innocent."

"Like kill. They're serious enough to kill people...money is the motivator," Kyle stated.

I nodded. "Yes. If they did indeed cause Jacob's death—which I believe they did—and they were ready to kill me, who knows how many other innocent people have died. And it makes sense for a company like that to have someone from NOAA on their board. If anything, it's mostly for show. To make the public think they're environmentally conscious."

Kyle set down his coffee cup. "Companies like this often have people like you on their board?"

"Yes and no," I replied. "Larger corporations would have someone like Derrick on the board. He could be their environmental consultant or expert. It's not as uncommon as you'd think, but I'm surprised Derrick would be associated with a company that builds the pipelines. I'm wondering if he owns shares in this company, and that is his motivation behind all of this."

Kyle pushed his fingers through his hair and let out a long sigh.

"I think we tell Bill about this, and he tells his dad. I mean, he's a freaking congressman," Hunter stated.

They both looked at me. I cleared my throat and gave my honest opinion. "Yes, but oil is a huge business, especially in Alaska. He might not do anything simply because it brings in money to his state. In my experience, most politicians aren't really looking out for the little people."

Kyle sighed. "Everly, we need to go to the police with this."

"I could go to my boss, or even *his* boss," I said, "but how do I know if they're not on some dark company's payroll? I mean, the man I was going to marry tried to have me killed! This is clearly about money—and I'm guessing *a lot* of money."

Hunter exhaled. "You two can't beat this on your own. The moment they find out where you are, Everly, they're going to come for you."

The three of us sat in silence for what seemed like forever.

"The newspapers," I said. "I could send the media info about this. Put it out there for everyone to see, and I could even say I'm in hiding for my life over it. We could name the company. I could give them Derrick's name, as well as this James guy and a description of him."

Kyle and Hunter exchanged a look before Kyle shook his head. "They'll want proof. Solid proof."

Hunter nodded. "I agree. I mean, we could maybe see if they'll leak the story, but..."

"We have the pictures that Adam took," I said. "Of me, after I was beaten."

Kyle shook his head. "I don't think that would be enough."

Hunter smiled softly at me. "I agree, Everly. I hate to say this, but you need to get the law involved."

I sighed because I knew they were right. This was something we couldn't do without getting them involved. "Do they come here, or do we go there?"

"I'll take you into the station after hours," Kyle said. "My dad can arrange for someone from Boston PD to be there, as well, since they're much larger than Boggy Creek."

The tears were starting to build in my eyes as I drew in a shaky breath. "Okay. I'll talk to your dad and whoever he trusts from the Boston PD."

Hunter and Kyle both let out a breath, and I could see them visibly relax a bit.

Kyle took my hand in his. "It's the right thing and the best thing to do, sweetheart. Trust me."

Smiling, I squeezed his hand. "I do. With my life. But after we talk to the police, I want to send out two emails if Hudson's friend can mask where they're coming from."

"To whom?" Kyle asked.

"One to Kristy, and one to my boss. I'm going to resign from NOAA."

Kyle and Hunter both stared at me with shocked expressions.

"Wait, are you sure you want to do that, Everly? You love your job," Kyle asked.

With a smile, I replied, "I've never been so sure of anything in my entire life."

# Chapter Seventeen

## James

"It's been over two weeks, Derrick. You said she'd be an easy mark. She hasn't even invited me back to her place yet."

I could hear the fucker sigh on the other end of the line. "Maybe she's become more careful with her random lays," he said. "After all, she fucked her best friend's fiancé. Can't you rough her up some and get the info out of her that way?"

Rolling my eyes, I said, "Everly's still out there. At any moment, she could reveal what happened to her to the public. And with one NOAA employee suddenly skipping town, the last thing I want to do is draw more attention."

Derrick sighed again. "She clearly doesn't trust the police. And as far as I can tell, no one has been sniffing around my business or asking questions. Her brother and parents clearly think she's at some stupid yoga retreat. I do remember she went to one once, but I can't remember the name, and I got nowhere calling up some retreats around the Arizona area. They won't give out any personal information at all. I can't ask Hudson because he'll know something's up if I come back into the picture again."

I rubbed at the tension in my neck. "Did you know she sent in a letter of resignation? She quit NOAA. I found out *that* bit of information from Kristy. She's pissed that she hasn't been able to get a hold of Everly. And no one has shown up to her apartment in DC."

"Wait, did you trace the email or whatever it is you do with that kind of stuff?"

"Of course. It was scrambled, which means she had help with it. So, now I'm thinking her family knows more than they're letting on. Possibly not the parents, but I'd bet the brother knows the truth. I've already got guys watching the parents' house in Boston and the brother is in New Hampshire, and they're going about life as if she isn't in hiding somewhere. Where the fuck is she, Derrick?"

"How the fuck would I know?" he whisper-shouted. "You don't think I'm on pins and needles here, too, James? We need to figure out where in the hell she is before she talks."

"I know that, asshole! I'm working on Kristy."

Derrick huffed. "She's most likely a dead end. You're wasting your time. Come back to DC and we'll figure this out. Besides, how much more time can you be away from your job, Detective?"

"Told my supervisor my mother passed away. It's kind of true; she died last year. Besides, my gut is telling me Kristy is the key to finding Everly. This is what I do for a living, Derrick. I get people to confess without them even knowing they're giving me information."

"Whatever, play detective with her," Derrick said. "I've got a meeting in five minutes I've got to get to. I'm flying out to the Arctic tomorrow or the next day."

"Why? I didn't think you did field stuff anymore."

"I don't, but there's some pretty troubling data coming in on a project, and my boss wants me there to personally look into it. I'll have my second cell on me. Don't use my work one."

I rolled my eyes again. "This isn't new for me. I'll let you know if I get any information from the best friend."

"Don't waste any more time on Kristy if you can't get any info from her."

I smiled. "It won't be a waste of my time if she finally lets me into her pants after all this fucking hard work. She hasn't even let me get into her goddamn apartment yet."

Derrick laughed. "Trust me, she's a fun ride and worth the wait. Gotta run. Talk soon."

After the call ended, I pulled out my other phone to see that Kristy had texted me.

*Kristy: "Dinner at my place tonight?"*

I leaned back in my chair and sighed. "Fucking finally."

*Me: Dinner at your place sounds amazing. What time and should I bring anything?*

*Kristy: Seven? And nope, just bring yourself!*

My gut was telling me that the answers to my questions about Everly Higgins would be revealed that evening. Kristy might actually have no idea where her best friend was, but I was positive if I had a chance to look around, I'd be able to find something, even if that meant playing a little dirty.

Smiling to myself, I stood and headed to the closet to find something to wear. "Dirty is always my favorite option."

I showed up to Kristy's house at seven on the dot. When she opened the door, she let her eyes do a quick sweep of me, and I saw a slight flush on her cheeks. She liked what she saw.

"Hope I'm not late," I said, lifting a bottle of wine.

Taking it from me, she replied, "You're right on time; come on in. Dinner has about ten minutes or so left."

I followed her into her apartment, took off my coat, and placed it in her outstretched hand. "Forgot how bitter cold it is in Alaska. How can you stand it?"

Kristy laughed. "You also forget my job literally involves working on glaciers."

I winked. "Sorry, I did forget there for a moment."

After hanging up my coat, Kristy turned and headed into the small kitchen. "I hope you like eggplant parmesan. My grandmother is a hundred percent Italian, so I make a pretty mean version."

Making my way around her apartment, I took it all in. She probably rented this place fully furnished since there was only basic furniture in the small living and dining areas. Paintings of views around Alaska covered the walls. There was a desk in the corner, and I made my way over to it. I causally bumped her computer, only to find it locked. I'd need to figure out her passcode. To the right of the computer sat a small stack of folders. Behind those were four small picture frames. I picked one up, looking at it.

"Is this your parents?" I asked, setting the first frame down. It was a picture of a younger Kristy with an older man and woman. The woman looked nearly identical to Kristy.

"Yep!"

The next photo was of Kristy and a guy. "Tell me this isn't a boyfriend who's waiting back home for you."

She laughed. "My brother, Mac."

The third photo was of an older couple. I was guessing maybe her grandparents. And the last one was of her, another pretty woman about Kristy's age, and Everly. They were standing on a beach, each of them in bikinis.

"That's Everly and another co-worker from NOAA," Kristy said as she walked into the room. "Her name is Jan Morrison. Everly and I met her at a class she was doing on the underwater melting of glaciers."

I nodded and took the glass of wine that Kristy handed me. I set it down and said, "Thank you." Then I sat when she motioned for me to take a seat. "You still haven't heard from her?"

Kristy's smile faded. "No. I'm really beginning to worry. I called her brother this morning."

"Really? Did he say what was going on? Why she quit her job?"

"He said Everly was making some major changes in her life, and he thinks she's been able to do some serious thinking on this retreat. I don't understand why she hasn't called me. I mean, she didn't call me during the last retreat, but she did email. But if Hudson isn't worried, then I guess I shouldn't be either. I do think if she's quitting it's because she wants to settle back in Boston, or maybe even Boggy Creek."

That made me sit up slightly. "Well, that's a good thing, right? She'd be near her family."

She gave a one-shoulder shrug, frowning. "I guess so. I've been racking my brain trying to think of why she would have left her job at NOAA. She loved it. Loved what she did, had a true passion for it. It feels..."

I picked up my wine and took a drink. "It feels like what?"

With a shake of her head, she replied, "Wrong. I asked Hudson if she was in trouble, and he said no. She simply told him she needed some time away."

"For what, I wonder?"

A ding came from the kitchen and Kristy stood. "That's what I asked. The only thing she told him is that she can't share what's going on, but she'll be able to soon."

My chest felt tight. What the fuck did that mean? "Well, hopefully whatever it is, she gets it figured out soon."

She smiled sadly. "Me too. I miss my best friend. Dinner's done."

I had to hand it to Kristy, she could cook one hell of an eggplant parmesan. We talked as we cleaned up after dinner, and then moved back to the living room to finish off the bottle of wine. I hated playing games like the one I was currently trapped in. I just wanted to get the fucking information I knew this bitch had. She was the key, my gut told me so. And twenty-five years of working for the DC police, one thing that it had taught me was to listen to my gut.

When a break in the conversation stretched a little too long, I cleared my throat. "Thank you for dinner, Kristy. It was delicious, and I've really enjoyed myself this evening."

If she didn't invite me to stay, I'd have to drug her and search her apartment.

She smiled. "I have too. How long are you in town for? I don't think you ever said. Or maybe you did, and I forgot."

"I, um...I leave tomorrow to head back to Washington."

"Tomorrow?"

I could hear the disappointment in her voice.

"Well, then, I'm sorry I waited so long to invite you over," she said.

I winked, then set down my glass of wine. "Maybe we should make the most of the time we have left."

She flashed me a sexy grin. "Maybe we should."

"Before we do that, do you mind if I check in for my flight? I've been trying to do it on my phone and it isn't working."

"Sure." She got up and made her way to her laptop. I followed and watched as she typed in the password.

"While you do that, I'll go...freshen up."

I winked. "I'll be waiting."

Once she was out of the living room, I opened up the website for American Airlines so that she would see it when she walked back in.

I went back to the sofa and sat down. Kristy walked out, glanced at her laptop and then made her way over to me.

It was soon clear to me that she wasn't one of those women who needed to be romanced first. She crawled on top of me...and fifteen minutes later, we were in her bedroom fucking.

After making sure I satisfied her a few times, I got up to get some water. I slipped a sleeping aid into the glass before I headed back to her room. I gave her enough to make sure she fell asleep fast—and would remain that way for at least a few hours.

Thirty minutes later, I was searching her place. She was neat and tidy, so going through everything was a breeze. I searched her phone to make sure she hadn't had any contact with Everly, and the only thing I saw were the calls she'd made to her cell after Everly had taken off. They were short calls, which told me she'd only gotten Everly's voicemail.

I sat down at her laptop and shook the mouse. Her screen came on, and I smiled as I typed in the password I'd seen her use earlier. "Should really be more creative with your passwords, sweetheart. *Iceberg* would have been one of my first guesses."

The first thing I did was open her email and type in Everly's work address. A plethora of emails loaded up, and I groaned internally. Sighing, I selected the newest one and started reading.

Most of the emails were about work, so I switched gears and looked for any emails from when Everly wasn't in Alaska yet. After reading through some of the emails she'd sent from Iceland, I paused when a subject line caught my eye.

*Boggy Creek is AMAZING!*

I clicked on it and read about how Everly had surprised her brother Hudson, who was staying in a small town they used to visit as kids. Boggy Creek, New Hampshire. I already knew Hudson lived there, so I closed it out and the next email popped up.

*You're not going to believe this!*

I raised my brows, clicked on the email, and started to read.

Hey, Kristy!

Hudson is doing great. He's totally in love, it's clear as anything. I simply adore Greer, and she has a brother who is...yeah... he's handsome. He took us all hiking, and you're not going to believe what he did. HE KISSED ME! Okay, honestly, I kissed him, but whatever.

Oh, Kristy...Kyle is...I don't even know what he is. But I found myself having crazy thoughts and weird feelings about him. We all went to his and Greer's parents' place for dinner and a family game night. You don't even want to know how crazy weird that family is when it comes to games. But Kyle disappeared onto the back porch and I followed. It is so unlike me, but I kissed him again, and I've got to tell you, I wanted to melt into him. Instead, I did the responsible thing and acted like a complete idiot. I told him my job meant everything to me and nothing could ever happen. He must have thought I was insane since I was the one who'd initiated both kisses. Thinking back, I wish I had gone for it. I really liked him, and he could kiss. Man, could he kiss. Oh, and he's a cop."

I dropped back in my seat and stared at the last sentence. Those five words turned everything all around. Pulling out my phone, I dialed the number of the guy I had watching Hudson's house.

"Hey, boss."

"Tell me, how many times have Hudson and Greer gone to her brother's house?"

He cleared his throat. "The cop?"

"Yes, the cop."

"Well, I don't think more than four times. Hudson went there for a guys' poker night, then he and Greer went over there once. They saw him last Sunday evening at their parents' house. Then I think they might have gone over there once more."

I nodded. "Is that right? And he hasn't ever brought a date with him to his folks for dinner?"

"No. I haven't really seen him that much, though. He does have a police dog he brings everywhere."

"Okay, does he park out on the street or in a garage when he goes to the parents' or the sister's house?"

"He parks on the street."

"I want you to start watching *his* place and not the brother's."

There was a long pause.

"Did you hear me, Bryce?"

"Um, yeah. You want me to do surveillance on a *cop*? Just so you know, boss, it's not going to be easy. Every time I've followed them to his place, I have to park down the road. He lives in a rural area on some land. I can't even see his house from the main road."

I could hear the reluctance in his voice. "He's a small-town cop, Bryce. Are you afraid of him?"

He huffed. "Fuck no. But why do you want me to watch a cop?"

"A hunch. When he leaves, I want you to keep an eye on the house. Don't follow him. Tell me if anyone else is there."

"Like I said, I can't see the house from the road. And if I'm parked on the street, it'll look suspicious."

"Then fucking park somewhere less suspicious and climb the fence or get to a spot where you can see the house, Bryce."

"Right. I'll move to that location tomorrow."

I closed out the emails and shut the laptop. "I want a full report on anything you see tonight. You can update me tomorrow morning."

"You got it."

Hitting End, I got up and headed for the front door when I paused and looked back toward the bedroom where Kristy was sleeping. I smiled and gave a slight shake of my head. My hunch was spot on about her. I knew she would be the key to finding Everly. My flight for Washington left at one in the afternoon tomorrow. Hitting another number, I started toward the front door.

"Change my flight tomorrow. Instead of flying into DC, book me on the first flight for Boston. And have a rental waiting at the airport."

I hit End again and started down the steps of the building.

"Smart girl, Everly. Running to your cop. But you can't hide forever."

# Chapter Eighteen

## Kyle

"**A**re you sure it's not a neighbor's car?" Hunter asked as we drove by the sedan that was parked about a mile down from my place. I'd seen it there last night as well.

"I'm positive. I know my nearest neighbors, and none of them have a car with Washington plates."

"You run them?"

"Yeah, got the name of a woman who lives in DC. She's a nurse."

Hunter didn't turn around to look, but instead glanced in his side mirror. "Stolen?"

"No. And the bad thing is, I saw this same car a week back, parked down the street from my parents' place. At the time, I thought it was weird to see DC plates. I got up early this morning to see if it was still here, and it was gone. When you and I left for the station earlier, it still wasn't here. Now it's back, which only means one thing."

Hunter turned to me. "Holy fuck, they know she's at your house. How?"

"I don't know. All I know is when we came back from the station last night, I saw it. I didn't mention anything to Everly. I did tell her not to turn on any lights or leave the house at all today."

Rubbing his hand down his face, Hunter whispered, "Fuck. What did the detective from Boston PD say?"

"He recorded everything Everly said, then wrote down all the information you found on the construction company. Don't worry, I didn't tell him where I got the information. He's having a tail put on Derrick, and called a friend of his who's a game warden in Alaska and asked if he could snoop around the Valdez PD to see if he can find the two guys who kidnapped Everly. She gave him a description of both. He filled in the game warden with as little information as he could. The guy only needed to hear bad cop, and he was on board. Dad is going to see if he can get a few state troopers to watch Hudson's house, as well as mine."

I hit the button for the gate I'd installed a few days after Everly showed up.

Hunter said, "He wasn't in the car, which means he's on foot, Kyle."

"I've got the perimeter alarm on. If anyone steps foot on my property, I'll know."

Before I parked, Hunter asked, "Does she know the house is being watched?"

"No. The last thing I wanted was for her to freak out. I did, however, tell her to keep the alarm set."

"What do you need me to do?" Hunter asked.

"Nothing, dude. As long as he thinks it's life-as-usual for me, then we're all good."

Hunter let out a bitter laugh. "I don't think it's all good, Kyle. Someone is watching your house, which means they've somehow tied you to Everly."

I nodded. "But I don't know how they did it. No one outside of Boggy Creek knew about our connection."

We both got out of the truck, and when we stopped at the bottom of the steps that led up to the porch, Hunter stated, "That you know of. What if Everly told someone about you?"

"Like who?" I asked.

Hunter raised a single brow. "The best friend?"

I looked away. "Fuck. I didn't even think to ask Everly if she might have mentioned me to anyone."

"Well, now's the time." Hunter motioned for me to head up the steps.

After we walked into the house and I shut the door, I set the alarm. "Everly?" I called out.

"In the kitchen!"

Cat ran from the kitchen to give me an excited greeting, then turned her attention on Hunter.

"Hey, Cat. How's the good puppy?"

"She's not a puppy!" I called out over my shoulder. Hunter let out a soft chuckle.

We walked into the kitchen to find Everly pulling cookies from the oven.

"I was bored, and nervous, so I started to bake."

When she motioned toward the other counter, my jaw about hit the floor. It was filled with brownies, at least four different types of cookies...and was that peanut brittle? How in the hell had she made all of that? I wasn't gone that long.

"How did you make all this?" I asked, heading straight for the peanut brittle. It was one of my favorites, and I was dying to taste it. If it was good, I was marrying her. Not that it wasn't fucking amazing to be with her in every other way possible, but the perfect peanut brittle would seal the deal.

Hunter took a piece of brittle too. We both bit into it at the same time.

"Jesus, this is good, Everly," Hunter said, grabbing another piece.

"I made it in the microwave."

I jerked my head to look back at her. "Come again?"

She laughed. "Yep. I found the recipe tucked into one of the cookbooks you have on the shelf there. It was handwritten, and at the top it said 'easy and oh-so-good.' So, I made it."

I looked around the kitchen. "I can't believe I had the ingredients for all of this."

Everly started to take the cookies off the baking pan and place them one at a time onto a cooling rack. "I was starting to get a hankering for baking, so a couple of days ago I asked Greer to pick up some stuff for me. She brought it with her when she and Hudson stopped by the other day."

I nodded. "That's right, I remember her carrying in bags. I figured she thought I was starving you."

Everly smiled as I winked at her. Fuck, I hated to break the news to her that someone was watching the place. The only good news was the perimeter alarm hadn't gone off, so that told me no one had actually gotten onto the property.

Hunter looked at me and raised his brows, silently urging me to tell her about the car.

"Everly, I'm pretty sure my house is being watched," I said.

She nearly dropped the cookie tray, but quickly recovered. "What? How do you know?"

"I saw a car parked down the road last night after we left the station, and I remembered seeing the same vehicle on the street near my parents' house. It wasn't there this morning, but now he's back—parked near the access road that leads to the trail along the creek."

Everly slowly turned and placed the baking sheet on top of the stove, then pulled off the oven mitt. She drew in a slow breath and exhaled before asking, "How did they find out I was here?"

The fear on her face nearly broke me in two. I tried to find the words to speak, but all I wanted to do was pack up and take her and Cat away until we caught these bastards.

Hunter cleared his throat. "Everly, did you happen to tell anyone about Kyle?"

She quickly shook her head. "I haven't spoken to anyone at all. I mean, besides everyone who has come to the house."

"No, I mean...maybe after the first time you met Kyle?" Hunter stated.

She turned to look at me and our eyes met. I knew the answer before she even said anything. "I, um...I sent a few emails about meeting you to Kristy...my best friend."

I wasn't sure if I should be happy or frustrated. Maybe I was both. Happy she'd told Kristy about me, but frustrated I hadn't thought to ask her if she'd told anyone about us. What in the hell kind of cop was I?

"What did you tell her?" I asked.

Everly's cheeks instantly went pink, and she looked at Hunter and then back to me. I nodded for her to go on.

"I mentioned how nice you were, how we'd kissed a few times."

Hunter pointed at me. "I knew it! I *knew* Everly was the one you've been pining for all these months!"

Everly's eyes went wide while I internally groaned and made a mental note to punch Hunter in the face later.

"Pining for me?" she asked with a slight smile.

Pointing back at Hunter, I said, "You, I'm going to punch when I find the first opportunity to do it, and *you*"—I turned to face Everly—"I'm going to kiss right now."

Before she could even utter a word, I pulled her into my arms and kissed her. Then I moved my mouth to her ear and whispered, "We're going straight to the bedroom when Hunter leaves."

She giggled and pushed me away.

Hunter sighed. "Can we get back to the whole people-trying-to-kill-your-girlfriend-who-now-know-she's-here thing?"

I grinned like a crazy fool. "I like that."

Everly tilted her head. "You like what?"

"You being my girlfriend."

Cat jumped up and proceeded to push her way between me and Everly, then sat down. She stared up at me like she was extremely unhappy.

Hunter popped something into his mouth. "It appears Cat isn't too thrilled with the idea. And holy shit, what is this? It's delicious!"

Everly laughed. "It's an Oreo ball. Crushed Oreos and cream cheese dipped in chocolate."

After popping another one in his mouth, Hunter tried to push one into mine. "Kyle, taste this. It's like crack!"

I pushed his hand away. "I think we have other things that are more important right now."

"I'm telling you, dude, you have to try one."

"I don't want one, Hunter."

"Try it! They're amazing!"

I started to tell him to fuck off, and he used the opportunity to shove a ball into my mouth. One bite, and I nearly let out a moan. He was right, it was good...but I wasn't about to tell him that.

"You know it's good," he said, "Say it."

Instead, I gave him the finger and focused back on Everly. "I think it's time you call Kristy."

"What?" Everly and Hunter said in unison.

"We need to know if anyone has contacted her about you."

"I don't think that's a good idea, Kyle." Everly took off the apron she was wearing and placed it on the counter. "We might be putting her in danger."

"My gut is telling me we need to call her, sweetheart."

Her expression softened, and she drew in a breath. "If you think we need to..."

I nodded. "We can use the phone I gave you. It can't be traced."

Everly nodded and pulled the phone out of her back pocket. Her hands shook as she dialed Kristy's number.

"She might send it to voicemail since she won't know the number." Everly put the call on speaker so Hunter and I could hear it.

"Hello?"

"Kristy...it's Everly."

"Everly! Oh my God, are you okay? What in the hell is going on? Your brother said you were at some fancy yoga retreat finding yourself, but you turned off your phone, and you never called, and I haven't heard from you, and I've been worried sick and—"

"Kristy, take a breath," Everly said with a nervous laugh. "I'm okay. But I'm not at a yoga retreat."

Putting the phone on mute, Everly asked, "How much should I tell her?"

"Whatever you feel comfortable with," I said.

She nodded.

"I kind of figured that," Kristy said into the phone. "What happened, babe? Did you fall into a depression over your brother getting married?"

"No. It's a really long story, and I'll tell you everything soon, I promise, but I need to ask you something."

"Anything."

Kristy's eyes darted from me to Hunter. I nodded and smiled, hoping it would give her the encouragement she needed.

"Has anyone been asking about me? Strangers, or someone saying they work for NOAA?"

Kristy paused. "No. I mean, Dan asked if you were okay, and a few of us were talking about how it's not like you to up and leave. And I met an old friend of yours, Martin. We talked about you a bit."

"Martin?" Everly asked in a shaken voice.

"Yeah, he said he knew you. He works for NOAA. You might not remember him, I think he said it had been awhile since he'd seen you."

I grabbed the notepad sitting on the counter and wrote down a note asking Everly to have Kristy describe this Martin guy. It wasn't a very common name, so for some guy named Martin to have called Hudson, and now this...it was concerning.

"Um, Kristy, what does Martin do for NOAA?" Everly asked.

"He never really said, come to think of it. He said he came back to Valdez every year for old time's sake and some project he was working on. We chatted for a week or two and had dinner at my place the night before last. The next day he left to go back to DC."

"Really," Everly said, clearly lost in her own thoughts. I got her attention and she looked down at my notes. "What does he look like?"

"Handsome as hell. Tall, at least six-two. Blonde hair with the cutest scar on his right cheek."

In an instant, Everly went white as a ghost and stumbled back. I reached out and grabbed her before she fell to the ground.

Hunter quickly brought a chair over and helped Everly sit down.

"Hello? Everly? Is everything okay?" Kristy asked.

Everly swallowed hard and cleared her throat. "You said he left Alaska?"

"Yes. I really wish I'd have invited him over earlier. I gave him my cell number and realized after he left that he never gave me his. I was actually hoping you were him calling."

"Kristy, I need you to listen to me—Martin isn't who you think he is."

"What do you mean?" her friend asked in a confused tone.

"I can't go into details, but I believe he also goes by the name James. He's not a nice person, Kristy, and if he does reach out to you, do *not* speak to him. And whatever you do, don't tell him I called you. Promise me!"

"What's going on, Everly? Are you sure you're okay?"

"Promise me, Kristy! You have to promise me you won't see or talk to that man again!"

Crouching down, I took Everly's hand in mine and gave it a squeeze.

"Okay, I promise," Kristy said. "But Everly, you're starting to scare me. What makes you think Martin is this James guy?"

"You described Martin—or I mean, James. And I think it's the same guy. He's the reason I had to leave. I can't tell you right now, but it's all going to come out soon."

"Wait, Everly, you're really confusing me!"

Everly met my eyes. "Kristy, I have to ask you another question. Did you tell Martin about Kyle? The guy I met back in Boggy Creek?"

There was a moment of silence before Kristy said, "I didn't say anything about him. But now that I think about it, he did ask a lot of questions about you, things that he should have known if he actually knew you."

Everly looked like she was in a state of utter panic, and I could only imagine what was going on in her head. The man who'd tried to kill her had been hanging out with her best friend and asking questions about her.

I took over the conversation by gently removing the phone from Everly's hand and taking it off speaker. Hunter immediately went to Everly's side.

"Hi, Kristy. This is Kyle."

"Kyle? The Kyle from Boggy Creek?"

"Yes, that's me," I said. "Listen, something really bad happened to Everly, and she had to leave Alaska for her own safety. I need you to do me a favor."

I could hear Kristy sniffle as she replied, "Yes! If it's for Everly, I'll do anything."

I glanced back at Everly. "It's more for *your* safety. Martin isn't who he says he is, and he's a very dangerous man. You said you invited him back to your house?"

"Yes. For dinner. We had a nice time. One thing led to another, and we slept together. I woke up, and he was gone. He did tell me he had a flight out that next day. I honestly couldn't have cared less because my head was pounding."

I frowned. "Did you drink a lot?"

"No, I only had two glasses of wine. Then some water Martin gave me after we...um...you know."

I drew in a breath and then exhaled. "He used you to try to figure out where Everly is hiding."

She gasped. "What? Are you sure?"

"Yes. You said you woke up feeling like you drank too much. I hate to ask a personal question, but do you *remember* actually being with him, or..."

"He didn't drug me. I never left my drink. I'm very careful about that, and I was very aware of what we were doing in my bedroom. He even..." Her voice trailed off.

"What? He even what?"

"Oh my God. Kyle…I think he drugged me *after* we had sex. He brought me water, and I drank the whole thing. I remember suddenly feeling very tired. Then I woke up early the next morning."

I walked out of the kitchen and cursed under my breath. "Do you have a password on your laptop?"

"Yes." She cursed. "He asked me if he could use my computer to check in for his flight. Something about not being able to do it on his phone. I typed in my password, and he was standing right there."

"Did you save the emails Everly sent you, the ones about me?"

I could hear movement, then the sound of keyboard keys. "Holy shit. He accessed my email!"

"How do you know?"

"My email is open on the laptop. I never check my personal email on my laptop, just my phone, since this is a work computer. It's a weird policy I have. And work emails are accessed through a secure company site." There was more typing before she added, "I still have all her emails."

I scrubbed my hand down my face. "Fuck. They must have been watching Hudson this whole time. They found out about me, and James told his guy here to watch my house for signs of Everly."

"Wait." Kristy's voice sounded shaky. "James, er, Martin, or whoever, is having Everly's brother watched? Why?"

I let out a breath and stepped out onto the porch. I didn't want Everly to know what I was about to tell her best friend—because it could potentially put Kristy's life in danger.

"Listen to me carefully. After we have this conversation, I want you to go someplace safe, Kristy. Maybe for three or four days. I finally talked Everly into going to the police, and I'm praying like hell we figure out who this James guy is and they all get arrested soon."

"Wait. They all get arrested? What did they do? And why is she only going to the police now? Kyle, what happened?"

Giving a backward glance at the house to make sure I was still alone, I went on. "She felt like she couldn't trust anyone. I don't want to tell you anymore, but once this all gets worked out, Everly will tell you everything. But I need you to get out of there."

"Oh my gosh—you're really scaring me. Should I go to the police or...what should I do?"

"Do not go to the Valdez police."

"Fuck," she whispered.

I tried to think of a solution, then said, "Can you go to a spa-type place? You know, the kind where you can stay for a week?"

"I have a job, Kyle! What am I supposed to tell my boss? No, I'm not going to do that. What I *will* do is stay with a friend of mine. He's a firefighter here, a really great guy. I'll tell him I met a guy, we hooked up, and I got a really bad vibe from him. He'll let me stay for a few days. And work shouldn't be an issue. I'm never alone, and I highly doubt anyone would go to a glacier to try to hunt me down."

"Make sure you're safe until you hear from Everly or me. Don't act like you found out any information, and don't tell anyone you heard from either of us."

I could hear the fear in her voice but was relieved to hear conviction as well. "I won't tell anyone."

"I do need to ask you one more thing. You said that Martin worked for NOAA. Are you sure?"

"I'm positive. Before I invited him to dinner, I called a friend of mine who works in personnel. She confirmed that a Martin Williams worked for NOAA and was some big, high-up guy. He's a climatologist, as well as an oceanographer, and he's Deputy Director of Climate Science."

My stomach dropped. If this guy worked for NOAA, how deep did this go in the organization?

"Can you get a picture of him?"

"She sent me his old badge picture. We used to have our pictures on our badges, but not anymore. I haven't opened it because I didn't see a reason to. I already know what he looks like. Hold on, let me log-in to my work email."

I paced back and forth, realizing I had walked outside without a coat on. There was an approaching cold front, and the temperature was dropping fast.

"Wait...this has to be a mistake. This isn't...that's not..."

"It's not what?" The silence on the other end of the phone was nerve-racking. "Kristy, talk to me."

"Kyle—this isn't the man who was here. This isn't Martin, or the man who *said* he was Martin."

This time, a feeling of sickness rolled through my entire body. "That's because his name is James. Take what you need and get out of your apartment. Make sure you're not being followed, and check back in with us in an hour. Call this number when you do. It's for a burner phone." I rattled off the digits.

"That's not the number that came up."

"I know. It's not meant to be."

"Wait, you're sure I shouldn't go to the police?"

I sighed. Everything in me *wanted* to tell her to go to the police, but we already knew at least one of the guys who'd kidnapped Everly was a cop there.

"Go to your friend's house, the fireman. Stick to the original plan. I think James got what he wanted from you and as far as he knows, you still think you had a one-night stand with a guy named Martin Williams."

The sound of drawers opening and closing indicated that Kristy was packing to leave. "Okay, I'll head over there and call you back in an hour."

"Kristy?"

"Yeah?"

"Make sure no one is following you. Check your rearview mirror often. They most likely won't be right behind you, but a few cars back."

Her breathing was getting more labored, and I wasn't sure if it was from moving around quickly or if the fear and panic were finally setting in.

"Stop and take a deep breath," I said. "Chances are James has already forgotten about you and his only focus now is finding Everly."

"Oh God, is she going to be okay?"

I looked back at the house. "She's going to be fine. I don't intend to let anything happen to her, I promise you."

I heard a car door slamming on the other end of the line and I started to head back toward the house. "You in your car?"

"Yes. I'll, um, I'll check in once I get to my friend's house."

"Okay, remember, act normal and don't mention anything about talking to Everly."

"Got it. Kyle, please take care of her. She's like a sister to me, and if anything happens to her because…"

Her voice trailed off, but I could tell she'd started to cry. "This isn't your fault, so don't even go there," I said. "I'm going to let you go now, so I can get back to Everly. We'll talk soon."

"Okay, talk soon."

The line went dead, and I walked back into the house and found Hunter and Everly in the living room. She jumped up the moment I entered. I immediately noticed that Cat had been sitting on the sofa next to her.

"Is she okay?" Everly asked. "What did you tell her? We shouldn't have called her!"

"Hey, calm down," I said, walking over and pulling her into my arms. "Let's sit down, and I'll tell you everything. But first, she's going to be okay. James got what he wanted from her, and he's gone. He has no idea we've spoken to her, and she isn't going to tell anyone. She's going to go stay at a friend's house; he's a fireman."

The corners of Everly's mouth lifted in a slight smile. "Oh, she really likes him."

I sat with Everly, keeping her close, and let out a long, deep breath. "Okay, we know how he found out about me. From what Kristy and I could piece together, it was after they slept together."

Everly snarled her lip, her entire body shivering. "She slept with him?"

I nodded and moved on. "It sounds like he gave Kristy something so she'd fall into a deep sleep. She said she woke up early the next morning and that he was gone. He'd told her he was getting on a flight to DC that day. My guess? He's already here in New Hampshire."

I could feel Everly's body tense up.

"How did he find out about you?" Hunter asked.

"He got on Kristy's laptop and read her email. She only knew because he'd left the email browser open. She hadn't noticed it until I asked if he could have checked her computer. Said she only checks her personal email on her phone, since the laptop's for work."

Everly nodded. "That's true. And to check work email, we have to log into a web server. It's not connected to the email app on our laptops."

"Kristy checked and she still had the emails you sent her about me. I'm guessing that's how he found out the information. He was smart, though, to think of checking her emails."

Hunter shook his head. "If he was willing to kill Everly, why was he so careful with Kristy?"

"Killer with a conscience, maybe?" I replied.

Everly gave me a thoughtful look. "You might be joking...but I think you're right. He truly seemed like he wasn't thrilled about killing me. Or at the very least, he seemed to want it done quickly, without actually having to meet me."

"My guess is they already had one missing woman, and two would cause people to start asking questions," I said.

Hunter sighed. "That makes two of us."

I looked over at Hunter and then back to Everly. "There's more. Before Kristy invited him to dinner, she called a friend of hers in human resources at NOAA to check him out. They confirmed that a Martin Williams worked there. She actually sent Kristy a copy of his old badge with his picture on it, but she didn't open the email until we were on the phone."

Hunter leaned forward, and so did Everly. "And?" they asked in unison.

"Martin Williams wasn't the man who was with Kristy. The man she described sounds like James."

Everly blinked as a stunned expression moved across her face. "So, he's using the identity of someone at NOAA?"

"It appears so. It's some director, Kristy said. He's pretty high up at NOAA."

Everly stood, and Cat sat up on the sofa to watch her pace back and forth. "It doesn't make sense. I don't know a Martin Williams. I mean, if he's a director, then he must've been promoted recently. Why would James use someone's name at NOAA?"

"Because he knew if he said he worked for NOAA, people would easily accept him," I said with a glance in Hunter's direction.

"What if they're not just watching the house, Kyle? What if he comes for me now that he knows about you?" Everly asked, fear transforming her expression.

Standing, I walked over to her and cupped her face in my hands. "He'll have to get through me and Cat first, and I promise that isn't going to happen. Trust me, okay?"

A tear slipped from her eyes, and I wiped it away with the pad of my thumb. "I do trust you," she said. "More than you know."

I smiled and kissed her forehead. "I think I have a general idea."

Hunter cleared his throat. "Kyle, I think we need to let your dad know this new development."

"I'll call him right now."

Everly wrapped her arms around her body and let out a soft sigh. She looked as if she was about to collapse onto the floor right then and there.

"Listen, I'm going to head on home, give you two time alone," Hunter said. "If you need anything, you'll let me know?"

I nodded and followed him out of the house and to his car. It was one of the rare occasions where he hadn't brought Jack with him.

Before Hunter got into the car, he looked at me. "You'll let me know if something seems off, right?"

"Yes, I promise. If I feel like Everly's in danger, you'll be the first to know. I think staying here is the smartest thing to do for now. I know I can keep her safe here. Plus, we should have some officers here soon."

He placed his hand on my shoulder and gave it a squeeze. "Let's hope this is almost over for both of you now that Everly reported it to the cops."

"More so for Everly. I can't even imagine what she's going through right now. I'm hoping that having Derrick tailed will lead us to this James guy."

"Me too." With a slap on my back, Hunter got into his vehicle.

"Tell Arabella I said hi, and give her a hug and kiss for me."

"Will do," Hunter said with a smile. I couldn't help but smile back. I was so happy for him and Arabella. They had to go down a long, miserable, and very bumpy road, but they'd finally found the happiness they both deserved. The two of them were meant to be together, just like Abby and Bishop.

I watched as he drove off and then turned to study the acres around me. Whoever that motherfucker was watching my house, he'd better be smart enough not to cross onto my property—or all hell would break loose.

# Chapter Nineteen

## Everly

I paced back and forth while I waited for Kyle to return to the house. When the door opened, I exhaled, feeling my body relax a bit.

"Maybe we shouldn't have called Kristy," I said when Kyle entered the room. "We may have put her in danger. What if James goes back, or he sends those two thugs to get her?"

Cat whined at my feet and started to paw my leg.

"Hey, take a deep breath, okay?" Kyle pulled me into his arms.

"I have been, and it's not helping."

He kissed the top of my head and then leaned back to look at me. "I honestly don't believe she's in danger. James left there thinking she was none the wiser, and the last thing he'd expect right now is for you to call her. She's going to be fine."

I nodded. "I'm sure you're right." Every muscle in my body was aching from being so tense. The second Kristy had described the man she thought was Martin, it felt like he was going to show up at any minute.

"So, the guy knows we kissed. That doesn't mean you'd come here."

I looked down at Cat and then back up at Kyle. "I know you're smarter than that, Kyle. You and I both know he suspects I'm here. That's why someone's watching the house. What are we going to do?"

He squeezed me closer. "We're going to sit tight and wait for all the puzzle pieces we threw out there to fall into place. And if he does show up, I'll be ready for him. I've got a perimeter alarm set up around my property. I don't normally use it, but I've had it on since you first showed up. If anyone steps foot on my land, I'll know."

"The wildlife won't set it off?" I asked.

"It's a sensor and it's set to sense for something bigger...like a person."

I pulled out of his embrace and headed back to the sofa to sit. "Your dad said they'd put someone on Derrick. Why can't they arrest him now?"

Kyle looked down at me. "Dad called, and the state police in Alaska are pretty sure they have the warehouse where they had you narrowed down. Hopefully James isn't too smart and left some evidence behind. We're going to get them, Everly. And we're starting with Derrick. They'll offer him some kind of deal in exchange for information on James and the other two guys. I promise it'll all be over soon."

I wrung my hands together. "Oh God, I should have gone to the police in the first place. I've caused such a mess!"

Kyle crouched down and took my hands in his. "You had something very traumatic happen to you, Everly. I'm not surprised you didn't trust anyone, and it's okay to still have that fear. Hopefully, Derrick and James will be held accountable for attempted murder—and if the police can prove that Jacob's car was tampered with, they'll be brought up on murder charges as well."

"Yes, but how do we find all the people behind the scenes? There had to be someone who worked with Jacob who deleted the report or stopped it from being filed."

"Trust me, we're going to get everyone."

I chewed nervously on my lip. "I just want this to all be over."

Kyle nodded and placed his hand on the side of my face. "I know you do. I wish I could take all the fear and uncertainty away. What can I do to help, sweetheart?"

I wanted to drown in his kind gaze. "Maybe we could go on a picnic...here in the house?"

He grinned, and I nearly sighed. The sight of that dimple on his handsome face was my undoing every single time.

"A picnic, huh?"

Nodding, I replied, "I could help with everything."

"I think you already helped with dessert."

Oh my gosh, I'd already forgotten about my marathon baking. "Crap, let me clean up the kitchen first."

"How about we clean it together?" Kyle stood and pulled me up. "Then you can go take a nice long, hot bubble bath, and I'll organize our picnic."

"A bubble bath sounds amazing. Let's go clean up."

Kyle laced his fingers in mine, and we headed to the kitchen. "What are we going to do with all of this food you made?" he asked.

Glancing around the kitchen, I let out a laugh. "I guess I must like to bake when I'm feeling nervous. Terrified. Worried."

Kyle leaned down and kissed me gently on the lips. "Come on, let's get this all put away. I've got some Tupperware in the pantry my mother bought last year. She wanted to have a bake-a-thon and give out holiday treats to family and friends. We can divide this stuff up and share it with all our friends."

My heart jumped when Kyle called his friends mine as well. I could totally see myself living this life. Here in Boggy Creek. It was a future I'd dreamed of, but I'd pushed it so far down because of my career, never allowing myself to think about it. That was, until Kyle Larson showed up in my life.

Once the kitchen was cleaned and all the baked goods were in containers, Kyle ushered me upstairs, where he drew a bath in his bathroom. He had a large soaking tub that I'd used a few times when my ribs were really bothering me.

"The bath is ready if you are," Kyle said, poking his head into the bedroom I'd been staying in. The last few nights I'd slept with Kyle in his room, much to Cat's displeasure. She was a good sport about it, but whenever Kyle and I started to kiss, she'd sigh dramatically, jump off the bed, and make her way to her own little spot in his room.

Quickly walking out of the bedroom, I replied, "I'm more than ready."

Kyle took my hand in his and led me to the bathroom. I gasped when I walked in. He'd lit candles and placed them all around the room. Soft music was playing and the tub was filled with bubbles. There was even a glass of wine sitting on the edge of the tub.

I turned and looked at him. "Why are you still single?"

He laughed and pulled me against him. I could feel him growing harder as he slipped his hand under my robe and grabbed my ass, nearly causing me to forget the bath in favor of going into the bedroom.

"I've never met anyone I wanted to do this for," he said.

Oh my. If that didn't make a girl feel special, I wasn't sure what would.

"Kyle," I whispered before he pressed his mouth lightly to mine.

"Enjoy your bath, sweetheart. I'm going to get things ready for our indoor picnic."

Smiling, I stepped back, opened the robe, and let it fall to the ground. It was Kyle's robe, which I had practically stolen. It smelled like him, and Lord, it was so soft and warm.

Kyle's eyes roamed down my body, and I could see the desire in his hot gaze. "If I was a weaker man, I'd crawl into that tub with you and do all kinds of naughty things."

I raised a brow. "If you think that's a threat, you're sorely mistaken."

He laughed and kissed me quickly on the forehead before stepping back and slipping both hands into his pockets. "I'm leaving now, you little minx."

With a shrug, I turned and slowly put one foot into the hot water. It felt like heaven. Glancing over my shoulder, I said in the most seductive voice I could pull off, "Your loss."

The moment my entire body was under the water, I let out a long exhale. I wasn't sure what Kyle had put in the water, but it smelled amazing. I was relaxed within seconds. All thoughts of James, Derrick, the plot to end my life, going to the police...everything slipped away until I was left with candlelight and...

"Christmas music?"

It was then I remembered the other night. After Kyle and I had made love, he'd asked me what my favorite kind of music was. I'd said Christmas music and mentioned that I listened to it all year round.

"Oh, Kyle. You have certainly stolen my heart," I whispered to myself. "Or maybe I gave it to you all those months ago after that first kiss."

I closed my eyes and dropped my head back, relaxing my entire body. The aroma that filled the bathroom was so soothing. A girl could get used to this kind of treatment.

Forcing myself not to think about the bad, I concentrated on the now. Being here in Boggy Creek with Kyle. Living with him, sleeping next to him, and waking up with him. The way he would whisper my name against my neck before he took my mouth in a searing kiss and pushed inside of me. All of it made me feel ways I'd never truly felt before.

Wanted. Loved. Cherished.

Smiling, I ran a finger down the side of my neck and over my lips. Kyle's kisses felt as if they left tingles on my skin for hours. And his smile. Letting out a soft laugh, I pictured him grinning as he pulled the black stick out on pick-up sticks. I couldn't help but smile back when he flashed those dimples.

I opened my eyes and took in the bathroom once again. I had never in my life met a man who was so romantic.

Grabbing the washcloth, I dipped it in the water and ran it over my entire body while I hummed the tune that was playing. Christmas this coming December would be different from years past. I could find a small little place to rent in town. Maybe even Greer's old place above her bookstore, if it was available. I wasn't sure what I would do for a job, but I'd figure something out. It was time to settle down, build a future...and I wanted to build that future with Kyle.

A soft knock on the door brought me back to the present. "Come in!"

Kyle opened the door and flashed that breath-stealing smile of his. "You almost done? I've got our picnic all set up."

I straightened. "Already?"

He laughed. "You've been in the bath for almost forty minutes. I'm sure you're turning into a prune, and the water has to be cold."

"Forty minutes! It feels like I just slipped in."

Kyle grabbed a towel and held his hand out for me. When I stood, I could feel the chill in the air and my nipples instantly hardened. Kyle did a quick sweep of my body and bit down on his lip.

*Okay, if that isn't the sexiest thing I've ever seen.*

"You on steady ground?" he asked before he let go of my hand.

"I am, thank you."

Kyle wrapped the large bath towel around me and then cupped my face with his hands. "You are the most beautiful woman I've ever laid eyes on, Everly Higgins. And you're *mine* now."

I felt my cheeks grow hot. I wanted to be Kyle's in every way possible. "I was thinking...when this is all over and done with, would you help me find a little place to rent? I wasn't sure if Greer's place above the bookstore might be available or not."

Kyle drew back and met my gaze. "You're staying in Boggy Creek?"

Nodding, I replied, "Yes. I don't want this...well...what I mean is, I don't want *us* to end."

A brilliant smile grew on Kyle's face. "I don't want it to end either. But I don't want you to give up what you love. What about the teaching position in Boston?"

"I won't lie, I'll miss my job. But I want something more. I want what Hudson and my parents have. And I really hope you feel the same way."

Kyle scooped me up into his arms, eliciting a bubble of laughter out of me. "What are you doing?"

He walked into his bedroom and gently put me down on the edge of the bed. "I'm going to make love to you. You smell delicious, and I want to taste every inch of your body."

Giggling, I asked, "What about our picnic?"

He shot me a wicked grin. "It can wait a bit longer. I have other things on my mind right now."

"I'm all wet!"

He winked and pulled the towel off me. "I sure as hell hope so. I better double-check, though."

Before I could even register what he was doing, Kyle lowered us to the bed and his mouth was on me. Hot and wet and kissing me into a rapidly building orgasm. I fisted the bedspread and arched my back, crying out his name as my orgasm came so fast, it nearly stole the air from my lungs.

Right as I was floating back down, Kyle grabbed my leg and lifted it before pushing inside me. He moaned and closed his eyes, stilling when he was all the way inside of me. "You feel so warm and tight, Everly."

"And you feel so warm and hard, Kyle."

His eyes opened, and he gave me a gentle smile. "I've been waiting so long for you. For that one woman who made me want things I never dreamed I would want. I'm falling in love with you, Everly."

I couldn't control my emotions and a sob slipped free. Then the tears came. Before I could tell him I felt the same, he continued.

"I think I fell in love with you the moment I saw you. There was something about you that made my chest squeeze with a feeling I've never experienced in my life. And that one feeling alone made me realize you were different."

Kyle pulled out of me, then pushed back in even slower. We both let out a soft moan of pleasure before he drew in a breath and kept talking.

"It made me realize you were the only woman I wanted in my life. The only woman I wanted to marry and have a family with."

Tears continued to slip down my face and Kyle gently kissed them away, whispering my name between each touch.

"Tell me you're mine, Everly. Tell me you won't leave again."

My heart felt as if it might explode right in my chest. This was what true love felt like—and I was head over heels in love with Kyle.

Wrapping my legs around him, I held on as tightly as I could while he moved inside of me. "I'm yours, Kyle."

"Promise you won't leave me."

Our eyes locked, and I felt the shift between us. It was the most beautiful moment of my life. "I'll never leave you. I promise."

# Chapter Twenty

## Kyle

"**W**hat do you mean, I can't open my eyes? Kyle, how am I supposed to walk down the steps?"

After Everly and I made love, we laid in bed for a few minutes and talked about our future. She'd only been in Boggy Creek for a few weeks, but they were the best weeks of my life. I knew without a doubt I was in love with her.

"I'll guide you," I said, "keep your eyes closed."

With a brilliant smile, she said, "Fine, but don't let me fall."

I held her tighter. "Never." I led her down the stairs carefully. "Okay, last step. Now walk this way."

Guiding her into the living room area, I stopped right in front of the quilt on the floor. Everly giggled with excitement while Cat sat across from us and glared at me. Apparently indoor picnics were not something Cat was down for.

"Okay," I said, "I need to do a few more things, so stand right here and do *not* open your eyes."

I grabbed the lighter and quickly made my way around the living room, lighting the few candles I had left over from setting up the bath for Everly.

Clicking play on my phone, the playlist I'd picked out started and Everly laughed once more. "You must have been taking note, Mr. Larson."

"What do you mean?" I asked, fixing where Cat had messed up the quilt and making my way back over to Everly.

"Well, I said I loved Christmas music, and you had that playing while I took a bath—which, by the way, really put me in the Christmas mood."

"Did it now?" I placed a kiss on her neck and watched her body erupt in goosebumps.

"Yes," she answered in a breathy voice before clearing it and going on. "I love Christmas, but I haven't been able to get a tree in years."

Smiling against her neck, I said, "Well, I happen to be best friends with a guy who owns a Christmas tree farm. I bet I could hook you up with a pretty nice tree."

"I bet you could. But I'm also impressed you remembered I liked this group."

I made slow circles behind her ear with my tongue before I whispered, "LANY is one of my favorite bands as well."

I stood behind her and wrapped my arms around her waist as I took one last look around the room. On top of a quilt I laid on the floor, I'd set a picnic basket filled with cheese, fruit, bread, crackers, wine, and a plethora of the desserts Everly had made. The candles added the perfect amount of light...but they couldn't compete with the sky outside. The sun was beginning to go down, and I knew when it went behind the mountains it would be a sight to behold.

I had gone outside and cut flowers from the garden that I'd sadly been neglecting lately, but it somehow kept producing the most beautiful blooms. I'd placed fresh bouquets around the room, including a rose on top of the next book we were reading: *Emma*.

Pressing my mouth to her ear, I whispered, "Open your eyes, sweetheart."

Everly gasped as she took in the picnic setup. "Oh, Kyle, this is so beautiful and romantic."

"You like it?"

She turned in my arms, those soft green eyes looking into mine. "I love it. It's perfect."

The song changed to "One Minute Left to Live," and I stepped back and held out my hand. "Will you do me the honor of dancing with me?"

Her eyes shone with an emotion I was really beginning to love seeing. I vowed to make them do that as often as I could.

After she placed her hand in mine, I drew Everly against me and we swayed back and forth to the song, while Cat sat to the side and watched, giving a small bark every so often.

"Do you want kids, Kyle?"

I pulled my head back and looked down at her. "Yes. Do you?"

She nodded. "Do you think Cat would be okay with it?"

My heart slammed against my chest, and I tucked a strand of hair behind her ear. "Knowing you want kids with me makes me the happiest man on earth."

Everly chewed on her lip. "I know talking about kids might be a huge leap in our relationship, but I figured it was something important to ask."

"I have something important to ask *you*."

She raised a brow and tilted her head. "Really?"

Nodding, I said, "Yep."

"Ask away."

I stopped dancing and called Cat over to me. Clearing my voice, I took her hands in mine and met her gaze. "Cat and I would really love it if you'd think about moving in here with us, instead of looking for your own place. I mean...no pressure or anything, but we'd both love that."

Everly's hand flew to her mouth as her eyes filled with tears. She nodded and let out a half sob, half laugh.

"Is that a yes?" I asked.

She threw her arms around me and cried out, "Yes! Yes, yes, yes! I would love to move in with you and Cat!"

Cat jumped up, and Everly and I both put an arm around her to include her in the hug.

"She said yes, girl."

Cat barked and then licked Everly, causing us both to laugh while the dog barked in delight.

Everly leaned up on her toes and kissed me. Cat only let that last for about twenty seconds before she nudged us apart with her nose.

"I think she wants us to sit down and enjoy that picnic," Everly stated, petting Cat.

We fell into light conversation while we took everything out of the picnic basket. We talked about her job, my job, Cat's training... and even negotiated the possibility of getting a cat.

Everly poured us both another glass of wine. "Hudson and Greer really love their little cat."

"I guess the cat would be up to Cat."

We both turned and look at my dog, who was currently sleeping on the blanket next to us.

"What would happen if she didn't like the cat?" Everly asked.

With a one-shoulder shrug, I said, "She'd probably eat it."

Everly gasped. "You're kidding, right?"

Laughing, I looked at Cat and then back to Everly and raised both of my brows.

"What does that mean, Kyle Larson?"

Cat lifted her head and put in her two cents with a soft bark.

"See? She said she'd never hurt a little kitty, would you, sweet girl?"

Cat practically crawled into Everly's lap, making her laugh. It was the sweetest sound I'd ever heard. And one I wanted to hear every day for the rest of my life.

The sun had sunk beneath the mountains, and the room was lit by the few candles and what was left of the daylight. I stood and stretched. "What do you say we clean up and sit on the sofa? We can either watch a movie or read."

"Listening to you read is so relaxing."

"Then reading it shall be," I said as we started to work together to clean up the picnic.

Just as we were about to sit down on the sofa, the soft sound of an alarm rang out.

"What's that?" Everly asked.

I reached for my phone on the side table and sent a text to Hunter. "Cat, here!"

Cat ran to meet me at the front door, and I opened the closet and pulled out a vest and put it on her. She started to whine and bark. She knew we were getting ready to work.

Turning to Everly, I said, "Wait right here. Do *not* move." I pointed at Cat. "Stay."

I had never moved so fast in my life as I ran up the steps and went into my closet. I opened the gun safe and pulled out my Glock, along with my AR-15 that had a night-vision scope. I put my bullet-proof vest on next.

After I strapped on my weapons belt, I put the Glock in its holster, swung the AR-15 over my shoulder, and headed back down the steps. Everly stood at the base of the stairs, a look of utter terror on her face.

"Everly, I need you to do me a favor."

"O-okay. But will you tell me what's going on?"

Taking her hand in mine, I led her to the kitchen and opened the pantry door. One quick push of a hidden button and a fake wall opened.

"Oh my God. You have a hidden room?"

I guided her in and turned on the light. "Here's the button to open the door, but don't come out, do you hear me? No matter what, do *not* come out."

"Kyle, you're scaring me."

I cupped her face in my hands and looked directly into her eyes.

She shook her head. "Don't you dare say it like it's the last time you'll be able to. Do you hear me? Don't you dare, Kyle!"

Instead of telling her I loved her, I kissed her. And I poured everything I could into it. Everything I was feeling and then some. I pulled back and said once more, "Don't come out of this room."

Turning, I quickly shut the door and turned off the few lights left on in the house. I blew the candles out and then slipped out the back door, Cat at my side.

I got down low to the ground, giving Cat the command to do the same, and made my way toward the trees.

"You're on my turf now, motherfucker," I whispered.

Once I got into the trees, I held my position, put my scope to my eye, and scanned. Two people were slowly moving through the trees that lined the east side of the drive. My heart pounded in my chest as I watched them get closer and closer to the house. I waited to see what they'd do.

The sound of a rifle being fired made Cat jump up, but I gave her the command to stay.

In a low whisper, I said, "Not yet, girl. They're trying to get us out of the house. They think we don't know they're here."

When there was no movement inside the house, they fired another shot. It was then I noticed the third guy exiting the woods ten yards from where Cat and I hid. He made his way toward the back of the house while the other two moved closer to the front.

"I don't think so," I said as I aimed and shot, causing him to drop to the ground. Turning the gun, I saw that the two guys out front had dropped to the ground. "That's right, assholes—you're one down now."

# Chapter Twenty-One
## James

### Thirty Minutes Earlier

I pulled up behind the parked vehicle and got out. Mac exited the other car, with rifle in hand and a pistol strapped to his side.

"Status?" I said, motioning for him to walk with me and Jim. I'd already pulled up the Google satellite image for the house and knew it sat on a bit of land. Jim and I would take the front and go down the driveway. Mac would head down the fence line and come in from the back.

"He's still there. Came home late last night. Another cop, Hunter Turner, showed up this morning. They both left in Larson's vehicle and were gone for a few hours; we checked and they went to the police station. One other car pulled up and a woman got out. She left a package in his mailbox."

"Do we know who she is?"

"She's in his book club."

I stopped and looked at Mac. "His book club?"

He nodded. "Yeah, overheard the brother, Hudson, and his wife talking about it. They meet once a week from what I can tell. Kyle showed up each time. It seems he's the only dude in it other than that brother of Everly's."

I glanced toward Kyle Larson's place. "He's either one hell of a smart son-of-bitch, or he's..." Letting my thoughts go with the breeze, I said, "We'll climb over the fence down there. Mac, you go into the woods about fifty yards and work around to the back of the house. Once we're close enough to get a shot, I'll fire a round and force him out. After he's down, we go in and get the girl."

"If she's even here," Mac said. "Boss, are you sure this is wise?"

I turned to Mac. "What?"

"Well, for one thing, he's a cop. If he does have her in the house, do you really think he'll come charging out? And you and I both know, if we kill a cop..."

He let his words hang in the air.

I scowled at Jim. "I don't give a fuck *who* he is. The police are involved now. Derrick said he has the cops following him, which tells me the little bitch finally went to the authorities. So now it's me or them. I pick me, Mac. Who do you pick?"

When he didn't respond, I went on. "And as far as whether the girl's here or not, I *know* she's here. My gut tells me she is."

Jim and Mac both looked like they wanted to argue with me, but didn't.

"What happens if the neighbors call the cops when they hear the gunfire?" Mac asked.

"We'll be long gone before they get here. They have a handful of cops in this small town, with only one deputy on duty usually. Your job is to let me do the worrying. Got it?"

With a quick nod, Mac said, "I got it."

"Good—now get the fuck going, and move slow and quiet. His house may sit back from the street a good way, but that doesn't mean we're in the clear."

Mac cleared his throat. "Boss, you need to know something about the perimeter of the place."

"Walk down the property line twenty feet, climb the fucking fence, and head to the back of the house, Mac."

He shook his head. "He has an alarm system and..."

Pointing my pistol at Mac, I said, "I know about alarms, Mac. Go."

"You disabled it, then?" Mac asked.

"For fuck's sake, dude, go before he kills you!" Jim stated.

Mac slowly shook his head. "Right, boss."

As Mac headed down the fence line, I tossed my bag over the fence and started to climb. Jim followed.

"What's in the bag?" he asked as we ran toward the trees to the right of the driveway. I was hoping the satellite photo was a more up-to-date one and we'd still have the cover we needed in order to make our way to the house.

"Ropes. Cloths. Zip ties. Everything we need to kidnap and kill a little nuisance."

Any guilt I had about killing Everly Higgins was long gone. She was nothing but trouble and a huge pain in my ass. Not to mention the time she'd caused us to waste while we were looking for her ass. Now she was going to pay for all of it.

We slowly made our way up the drive until we were about twenty or so feet from the house.

"Fire a shot in the air," I said quietly to Jim.

He did as I asked—and we waited.

When no one came out of the house, I cursed.

"What if he isn't here?" Jim asked.

"Then it'll be even easier to take the girl."

Mac fired his shot in the air, and there was still no movement from the house.

"What the fuck," I mumbled, and we started toward the house once more.

The sudden sound of a gunshot came from the direction where Mac was supposed to be moving toward the back of the house. We both dropped to the ground.

"Sounds like he knows we're here," Jim whispered.

"No fucking shit," I stated as I looked around. "Let's go around this way. Sounds like he's on the opposite side of the house now. Look for a basement access."

I could barely see him nod as we made our way low and slow through the woods.

Another shot.

Jim and I paused.

"Do you think it's Mac?" Jim asked.

I took another glance at the house and couldn't see a single light on inside. "I think it's him, fucking around with us."

# Chapter Twenty-Two
## Kyle

Cat and I stayed low to the ground as I looked through my night-vision scope and saw Hunter shoot in the direction of the two men. He missed.

"Fuck," I whispered as we hustled toward the house. They were getting closer to the back door, which meant they were getting closer to Everly.

The normal protocol was to announce that we were police and warn them we were letting the dogs loose. The problem was, if we warned these guys about the dogs, they'd shoot them. And that was the last thing I wanted.

There was a noise coming from behind me, and both men stopped and turned my way. It was then I saw Jack come barreling out of the woods. Cat whimpered, but I held her back.

"Get 'em, Jack," I said. He growled viciously before jumping on one of the men, taking him down.

"Get him off of me, James!" the man cried out. "Get him off!"

My heart nearly jumped out of my throat. James. The fucker was here.

The dog was shaking the man like a goddamn rag doll. James

turned to point the gun at Jack, and I took aim and shot. He spun around and hit the ground.

Fuck. It looked like I got his shoulder.

I could see movement in the trees, and I knew it was Hunter heading for Jack and the other guy. He yelled out a command for Jack, and I jumped up and started running toward James, who was slowly getting back up.

He saw me coming and lifted his gun and shot. Cat yelped and stumbled before she fell.

"You motherfucker!" I cried out as I lifted my AR-15 and shot back, hitting James.

James dropped down to the ground again as I heard Hunter yelling for Jack to release the man.

"Release, Jack! Release!" Hunter shouted.

"Your fucking dog nearly ripped off my arm!" the man whimpered. "I need an ambulance! I'm going to bleed to death!"

Jack stood over him, barking while Hunter held him back.

I looked down at James and then dropped to look for a pulse. It was barely there. He opened his eyes and looked at me. He tried to speak, but I spoke first.

"You lose," I said. "She's safe, and Derrick and your other henchmen are going to rot in jail while you rot in hell."

"No," he gasped. "No."

I stood and turned to look at Hunter who had now fully detained the other man. Before I could say a word, I heard a gunshot and a sharp pain hit my upper shoulder and arm.

Fuck. The motherfucker shot me.

# Chapter Twenty-Three
## Everly

"Lord, please don't let anything happen to Kyle or Cat. I love them both so much. Please don't let anything happen to them."

I paced back and forth as I looked around the nearly empty room. There were no windows, just a large shelf on one side with non-perishable foods. There were a few lanterns, flashlights, and bottled waters.

"Good Lord, he has a safe room in his house."

I closed my eyes and squeezed them shut, as I once again prayed to keep Kyle and Cat safe.

Then I heard a gunshot and jumped. I stood in the middle of the room and cried when I heard another shot. Then another.

"Kyle," I whispered.

I waited for what felt like forever before I heard another gunshot. My heart felt as if it stopped.

*Kyle.*

"Oh my God! Oh my God! Kyle!"

Spinning around, I pushed the button that opened the door to the safe room. It was heavier than I thought, and I had to pull hard.

Once the door was open, I ran outside. The first thing I saw was Kyle, on the ground, and Cat next to him.

"Oh my God!" I cried as I ran to them both.

I could hear Hunter, another dog barking, and voices calling out different things. But all I could focus on was the blood stain growing larger across Kyle's upper arm.

"You've been shot. You've been shot!" I shouted.

Kyle grabbed my hand. "I'm okay, Everly. Cat, he shot Cat."

I moved to Cat and tried to find a wound, but it was so dark. Then I felt something sticky and I gasped.

"Kyle, she's bleeding!"

"Get the medics to her, Everly."

"What about you?" I cried out.

Right at that moment, the EMTs came running up. Hunter called out, "They've both been shot!"

"Help them!" I shouted as one of the men dropped down to help Cat, and the other began to help Kyle.

Crouching back down next to Kyle, I felt my tears pouring out. "I love you, Kyle. Please don't leave me! Please."

He smiled and reached for my hand. "I love you, too, Everly. It's going to be fine. Make sure they take care of Cat. Make sure!"

I wiped at my tears with my free hand while I held onto Kyle's hand, trying to stay out of the way of the EMT. "I swear to you, I will. She's going to be fine, just like you are."

His eyes met mine. "Do you...do you think...it played for a reason?"

I shook my head. "What do you mean?"

I could see the energy slipping away from him. Kyle was about to pass out. It was then I heard Cat let out a little bark and hope filled my entire body. Hopefully that meant she was okay.

"The song, sweetheart. That we danced to. I really hope I have more than a minute left."

My tears started to come faster as I shook my head. "No. You are not going to die, Kyle. You won't die!"

"Everly. Everly! You have to let go of his hand." Hunter tried to pull me away from Kyle.

"No, wait!"

"He's okay. He'll be okay," Hunter said.

One of the EMTs from behind me started to speak into a radio. "We've got two officers down, one a K9."

"Where are they taking her? I promised Kyle I'd make sure she was okay!"

"Shhh, it's okay, Everly, they're taking her to the emergency vet. They'll take care of her."

I looked at him. "Jack?"

"He's fine."

"But...but...Kyle put a vest on Cat. He put a vest on her!"

The EMTs and one other police officer who had recently arrived, lifted Kyle onto a gurney and started for the ambulance. "Officer with a gunshot wound to the upper shoulder and arm. Blood pressure is dropping."

And that was when my knees buckled and everything went dark.

"Everly?"

I opened my eyes to see Greer standing before me, a Styrofoam cup in her hand.

"I thought you might like some coffee and a blueberry muffin. You haven't eaten a thing."

I sat up and took the coffee and muffin from her. "I'm sorry, I guess I fell asleep." Glancing around the waiting room, I noticed we were alone. "What time is it?" I asked.

Greer sat down next to me. "It's almost nine."

I nodded and covered my mouth as I yawned. Sleep had been hard to come by in the last twenty-four hours.

Kyle had been lucky; the bullet hadn't pierced any arteries. Hunter said it also helped that it was a low caliber gun. They did do surgery to remove the bullet and to make sure Kyle didn't have any other injuries, such as nerve damage. He was going to be fine, and so would his arm.

I had never been so relieved.

"I thought I might be able to catch the doctor," Greer said, "but the nurse said he already came by this morning."

I chewed my muffin and then swallowed. "Yes, he did. He said Kyle should be able to go home either today or tomorrow. He'll be on some antibiotics. She wants the wound to stay as clean as possible, so she went over his care with me."

Greer's face relaxed. "I know last night Dad said Kyle would be fine...but I needed to hear it from someone else."

I smiled tiredly and took another bite of my muffin.

"How long will he be off work?" she asked.

"The nurse said she'd like him to take a few weeks off. Kyle didn't argue with her."

Exhaling on a soft laugh, Greer said, "He's probably glad he gets time off to hang out with you and Cat. How is she, by the way?"

"She's doing well. The vest Kyle put on her saved her life. She'll be a little sore from where the bullet grazed her, but nothing too bad. She's staying with your parents, and Lance is spoiling her."

"Of course he is."

I closed my eyes and let out a sigh of relief. "Thank God. It scared me when she yelped and then fell to the ground."

"I'm sure it gave her a good jolt, and she dropped because she was so stunned."

Nodding, I took another bite of the muffin, and we sat in silence for a few minutes. "I hate that the first time I saw your parents again was in the hospital with blood all over me and the police asking me a million-and-one questions," I finally said.

Greer took my hand in hers. "All they cared about at the time was whether Kyle was going to be okay, as well as you and Cat. Don't be surprised if my dad hires a bodyguard for you, though."

Frowning, I asked, "Why?"

"Call it over-protectiveness."

I smiled softly. "I don't mind at all. Do you know anything about Derrick?"

She nodded. "Yes, Hunter told my dad earlier this morning that they arrested Derrick. They found the warehouse, and Derrick ratted out the names of the two Valdez cops who kidnapped you. They were arrested as well."

I set the coffee and muffin down and let out a sigh. Then I looked at Greer. I hadn't asked anyone about James, and wasn't sure if she would know. "Did James survive?"

She shook her head. "No. Kyle fatally shot him."

I released the breath I hadn't even realized I'd been holding and sagged back in the chair. "Thank God. I need to let Kristy know it's over, that she's safe."

"Your friend in Alaska, right?"

I nodded. "It's over. It's finally over."

Greer put her arm around me and pulled me to her side. "Yes, it's finally over."

We both turned at a noise to see Hunter standing there. I stood. "Hunter...how did you know to come? Everything happened so fast."

"I got a 9-1-1 text from Kyle last night, and I instantly knew what it was. Jack and I weren't that far from Kyle's place, so I got there pretty fast. It was honestly plain luck I was as close by as I was."

"The two men who were with James..." I asked, "do we know who they were?"

Hunter looked at Greer and then at me. He swallowed and cleared his throat. "Old military friends of James. He would hire them to help him out with...jobs. They're both in the hospital and have already been placed under arrest. They have a cop watching them at all times, so you don't have to worry about those two."

Greer shook her head. "I still can't believe your ex-fiancé was in on this."

I sighed. "You and me both. Turns out Derrick was going to make some serious money with the building of the pipeline. Enough that he turned into a cold-blooded killer. And poor Jacob. Do they know if his death was intentional?"

"They're looking into it, but I'm guessing it'll take a few weeks," Hunter stated.

I rubbed my temples. My head was pounding, and I was exhausted.

"Why don't you come back to my house, Everly?" Greer said. "You can take a shower and get out of those extra clothes Hunter gave you last night. Eat a real meal and get a few hours of sleep."

Smiling, I took Greer's hand in mine. "Thank you so much, Greer. But I think I'll run back to Kyle's place, take a quick shower, change, and come back here. Did you just come from Kyle's room?" I asked Hunter.

He nodded. "Yes, he's sleeping. Looks like he won't be leaving until tomorrow. The nurse gave him something for the pain. He'll probably be out for a good couple of hours, so if you want, I can drive you to Kyle's place and then bring you back."

"No," a voice from behind Hunter said. He turned, and I saw Brighton standing there. "You go home to your pregnant wife. I'll take Everly back to Kyle's place. Besides, I have some more clothes for her. I went shopping for you the other day and found the most adorable fall and winter outfits."

I stood and walked over to Brighton, holding my arms open to hug her. "Thank you so much, Brighton." Glancing over my shoulder, I said to Greer, "That goes for you as well. And Arabella. The three of you helped make sure I didn't lose my mind through all of this."

Brighton hugged me again, then pushed me back and gave me a long look. "Jesus, you look like shit. Has Kyle seen you like this?"

I looked down at the borrowed, oversized sweatshirt and pants. "Um, yeah."

With a firm shake of her head, Brighton took my arm and started toward the elevator. "Oh, this is not going to do. We're going to get you all fixed up and taken care of. This is going to be a joint effort."

"Don't worry, Everly!" Greer called out as Brighton led me toward the elevators and pulled out her phone. "It will be painless!"

"Candace, we have a situation. Gather up all your stuff and meet me at Kyle's. Yes, you heard me right: Kyle's. Yes, this has to do with Everly, and Kyle and Cat getting shot. You should see the circles under this girl's eyes."

I looked at Greer, who was standing next to Hunter with a shit-eating grin on her face. She laughed and, just as we stepped in the elevator, called out, "Good luck!"

As Brighton went on about creams and hair products, I leaned back against the elevator and took what felt like my first full breath in hours.

Kyle and Cat were okay.

They were both okay.

# Chapter Twenty-Four
## Kyle

I opened my eyes and instantly felt warmth surrounding me. Turning to my right, I saw Cat curled up in a ball on the bed, fast asleep. To my left was Everly. She was on her side with her hand tucked under her cheek. She looked so damn adorable. Her hair was back to its natural color, thanks to Brighton and Candace. She had it pulled up into a ponytail. Her bruises were completely gone, and that beautiful face of hers looked at peace, finally.

After the night of the shootings, things moved quickly.

Derrick was arrested when he tried to catch a flight to the Arctic. After Everly gave a description of the two men who'd kidnapped her to the Valdez Police Department, they knew exactly who she'd been talking about. They were both cops, as she suspected; which didn't look too good for their department. No wonder that one guy was so upset when Everly had seen their faces. I hated bad cops.

Unsurprisingly, the oil company released a statement that Derrick and James had been working alone, and that they'd had no idea the two of them were involved in criminal activity. The same went for the pipeline construction company. I knew it was bullshit, as did everyone else, but with no other proof, the company wasn't charged.

Their pipeline was dead in the water, though, and I highly doubted the state of Alaska would be doing any work with them in the future.

I drew in a deep breath, staring at the ceiling as I slowly exhaled. It was over...and Everly was safe. That was all that mattered.

Glancing back at her, I smiled at my sleeping beauty. I'd been home from the hospital for two weeks and Everly was still treating me like I'd been injured far worse than I really had been. I was lucky, and I knew it. Hell, Cat was lucky as well.

Still, when my father suggested I take a few weeks off at my doctor's insistence, I wasn't about to argue with him. The idea of spending all that time with Everly was something I'd never turn down. We were finally able to leave the house, go for long walks, eat out, go to my parents' for Sunday dinner, and generally get to know each other more. I'd finally convinced her to go hiking with me. She had, of course, called my doctor to make sure it was okay. Once Everly got the okay from the doctor, I started making plans. Everly needed hiking boots and warmer clothes. It was the first week of November, and it would be cold up in the mountains.

My phone buzzed on the side table, and Everly instantly turned and grabbed it. Most likely hoping it wouldn't wake me.

"Hello?" she whispered. She slowly sat up and smiled. I sat up, as well, while Cat stretched next to me and let out a yawn. "Sure, let me get him." Everly turned to look at me. "Yes, he's right here."

Handing me the phone, Everly smiled. "It's Hunter."

I took the phone and cleared my throat. "Hey, Hunter, what's up?"

"How are you feeling?" he asked.

"Great. Everly insisted I take a nap, and I woke up."

"Good, I'm glad you're resting. Did you have plans for this afternoon?"

Looking at Everly, I replied, "Not really. Everly and I were going to go up to Cloudland Falls, but I wasn't planning on hiking all the way up. Doctor told me to take it easy."

Everly got out of bed, and I admired her backside as she walked to the bathroom, with Cat hot on her trail. I couldn't help but smile. The two of them had grown so close. I adored how Everly loved my sweet Cat, and Cat loved her just as much.

"If you don't mind holding off on that hike, there's something else I think you might want to do instead."

I lifted a brow. "Well, that certainly piqued my attention. Tell me what it is."

"Thought you might like to come and meet your godchild."

For a moment, I sat there in silence while I tried to work out in my head what Hunter was saying. "Wait, what?"

Hunter laughed. "Arabella had the baby about an hour ago."

I nearly sprang out of bed. "What? Oh my God! What?!"

Everly came rushing out of the bathroom. "What's wrong?" she asked.

Laughing and trying not to cry, I said, "Arabella had the baby!"

Everly's hands flew to her mouth. "What did she have?"

Hunter heard the exchange and laughed on his end. Hunter and Arabella had decided that they wanted the birth of their child to be a private thing. Not that they didn't love all of us, but it was important for them to share this together, alone. And we all got it. Arabella had been through hell and back and had spent years hiding from her one true love, Hunter. If they wanted to welcome their child in private, we all supported it.

"Hunter, congratulations, dude! You're a dad!"

Now he half laughed and half sobbed. "I would really love for you to come meet the baby."

Grinning, I said, "And you're not going to tell me if it's a boy or a girl?"

"You'll find out when you get your ass here."

Everly was already changing. "We'll be there as fast as we can."

"Take your time, we'll be here," Hunter said. "Hey, can you do me a favor and pick up a peppermint milkshake at The Queen Bee Café? Bella really wants one."

"Sure. Does Candace not know yet?"

"We've only told our immediate families as of right now. And I called you right after I called Willa, since we want you and her to be the godparents."

Oh fuck. I was going to break down and cry. "Dude...that really...I mean...that means...that means a lot."

"You mean a lot to me and Bella. Now get here so I can introduce you to my firstborn."

I wiped a tear away. "On my way. See you soon."

"See you soon," Hunter said before he ended the call.

My eyes met Everly's, and she smiled as she walked up and put her arms around me.

"Hunter and Arabella are parents."

She grinned. "Let's get you dressed, so we can go meet the baby. Should I call and see if your parents will watch Cat?"

Cat barked, and I looked down at her. "You know you can't go to the hospital, Cat."

Dropping to the floor, she let out a huff and then pretended to fall asleep.

"She's something else," I said with a laugh. I then made my way to the bathroom to get ready to go meet my new godchild.

After dropping Cat off at my parents' house, Everly and I headed to the hospital. "I'm sorry we have to put off our hike until tomorrow," I said.

"Don't be. This is even better. Do you think they had a boy or a girl?"

I thought for a moment. "I'm going with a girl."

Everly smiled and took my hand in hers. I'd had to practically wrestle my keys from her so I could drive. I was perfectly fine and not even in any pain anymore and was more than capable of driving. Plus, it was time for my life to get back to normal.

Bouncing in her seat, Everly said, "I think they had a girl too. I can't wait to hold the baby. Ever since Bishop and Abby brought Noah over, I've had baby fever."

I turned to give her a quick look before I focused back on the road. A warm feeling rushed through my body, and I instantly pictured Everly pregnant with my baby. "Baby fever?"

"No, wait...I didn't mean it like that, Kyle," she replied with a nervous laugh. "Don't go running for the hills."

"I'm not running; I want kids, too, remember."

She squeezed my hand. "I know, I didn't mean it how it came out. Who doesn't love a baby? The sweet sounds they make, the way they smell. They're so cute."

"They are—I'm not going to argue with you on that one."

We pulled into the small parking garage of Boggy Creek Medical Center and parked on the top floor. While we were walking into the center hand in hand, an idea hit me. I glanced over at Everly as she watched the numbers on the elevator light up.

*Ding.*

The elevator doors opened and Everly started to walk out, but I pulled her back in and quickly kissed her. "I love you, Everly."

She slowly opened her eyes, her smile turning into a full-on grin. "And I love you, Kyle."

After a quick kiss on her forehead, we walked out of the elevator and to the nurses' station. Hunter had failed to tell us which room Arabella was in. Once the nurse told us, we walked quickly to her room. Everly held a basket with a newborn arrival kit. She'd made one for Abby, as well, and Candace had loved it enough to ask Abby where she'd gotten it. When Candace found out Everly made it, she'd asked her to make a few for The Queen Bee. They'd sold out in two days.

"So, did you and Candace talk about more baskets?" I asked, pointing to the one Everly carried.

With a wide grin, she replied, "Yes! I told her about some other ideas I had, and she wants me to make those too. She really freaked out about the new-mom pamper-basket idea."

I laughed. "I'm sure she did."

Seeing Everly happy and with a newfound purpose made my heart feel like it might burst from my chest. When she'd told me she wasn't going back to her job, I'd had a hard time imagining what she would do in Boggy Creek. Turns out, NOAA *really* didn't want Everly to leave and convinced her to stay on as a consultant. There would be some traveling involved, but she could basically make her own hours. Now with the baskets, Everly had found herself a new side career.

We stopped outside the door to the hospital room and looked at each other. Everly let out a little giggle. I smiled back, then knocked and opened the door with my hand that wasn't freezing from holding the shake I had gotten.

Arabella sat up in the bed, her hair pulled up with stray curls falling around her face and neck. She had a glow about her that screamed she was the happiest woman on the face of the planet. In her arms was a beautiful baby, sound asleep.

"Oh," Everly softly said as she stepped into the room and set the basket down on a table near the window that already held flowers, candy, and various other gifts. News had clearly spread that Hunter and Arabella were now parents.

Taking a step closer, I peered down at the angel in Arabella's arms. Hunter sat on the bed with his arm around his wife, gazing lovingly down at his child.

I slowly shook my head in awe. "Look at that precious little thing. The baby is beautiful, Arabella."

With a beaming smile, she replied, "She really is."

I jerked my head up and caught Everly's eye. We both let out a soft laugh before I looked back down at the baby.

"Have you decided on a name yet?" Everly asked as she walked up to stand next to me. We both stared down at the little princess in her mother's arms—and I knew in that moment, I wanted this. I wanted it more than I'd already thought I did. And I wanted it with the woman standing next to me.

Arabella looked up at Hunter, who smiled and turned to Everly and me. "Her name is Genevieve Faith Turner."

Everly wiped a tear away and looked down at the baby. "Genevieve means God's blessing in French."

Arabella nodded and sniffled. "That's right. She's our little blessing from God."

I swallowed to clear the lump in my throat and then realized I still had the shake for Arabella in my hand. "It's a beautiful name for a beautiful little girl."

Arabella looked at me and smiled. "Would you like to hold her?"

Nodding, I replied, "More than anything. I've had a lot of practice with Noah. Here, let's trade. One milkshake for one precious baby."

Hunter and Arabella laughed as Hunter took the shake. I scooped Genevieve into my arms and smiled down at her. Her little eyes looked up at me in wonder.

"Hello, little angel. I'm Uncle Kyle, and I'm going to spoil you and teach you all kinds of fun and naughty things to do. You'll be the best pick-up sticks player there ever was."

Laughter filled the room while I walked over to the window. It was a beautiful day, and you could see the mountains in the distance covered in reds, oranges, and yellows. "Best of all, I'm going to take you hiking up in those mountains. I'll teach you all about the different trees and birds. You'll be the best fisherwoman in Boggy Creek Valley."

Sitting down in a nearby rocking chair, I slowly rocked as the rest of the room faded away and it was just me and Genevieve.

# Chapter Twenty-Five
## Everly

The sight of Kyle holding the baby nearly had me full-on sobbing. I somehow managed to hold it in, except for the one stray tear that slipped free. I wiped it away as I watched Kyle rock Genevieve in the chair and softly whisper to her.

Turning to face Arabella and Hunter, I smiled when I saw they were watching *me* watch Kyle.

Arabella reached for my hand and squeezed it while she gave me the kindest smile. "He's an amazing man. One of a kind and fiercely loyal to those he loves."

I nodded and wiped another tear away. To think I could have lost him. That night changed everything. I knew that I wanted to spend the rest of my life loving Kyle Larson.

When I looked back over at him, his gaze met mine. "Want to hold her?" he asked. "I know you want to give her a good smell."

A bubble of laughter slipped free, and I nodded and made my way over to Kyle and Genevieve. He stood and placed her in my arms. I got the same feeling I did whenever I held Noah. The internal need to have this. The desire to have a child of my own was so strong, it nearly left me breathless.

"Hello, sweet girl," I said. "Welcome to the world."

I couldn't help but lean down and smell the soft peach fuzz on her head.

"So, does she have the smell?" Kyle asked.

Closing my eyes, I drew in another deep breath. "She does, indeed!"

Hunter walked over and looked down lovingly at his daughter. "My mother says it's the angel dust on them; that's why all newborns smell that way."

Slowly rocking her back and forth, I replied, "I love that explanation. I think it's my favorite one ever."

Our eyes locked, and Hunter winked. "Mine too."

After rocking Genevieve a bit more and then giving her back to Kyle, Willa and Aiden showed up.

Kyle and I said our hellos and goodbyes before we headed out of the room.

"She's beautiful," he said. "There must be something in the Boggy Creek River water that makes all the babies here so adorably precious and stunningly beautiful."

"What?" I said with a laugh. "The water in the river?"

He nodded and slipped his arm around my waist, the glare from the elevator walls shining on his face. "Yes, think about it. Willa's kids are all beautiful. Bishop and Abby's son is beautiful. Hunter and Arabella's daughter is beautiful. It's the water, I'm telling you."

"Some would argue that all babies are beautiful," I countered.

Kyle faced me. "I can tell you one thing for sure, our baby will be the most beautiful baby ever born."

My heart did a little jump in my chest. "I like that."

He smiled and his dimples popped out. "You like what?"

"The sound of *our baby*."

Leaning down, Kyle brushed his lips softly over mine. "So do I. Let's go home. I believe we need to do some baby-making practice. One can never start too soon."

I stopped and pulled out my camera to take more pictures. Kyle stopped a little bit ahead of me.

"Are you okay?" I called out.

He turned and gave me a look that told me to stop asking him if he was okay. The man was in better shape than I was, despite being shot nearly three weeks ago.

I snapped a few pictures of the colored leaves that were meandering down the river, and then got low to the ground.

"What are you doing?" he asked.

"I'm taking a picture of these leaves on the trail."

Kyle laughed. "Why?"

Glancing up from my position on the ground, I replied, "You'll see in a second."

The leaves up close were focused, and the leaves down the trail were out of focus. It was a beautiful shot.

Standing, I walked over and showed Kyle the picture in the preview window. "This is why."

His eyes went wide. "Wow, you really know your way around a camera."

I gave a half shrug. "Well, when your father is a photographer whose work has been published in *National Geographic*, you pick up a thing or two."

"Have you ever thought about getting some of your photos published in there?"

With a chuckle, I said, "Where? *National Geographic*?"

"Why are you laughing, Everly? I've seen some of your other photos; they're beautiful."

We started walking up the trail, but I stopped again. "Where have you seen my photos?"

"I might have looked at your Instagram a time or two. Some of those pictures are breathtaking."

245

My cheeks heated with embarrassment, and I looked up the trail. "My father has been pushing me for years to send in some of my work. I guess I've always worried that if I sent them in, they'd publish them simply because of who my dad is."

"Hudson told me he's submitted photos, and they've never picked them up."

I looked at Kyle in surprise. "What? Hudson never told me that."

Kyle winked. "He's a man—no way is he going to tell his little sister that."

I could totally hear Hudson saying the same thing. We'd never really been competitive, but I could see him choosing not to tell me something like this, if only because he wouldn't want to discourage me from trying.

"There's a picture you took of one of the glaciers you were study-ing," Kyle said. "It's one that's melting faster than it should. The ice actually looks greenish-blue. It's beautiful. And the pictures you have of the northern lights...you could definitely sell those."

I smiled. "You're very good for my ego, Mr. Larson."

He shook his head and placed his hand on the side of my face. "No, I know talent when I see it."

I laughed, and Kyle joined in. "Are you sure you want to go all the way up?" I asked.

"I'm positive," Kyle said, taking the lead as we started back up the trail. "Speaking of *National Geographic*, did you know they once named Franconia Ridge one of the top ten best trails to hike in the world?"

"I did know that, as a matter of fact. My father told me about it. I can totally believe it. The view from the top is one of the most beautiful I've ever seen."

He glanced back at me. "I do believe we've had this conversation before."

"I do believe you're right," I replied with a chuckle.

The hike up to Franconia Ridge wasn't very challenging, but it was full of the most beautiful things I'd ever seen. The fall colors were stunning, even though I could tell we were on the tail end of them.

"Almost there!" Kyle called out.

Another few minutes and I found myself looking out over a sea of colors. After taking in the moment—and allowing Kyle to kiss me nearly senseless—I took out my camera and started to take pictures. "Look at the yellow over there, Kyle, how it pops." I pointed in the distance. "And there, with the bits of red poking out. The water looks like glass when it reflects the sky and clouds like that." I snapped more pictures. "That orange up against the blue sky—it's so beautiful."

Kyle let out a soft laugh. "Yes, it's all very beautiful."

"I'm sure you've seen this so much it's probably blasé to you now."

"Actually, it's the opposite. Just when I don't think it can't get any more gorgeous up here, I hike up and I'm proven wrong all over again."

I looked at the preview window and nearly gasped at the photo. It was stunning.

Taking another picture, I replied, "I can see that. It's even more stunning this year than it was when we were here last year."

"The foliage is a bit better this year."

Looking out over the vista, I nodded and mindlessly replied, "Maybe."

I stepped a bit farther out, taking in the expanse of the White Mountains. They looked like they went on forever. "It would be fun to own a little cabin up in the mountains."

"My parents have their cabin. We can go anytime you want."

I turned to suggest we have a picnic there—and immediately froze in place. Kyle was down on one knee, a box in his hand.

"I didn't think you were ever going to turn around," he said. "My knee is on a rock and it's killing me!"

I pressed my hand to my mouth to hide both my laughter and surprise. "I love that that's how you start off a marriage proposal."

Kyle laughed and stood. We both moved toward each other until we were mere inches apart.

Taking my hand in his, Kyle gave me a crooked smile, and my knees nearly buckled. "This is probably way too fast," he said, "but I let you slip away once, and I have no intention of doing that again. And when you get shot, you kind of start to think about things. And all I've been able to think about is making you my wife and giving Cat a mom."

A sob broke free. I didn't even bother to wipe away my tears.

"From the moment I first saw you, Everly, I knew you were my Elizabeth Bennet."

I closed my eyes and laughed before focusing back on Kyle's beautiful green eyes.

"I want to spend the rest of my life taking you on picnics, and reading you books, and making bubble baths for you. I want you to take pictures of our babies on the sofa with Cat laying nearby, guarding them like the great big sister I know she'll be."

Kyle closed his eyes and drew in a slow breath. He exhaled and then looked back down at me. "I want to wake up and fall asleep every night with you in my arms. I love you, Everly Higgins."

"Most ardently?" I softly asked.

Placing his hand on the side of my face, Kyle nodded slightly. "Most ardently. Will you marry me?"

I wanted to scream out *yes*, but I had one question for Kyle that had been driving me mad—and I needed it answered.

"Let me ask you one question first."

He drew his brows in, but his eyes were dancing with amusement. "Ask away."

"Do you remember coming into my room that night of the poker game and kissing me? Because the next morning, you acted like you didn't remember."

Stepping closer to me, Kyle pulled me into his arms. "I was stupid and slightly embarrassed, so I pretended I didn't remember. But I knew exactly what I was doing...and I laid awake almost the rest of the night thinking about that kiss."

I bit down on my lip. "So did I."

"Don't tell me that one kiss is going to sway your answer," he said with a wink.

Grinning, I wrapped my arms around him and reached up onto my toes. "A thousand times..."

He pressed his finger to my lip. "Jane said that, not Elizabeth."

I crinkled my nose. "Oh, that's right." Thinking about the book and movie, I looked back at Kyle. "I never wish to be away from you—"

Kyle shook his head. "Parted from you."

"Right. Parted from you this day on?"

I could tell Kyle was fighting to hold back a laugh. "Close enough, sweetheart."

Rolling my eyes, I said, "Maybe I should stick with yes. Yes, I will marry you."

Kyle captured my mouth with his, and soon we were both lost in the kiss and the moment—which was the most romantic one of my entire life.

I slid my fingers into his hair, groaning when he sucked on my tongue and then nibbled my lip. A part of me wished we had that quilt right now.

"Um, excuse me, are you guys almost done? We hiked all the way up here for engagement photos."

Kyle and I broke apart to see a woman with a backpack next to a young couple, and all of them were giving us goofy smiles.

"Oh my God! Congratulations, you guys!" the young girl said. "Though, I was really hoping you'd get that *Pride and Prejudice* quote right!"

Kyle and I both fell into a fit of laughter before we vacated our perfect spot to allow the couple and their photographer to capture a special moment as well.

As we started down the trail, Kyle stopped. "Hold on. I never put the ring on you!"

"That's right!"

Kyle pulled the ring back out of his pocket and opened the box. It was the first time I was actually getting a good look at it, and I nearly fell off the trail. It was a beautiful oval-cut ruby surrounded by diamonds and so breathtaking I could hardly speak. Once I found my voice, I looked up at him.

"Kyle, oh my goodness. This is stunning. I...I don't know what to say. I've never seen a more beautiful ring."

A brilliant smile appeared on his face, and he ran his finger lightly over my lip before he tilted my chin up and kissed me. He rested his forehead against mine, almost seeming relieved.

"The ring has been handed down in my family," he said. "It was my great-great-grandmother's ring. My mother gave it to me to give to the woman I want to spend the rest of my life with."

Kyle took the ring out of the box, grasped my hand, and slipped the ring on. "Now I give it to you, Everly, as a symbol of my eternal love."

I searched my brain for the right words, something to express myself in as beautiful a way as Kyle had, but I came up with nothing.

"If only I could take the way my heart feels right now in my chest and put it into words," I said. "I can't, though. All I can come up with is: I love you. Most ardently."

Kyle tossed his head back and laughed while I smiled.

"Come on, sweetheart," he said. "Let's go start working on our happily ever after.

# Epilogue
## Kyle

*Five years later*

"**C**at! Cat!"

I opened the back door of the SUV and Cat jumped out and ran straight for Jane. Laughing, I watched as my three-year-old wrapped her arms around my K9 partner and our family dog.

"Missed you, Cat!" she said. "Missed you!"

I walked over and crouched, giving Cat a scratch behind her ears. "Good girl, Cat." Turning to my daughter, I asked, "What about me? Did you miss Daddy?"

Jane looked up at me and smiled so big and bright, my heart nearly burst from my chest. I scooped her up and put her on my shoulders as we walked over to where Everly was standing by the side of the house. She was smiling, and her blonde hair was pulled back in a ponytail.

I leaned down and kissed her softly on the lips. "Hey there, beautiful."

Jane giggled. "Me now!"

Tickling her, I said, "I gave you a kiss, but I'll give you another one because I love you so!"

After receiving a sloppy kiss from my daughter, as well, I followed Everly around the side of the house to the garden. It hadn't taken her long to fall in love with gardening. She had a much better green thumb than I ever did.

"I picked so much today, it's unreal," she said. "Hunter and Bella are coming over for dinner with the girls, so I'll make them up a basket."

I smiled. Genevieve had recently turned four, and Rachel was about to turn one. Hunter adored his daughters, and they clearly felt the same. They were also the only two little girls I'd ever met who weren't afraid of bees.

Hunter once thought he wanted to become the local game warden, but after having Genevieve, he'd decided to leave law enforcement entirely. Now he helped Arabella with the apiary and helped Willa run their family's apple orchard. It wasn't a decision he'd made lightly or easily, but ultimately it had been the right one for him.

"I'm sure they'll love that," I said. "Speaking of baskets, how was the meeting today?"

Everly grinned at me, and I could tell she could hardly contain her excitement. "They loved the line I pitched them."

"I knew they would. What else?"

She did a little excited dance—which was adorable, considering she was nine months pregnant with our son, Darcy.

"They want to carry the product line."

"Oh, Evie, I'm so freaking proud of you!"

Everly had been making baskets for all different occasions, and she'd been doing so well with the business that she'd had to hire on some people to help her. I'd built her a workshop behind the house, and now she ran her business out of it. She currently had six employees, and her baskets shipped worldwide.

"I cannot believe my baskets are going to be in retail stores!" she exclaimed.

"I can believe it. I always knew you'd be successful at it."

Smiling, she reached up on her toes and kissed me quickly. "Thank you for always believing in me."

"Always."

"How was your day?" she asked as she tapped Jane on the nose.

"It was good. Stopped by Willow Tree Inn for my weekly cookie fix."

"How's everyone there?"

"They're good. Brighton and Luke have their hands full with that little girl of theirs. I'm telling you, Lucy is a mini-Brighton. She's almost five going on almost thirty. I actually feel sorry for poor Luke."

Laughing, Everly hit me lightly in the stomach. "She's an angel, but you're right. She *is* very much like her mother." Everly turned and walked into the garden. "Did you happen to talk to Aiden today?"

I grinned and lifted Jane off my shoulders, so she could help her mommy pick veggies. It was one of her favorite things to do. "I did. How long have you known Willa was pregnant?"

Glancing over her shoulder at me, Everly played all innocent. "Whatever do you mean? Willa's pregnant?"

"Ha ha. You knew."

She nodded. "I'm sorry, Willa asked me not to tell anyone. We happened to run into each other at the OB's office."

I rolled my eyes. "I thought we didn't keep secrets from each other."

Everly met my gaze. "Do you really want to go there? Or should I remind you about that ice fishing trip last winter with the boys?"

"What were we talking about again?" I asked with a wink.

"Thought so. Is Aiden excited?"

"He is, but I think this is the last one. With Ben, Ciara, and Merit already, four is their magic number."

Everly grinned. "I can't imagine having four!"

I placed my hand on her stomach, then kissed it. "How was your day, Darcy?"

"He's been active. I think he knows his due date is in a few days."

"Bishop said Abby is about to go insane. I still can't believe the two of you are due on the same day. And that they decided to find out the sex. I'm glad it's a little girl, though."

Everly giggled. "We all know what we were doing on the same day! I think after having Noah and Bryce's gender be a surprise—and doing unisex themes and clothes because of it—they really wanted to plan for this one. I'm glad they did, or their new little one would be wearing boy clothes home from the hospital."

I chuckled. "Has Abby told you the baby's name yet?"

"No! Has Bishop told you?"

Shaking my head, I replied, "Nope. I don't think they can agree on one."

"They'll know the moment they meet her."

"Hello?" a voice called from the front of the house. "Where is my sweet little baby Jane?"

Jane squealed in delight when she saw Candace walking down the pathway, dressed in high-heeled shoes and looking like she was about to hit a runway.

"Mandice! Mandice!" Jane screamed, making her way to the gate. Once Candace opened it, she lifted Jane and started to cover her in kisses.

"Seriously, when do I get to take her shopping in Boston?" she asked us.

"She's three, Candace," Everly said wryly.

Candace smiled at our daughter as she replied, "One can never be too young to learn fashion. See how she loves my cashmere sweater? She knows."

"She likes it because it's soft," I said, "and that's the only reason."

With a look that said I could go to hell, Candace turned back to Jane and smiled again. "Don't listen to him, my little protégé. You'll be designing clothes in Paris when I'm done with you."

Everly laughed as I rolled my eyes.

"You two go do whatever it is you do to keep popping out babies," Candace said while she put Jane down and took her hand. "We're going to the creek to talk the latest in toddler fashion."

I shook my head and watched the two of them head to the trail that led down to the creek. "You *have* noticed Everly's already pregnant, right?"

"Small details, Larson."

Smiling, I called out, "High-heels, Candace? Want to borrow a pair of Evie's boots?"

Candace lifted her hand and shot me the finger as she continued to talk to Jane about what colors were in for the season, and how there was a pair of high-heels made for every occasion.

I turned to Everly, who was watching Candace and Jane make their way farther down the path.

"How about a picnic?" I asked, pulling her to me.

She smiled up at me. "A picnic, you say?"

"Yep. I'll run in, make up something quick, and meet you back here in the garden."

Everly wrapped her arms around my neck and peeked over my shoulder. "I think we have a good thirty minutes before they get back. One good orgasm and this baby will probably pop out."

"Oh, I like your idea much better."

Lacing my fingers with my wife's, I gently tugged her into the house and up to our bedroom, where Cat dutifully stood guard from the corner of the room while I fulfilled my wife's desires...quickly and quietly.

"Wait," Everly said as I was about to make love to her again, this time with my mouth. "You should turn on *Pride and Prejudice*...just in case Candace comes back early!"

For more love stories please visit Kelly's website.
www.kellyelliottauthor.com

# Other Books by Kelly Elliott

**What's next from Kelly?**
*Returning Home (The Seaside Chronicles #1) July 12, 2022*
*Part of Me (The Seaside Chronicles #2) September 6, 2022*
*Lost to You (The Seaside Chronicles #3) November 1, 2022*
*Someone to Love (The Seaside Chronicles #4) January 3, 2023*
*House of Love series, coming 2023*

**Stand Alones**
*The Journey Home*
*Who We Were\**
*The Playbook\**
*Made for You\**
\*Available on audiobook

**Boggy Creek Valley Series**
*The Butterfly Effect\**
*Playing with Words\**
*She's the One\**
*Surrender to Me\**

*Hearts in Motion\**
*Looking for You\**
*Surprise Novella TBD*
*\*Available on audiobook*

**Meet Me in Montana Series**
*Never Enough\**
*Always Enough\**
*Good Enough\**
*Strong Enough\**
\*Available on audiobook

**Southern Bride Series**
*Love at First Sight\**
*Delicate Promises\**
*Divided Interests\**
*Lucky in Love\**
*Feels Like Home \**
*Take Me Away\**
*Fool for You\**
*Fated Hearts\**
\*Available on audiobook

**Cowboys and Angels Series**
*Lost Love*
*Love Profound*
*Tempting Love*
*Love Again*
*Blind Love*
*This Love*
*Reckless Love*
\*Series available on audiobook

**Boston Love Series**
*Searching for Harmony*
*Fighting for Love*
*Series available on audiobook

**Austin Singles Series**
*Seduce Me*
*Entice Me*
*Adore Me*
*Series available on audiobook

**Wanted Series**
*Wanted\**
*Saved\**
*Faithful\**
*Believe*
*Cherished\**
*A Forever Love\**
*The Wanted Short Stories*
*All They Wanted*
*Available on audiobook

**Love Wanted in Texas Series**
Spin-off series to the WANTED Series
*Without You*
*Saving You*
*Holding You*
*Finding You*
*Chasing You*
*Loving You*
Entire series available on audiobook
*Please note *Loving You* combines the last book of the
Broken and Love Wanted in Texas series.

## Broken Series

*Broken**
*Broken Dreams**
*Broken Promises**
*Broken Love*
*Available on audiobook

## The Journey of Love Series

*Unconditional Love*
*Undeniable Love*
*Unforgettable Love*
*Entire series available on audiobook

## With Me Series

*Stay With Me*
*Only With Me*
*Series available on audiobook

## Speed Series

*Ignite*
*Adrenaline*
*Series available on audiobook or coming to audiobook soon

## COLLABORATIONS

*Predestined Hearts* (co-written with Kristin Mayer)*
*Play Me* (co-written with Kristin Mayer)*
*Dangerous Temptations* (co-written with Kristin Mayer*
*Available on audiobook

Made in the USA
Las Vegas, NV
20 May 2022